Hellish Witch

Playing with Demons, Book 3

Sakura Black

Editor: Lyss Em

Book Cover: Artscandare

Interior Art: Etheric Designs

Contents

Foreword   VI

1. Prologue   1

2. Chapter 1   10

3. Chapter 2   16

4. Chapter 3   25

5. Chapter 4   35

6. Chapter 5   43

7. Chapter 6   50

8. Chapter 7   57

9. Chapter 8   67

10. Chapter 9   76

11. Chapter 10   87

12. Chapter 11   94

13. Chapter 12   99

14. Chapter 13   104

15. Chapter 14   112

16. Chapter 15   120

17. Chapter 16   132

18. Chapter 17   141

19. Chapter 18   150

20. Chapter 19   160

21. Chapter 20   168

22. Chapter 21   175

23. Chapter 22   181

24. Chapter 23   187

25. Chapter 24   195

26. Chapter 25   204

27. Chapter 26   214

28. Chapter 27   221

29. Chapter 28   228

30. Chapter 29   234

31. Chapter 30   246

32. Chapter 31   255

33. Chapter 32   264

34. Chapter 33   272

35. Chapter 34   280

36. Chapter 35   286

37. Chapter 36   294

38. Chapter 37   303

39. Chapter 38   311

40. Chapter 39   320

41. Chapter 40   328

42. Chapter 41   332

43. Epilogue   338

Afterword   348

Acknowledgments   349

Also By Sakura Black   350

About the Author   352

Foreword

Thank you for picking up this book!

Just a little word of warning, the book you are about to read contains swearing, violence and steamy scenes (monsters need love too). It is intended for mature readers.

Head to sakurablackbooks.com for the full list of trigger warnings.

Prologue

Bang. *Screeeeech.*

Pop. Pop. *Screeech.*

My heart thundered as gunfire and twisting metal resonated through the concrete walls surrounding my cell.

A scream stabbed the distant chaos.

I could relate.

Pain blared through my puffy cheek and stiff jaw. My eye socket throbbed in time with the blood surging through my battered veins. Hunger clawed at my middle like some feral beast.

I could hardly summon the energy to get excited about whatever drama was going down beyond the plain walls of my prison.

Screams weren't uncommon here.

Another round of pain surged through my ribs, cold air stuttering in my lungs as I fought to breathe through it.

I leaned my forehead against the icy bars of my cell. The tips of my short horns clanged against them as a curtain of my ruby curls swung past my face.

The smooth metal practically froze my hands shut around them, until I couldn't even feel my claw tips digging into my palms, despite the small streaks of blood dripping down my hands to splatter against the filthy concrete floor. The human realm was cooler than Hell, and England was especially chilly despite the time of year.

My skinny frame shook from the effort to keep standing, but I refused to let my captors see me cower on the floor like meek prey. Whatever fun was happening beyond my cell, it wouldn't be long until it found me too.

My thoughts drifted as I nudged them away from the pain assaulting my body and the reality of being trapped squeezing my throat.

Both my demonic energy and mage magic were so low I'd stopped being able to heal myself days ago. I'd used the last of my magic in the bigger cells, healing the deep gashes and broken bones of an elderly demon chained next to me.

It hadn't been enough to save him.

Another scream echoed in the distance. Darkness writhed just beneath my skin in reply, and I shuddered at the unnatural sensation.

I didn't know how long it had been since the festering maggot I'd dated had sold me to demon hunters, but I wasn't sure how much more of their *hospitality* I could take.

Especially now they'd locked me away in my own special room. Funny how they were so touchy about me slaughtering a few of them, given what they were doing to my kind.

Both sides of my heritage.

The sole door to my solitary prison burst open with a roar of sound. A sweaty mage spilled inside, pistol raised. The door slammed shut behind him, smothering the clamour of battle.

Recognition burned through the fog of exhaustion and bled fire through my veins.

"Fenton," I hissed, yanking at the bars. "You fangless rat! I will tear your throat out and shower in your weak blood."

"Fuck!" The mage searched the room, frantic gaze sweeping past me like I wasn't even there.

His brows creased as his attention finally turned to me.

The last time he'd seen me, I was covered in a lot less blood and bruising. Unfortunately, I was still in the same tight jeans and cute low-cut top as the night he'd tricked me.

In contrast, he was still a golden-hued human with his unmarred skin, wearing a pristine white shirt. The only signs of distress were the sweat dotting his brow, and the slightly ruffled look to his short hair.

Hopefully, I could turn the metallic brown as red as my own curls when I clawed his face off.

"Oh, look, it's..." His straight nose wrinkled as he waved his gun. "I don't even care, you'll fucking do."

I hissed, baring my fangs. Darkness bucked under my skin, but I didn't dare answer its demands. It would be the last thing I did.

"Don't be sour, pretty demon," he chuckled, the sound edged in hysteria as he let the door slam shut behind him. "You're not all used up yet."

How had I not noticed the evil crawling beneath his pretty exterior when he'd first summoned me?

I'd never forgive myself.

You'd think my brutal upbringing would have come in useful for once, and given me trust issues or at least a healthy dose of scepticism, but apparently the only thing my cruel succubus aunts had beaten into me was stupidity.

"Oh, goodie, come here and let's find out, shall we?" I grinned, running my tongue along a fang to draw his gaze, desperately hoping he couldn't hear the shake in my tone.

As much as I wanted to, I was in no state to take on a mage. Even a rodent like Fenton. He seemed ruffled, like he hadn't been enjoying his time here either. I hoped the very monsters he'd sold me to had turned on him too.

His pouty lips twisted into a smirk, and he glanced at the key card hanging off a hook right beside the door he'd burst through.

"Everyone is so fucking stupid," he muttered, grabbing the white plastic and stepping towards my cell.

My lungs squeezed at the thought of him letting me out, even though I knew it wouldn't be for anything good. I might be as weak as a newborn unicorn, but he wouldn't be taking me anywhere without a fight.

Not again.

"Look at the adorable glimmer of hope in your big red eyes." He chuckled. "Unlike your kind and these moronic hunters, I'm not that dumb."

He lifted his palm, wreathed in a bronzed glow.

Pain bit through my skull and swallowed me whole.

Red fluttered across my vision as I forced my eyes open.

The world rushed in with a pained groan and blinding light. The noise fell again from my numb lips as the acrid scent of blood, gore, and magic smacked me in the face.

Saliva pooled in my mouth as every sense screamed at once.

I couldn't make sense of the shiny bars blurring past my face until I felt the heat banding around my waist. My stomach lurched as the mage tightened his hold and dragged me from my cell to the only door in the cramped room.

Beyond my solitary prison were the main holding cells I'd once stayed in. With a rough grunt, my ex turned the handle.

And dragged me straight into chaos.

Sharp light stabbed through the migraine hammering my skull. The dim screeches and gunshots now roared.

I released another pained snarl and tried to get my feet under me, but my entire body felt weak. I didn't know what that fucker

Fenton had done to me, but it was like my limbs no longer understood the commands my brain was sending.

Bodies littered the vast space, demons and hunters alike. Most captives remained trapped in their cells, though a handful of freed demons battled their way towards the other cages.

Across the room, a familiar grey demon with flame-coloured hair and double horns slashed his claws at a pair of hunters. Panic emptied my lungs. Blood covered his bare chest, peppered with cuts and bullet wounds.

"Let me through or I'll fucking kill the bitch!" Fenton's breathy voice snarled, far too close for the ache in my skull.

The cold barrel of a pistol pressed to my temple, but I could hardly focus on the mage's threat.

Rex was *here*.

My brother by choice. The only real family I had, blood or not.

And he was hurt. Because of me.

"Uncle!" My nickname for him escaped on a cry. "I'm sorry, I-I should never have left with him." The words fell from my bruised lips as I struggled against Fenton's steely hold on my weak body.

Every demon in the room seemed to hold their breath. Too many eyes raked me in my pathetic state.

A hunter's body fell with a wet thump, loud in the echoing silence.

The psychotic mage dragged me out past the cells framing the door and towards the open space of the room, my thrashing barely slowing his stride.

"Eve." Rex stepped forwards, pain creasing his blood-smeared face. "It's okay. Everything's going to be okay."

My heart stuttered at the sight of him.

By his side, as usual, were his enforcers: powerful demons who'd do anything for Rex and our kingdom of outcasts.

One in particular strangled me with terror. I'd never forgive myself if any of them were hurt, but especially not Killian, the vicious incubus with more scars than most.

"That's the piece of shit she was dating," Killian hissed, blood-splattered wings flaring to frame his dark-purple skin, inked in tattoos.

"More fucking trouble than you were worth, you useless slut," Fenton snarled in my ear, yanking my loose curls hard enough to knock a gasp free. "Should have doubled the price. Lousy fuck too."

The watching demons blurred as my eyes watered from the harsh sting joining the dull throb in my fuzzy head.

Shame smothered me. I'd let this idiot mage talk me into his bed, and now everyone here knew what a fool I'd been.

Rex snarled, a vicious growl rumbling his chest.

Killian's eyes flashed silver with menace. "You'll know pain like never before," he promised, voice silky with threat.

"You're all so fucking stupid, I love it." Fenton dug his gun harder into my skull. "I'm a sin eater. I can end this bitch even without the spelled gun. A single bite of my magic and she's brain-dead."

My body locked up in his grip. Was that what he'd already done to me? How he'd knocked me out with his magic?

The mage pulled the gun from my temple and swung it across the semi-circle of demons as they tried in vain to shift closer. He paused on Rex, aiming right at the bristling grey demon. "I've seen you before."

A woman appeared in the smashed doorway, stepping over charred bodies. Stunning lilac hair matched her glowing eyes. I'd have said she was a witch, if it weren't for the black claws tipping her fingertips as she gave Fenton a tinkling wave.

Could she be like me?

"Oh, hello, Fenton dear. Fancy seeing you here. Again." A vicious smile graced her lips as she strolled towards us.

Her gaze met mine. A strange kinship flowed between us for a single moment of connection before her eyes locked back onto the mage behind me.

"Take me," she said.

"No!" Rex snarled, whirling to face her. Fear contorted his features.

"Leave her here and take me instead," she repeated, ignoring my frantic brother.

I shook my head, silently pleading with her not to do this. She didn't even know me. She didn't know I was already broken. With all the damage done, I probably wasn't leaving here alive anyway.

"And why would I do that? A hostage is a hostage," Fenton scoffed.

He shook me hard enough to knock another pained whimper free as my tender brain rattled around my skull.

The demons in my periphery stilled their subtle movements. Fenton dragged me towards the broken doors at the other end of the room, staying just out of reach of the captives, trying to strike at him through the bars.

"I'm the only one who knows who you really are. What happens when you leave here without me? I'll lead all these blood-thirsty demons straight to your coven's territory." The feral witch moved with us, angling herself in front of the only exit. "You can't afford *not* to take me with you."

"Or I could just shoot you now and still have this bitch." Fenton shook me again.

This time, I was ready, trapping pained noises behind clenched teeth as agony spiked through old injuries and new.

The witch smirked. "You think you can shoot me and get that pistol back to her head before one of these demons is already wearing your blood? You've seen how quick they move."

"Zoella, no," Rex pleaded, the agonised sound stabbing my heart. "Don't do this. We'll find another way."

Fenton snarled. "Fine. Come here."

The witch strode closer, and Fenton dragged me to meet her, gun digging painfully into my temple. He released his grip on my hair, and I stumbled forward, legs threatening to give out under my full weight.

Something slammed into my back, sending me flying as I tripped over an unmoving body. Before I hit the ground, powerful arms caught me, pulling me into the safety of a muscular chest.

Killian.

"You're okay, Eve. I've got you now. Nothing will ever take you from me again."

Chapter 1

Two months later...

A feral hiss cut through the night.

I paused mid-stride, searching the quiet path for any sign of danger. Nobody was around at this late hour, especially not wandering the edge of the Bloodwood on a midnight stroll. It had become my regular route. A way to chew through the long hours.

These days, sleep was overrated.

My heart thudded, but nothing jumped out from the towering trees or the shadowed cottages set back safely beyond them.

A low chuckle underscored another distressed hiss.

I tilted my horns aside, listening intently.

"What's the matter, pussycat? Don't wanna be a cloak?" A scratchy male voice reached me again. "They fetch such a good price."

I turned to a cabin jutting out from the neat row with a frown. It was one of the older structures: a basic wooden square with a thatched roof. The Hybrid Kingdom had only been around for a decade, though, so even our oldest building wasn't that shoddy, just simple.

The cabin sat away from the others, too close to the forest for most, making it an ideal temporary residence for new hybrids seeking sanctuary in our hidden village.

No lights were on, but a dark figure fell from the shadows behind the building. He stumbled across the open grass that made up a makeshift communal garden, waving a bottle in one hand and something metallic in the other.

Steel glinted under the moonlight. A shiver trickled down my spine at the sight of his blade.

A hiss lashed out again, scraping at my ears. My pathetic night vision finally kicked in enough for me to make out what the male loomed over.

A mass of fur and fury raged behind bars. Claws swiped out through gaps in the cage, but the cackling demon stayed just out of reach.

My thoughts took a slow slide into a dark place. With barred cells and blood. Sneering faces and sharp blades. Fear and pain.

Before I knew it, my feet carried me from the dubious safety of the bleeding trees.

"How about a mop, then?" The demon upended his bottle, tipping the dregs of some cheap spirit over the trapped creature.

It hissed with a ferocity that set my pulse drumming, almost loud enough to drown out my thoughts.

The demon spluttered out a laugh. He narrowly avoided cutting himself as he doubled over with drunken mirth, the handle of his blade whacking his thigh.

"Or I could just *stab, stab, stab*." He punctuated the words with the jab of his blade towards the bars. "I've always been good at making pussies squeal."

A darkened lab replaced the hushed village with each blink. Memory and reality blurred back and forth in a nauseating swing as I struggled for control.

My claws ached from blunting them on metal bars. My flesh bled with too many cuts from glinting blades, mocking jeers from my captors just as sharp.

Screams echoed so loud I couldn't think straight.

I clenched my fists, willing the bite of my claws to anchor me here and now, but my thoughts were slippery. Oily and dark.

My feet carried me towards the cage with a single-minded intensity that strangled any logic. Saliva pooled on my tongue as my stomach roiled.

"Ooh, look! Another pretty creature to play with!" The tall demon slurred, waving his bottle at me in greeting. "The Hybrid Kingdom is just full of treats. Maybe I'll visit this pile of dirt more often."

Time skipped, and I was already standing before him, the cage looming between us.

He paused, glassy eyes narrowing. "Heh, the half-mage mutt, right? The *healer*? I've got something you can work your magic on, witch." He pointed his blade towards his crotch, snorting with laughter.

I couldn't unclench my jaw to reply. Instead, I reached a shaky hand for the cage bars, scrabbling at the bolt that held the rusted thing closed. Inside lurked pitch-black fur and feline eyes burning the shade of fresh blood.

A sweaty palm clamped my wrist, squeezing hard enough for my bones to creak. "Fuck off, girl. Or I'll put you in there with it and sell you in the next kingdom."

The feeling of someone else's skin froze me in place.

And then everything happened at once.

Something hungry burst from deep in my chest. Ravenous power lashed out with invisible force. It latched onto the demon with glee and hooked my chest, pulling at me with an awful tugging sensation that stuttered my heart.

Red edged my vision. It matched the blood pouring from the demon's mouth and a hundred lines soaking through his shirt. Cuts covered his bare arms, widening like screaming mouths. His nose shifted with a crack, blood gushing down his chalky face.

He couldn't even scream. A wet gurgle of pain spilled from his pale lips. Eyes wide with terror, he struggled to get away from me, slipping in his own blood.

I stumbled back, horror curdling my stomach. But foul magic had me in its grip, wrenching at my chest and strangling my throat.

"No," I whimpered, scrambling internally to call on my healing magic instead. But no warm glow responded to my desperate cries, my hands unlit and lifeless.

Once bright eyes drained of the last spark of life. The demon collapsed onto the wet grass. His own blood splashed up his cheek.

Dead.

I'd killed him.

Dead. Dead. Dead.

"Shit." My hands shook as I pushed loose strands of my red hair back between my horns. Power sloshed around in my chest as I struggled to take in what I'd done.

I got my first good look at the male. A middle-aged fear demon, a pureblood merchant likely visiting on his way to a nearby kingdom. He had sky-blue skin and unseeing green eyes. Ram-like horns curled around pointed ears stuck through with countless brass piercings. A smooth tail sagged down to his ankles, no bulbous end to hint at any surprises hidden within the tip.

His face would star in my nightmares. Along with the others.

I turned back to the silent cage, hands trembling as I fought with the lock. It gave with a metallic groan.

The giant beast inside slunk through the tiny opening, unhurried in its escape.

My lips parted, the bizarre sight enough to yank me from my panic spiral.

A *hellcat.*

I'd never seen one in person, but I'd heard the warnings about them.

The deadly feline straightened until her head reached my middle, all sleek power and vicious grace. Glossy black fur covered her lean frame, damp from the alcohol splashed over it. Crimson tufts lengthened her triangular ears and fuzzed out the tip of her dangerous tail.

She held completely still, blood-red eyes boring into mine.

I frowned. They were the same shade I had. For some reason, that felt important.

Something passed between us, and the night seemed to hold its breath.

"It's all going to be okay," I murmured, trying to soothe us both.

I may have just killed a man, but how could I regret saving such a majestic creature?

Her lips peeled back, revealing razor-sharp fangs.

And she struck.

Chapter 2

I lurched away from the feral hellcat, but my feet slid out from under me, and I landed in the blood-soaked grass with a squelch.

The beast's jaws locked around my forearm, fangs puncturing my skin.

I yanked out of her maw with a yelp, shoving her off and scrambling to my feet.

"Ow, you fuzzy traitor!" I clutched my arm and bared my own fangs. "Why?!"

Poison rushed through my veins, straight towards my chest in a wave of heat.

The hellcat licked her chops, swiping traces of my blood as she sat back on her haunches with what could only be described as a self-satisfied grin.

I glared at the smug beast.

She rose, turning her snooty cat butt on me, and whacked me in the face with her deadly red tail puff.

I clutched my cheek at the ticklish thwack, but thankfully, the pierce of a stinger was absent. At least the evil furball had only poisoned me once.

She sauntered towards the Bloodwood, and I hissed after her retreating form, "Ungrateful ball of fluff!"

I clamped my mouth shut.

Probably best not to shout in the middle of the night at my own crime scene.

Warmth throbbed along my arm from the fresh wound. A neat ring of pointy marks cut my wrist but, oddly, didn't bleed. Even with my rapid healing, a bite this deep should have. Instead, it shimmered, an almost glittering crimson.

The warm tingle of her poison worked its way to my chest, pooling around my heart. The adrenaline rush left me strangely energised. Whatever she'd intended for the venom in her fangs, it didn't seem to have worked.

Another toxin I was immune to, I supposed, thanks to my witchy healing magic.

I blew out a shaky breath and forced myself to deal with my real problem.

Blood and cuts covered so much of the body at my feet that it was hard to tell what he really looked like. The familiar metallic scent was at least partially covered by the sharp booze from the bottle shattered beside him.

Guilt bit me harder than the hellcat. He'd clearly been a mean drunk, but had he deserved to die in such a painful way?

Maybe, maybe not.

It should have been a conscious decision though. You shouldn't just murder people by accident.

I might have been raised in the alternating neglect and violence by my cruel aunts, but even I'd learned that lesson.

An uneasy feeling swam through my middle as I thought of *how* I'd killed him. There was something wrong with me. Twisted. Broken.

Had been for months now.

I stuffed down the fear and grabbed the demon by his ragged boot. Heaving with all my might, I followed the sassy hellcat, dragging her captor towards the woods.

The bastard was heavy given how lithe his frame was, and his curled horns kept snagging clumps of mud, soft from the day's rain.

It took me long minutes to haul the corpse through the grass to reach the dark tree-line. Minutes where I was convinced any of my neighbours would look out their cabin windows and see me. More than a few hybrids had great night vision, and some were even nocturnal.

The darkness of the forest cradled me as I finally passed the first bleeding tree. I took a second to catch my breath, searching for a way to make a fully grown male disappear.

The betrayer waited for me.

The hellcat who'd bitten me lounged along a low branch not a few paces away. My eyes narrowed, but she held my gaze, unblinking, for a long moment, before looking pointedly to the base of the tree she was snoozing in.

A large hole had been clawed out near the roots. Not big enough to roll the body into, more like an animal's den had been widened for better access. I frowned at the hellcat, but there wasn't a speck of dirt on her precious paws.

I didn't have long. Someone else might be taking a late night-time stroll like me. Or another creature of the forest might be hungry enough to finish the job the hellcat had started.

I heaved the body to the hole. Cursing under my breath, I shoved the demon in head first.

A faint hissing hack, almost like a cough, sounded above.

"Oh yeah, laugh it up, fluff face!" I shot a glare at the beast lurking on her branch above me, laughing at me kitty-style.

She licked her paw, tufted tail dangling down and swaying above me, just out of reach. Another taunt. I was half-tempted to jump up and snatch it, yanking the rude furball down into the mud with me.

"First you *bite* me, and now you're mocking me," I huffed, trying to shove all my weight down on the corpse, but his damned shoulders wouldn't fit through the hole. "You could at least be a little grateful I saved you from becoming an accessory."

A vague sense of amusement seemed to radiate from the hellcat, blood-red eyes glowing with mirth.

I glared harder.

I wasn't sure how I knew the hellcat was a female, exactly. Maybe it was the bitchy energy she radiated. Only a female could mock their saviour with such ruthless efficiency without a single word.

Or maybe I was projecting because I had mommy issues.

Well, I had a lot of issues.

Like accidentally ripping a person's flesh apart with magic until they bled out and died on me.

"Need a hand?" A sultry voice purred behind me.

I screamed, dropping the bloodied leg and leaping back. The body splatted against the mud, head stuck in the hole, leaving his spine bent at an unnatural angle.

A rich chuckle filled the night.

I whirled on the newcomer, heart in my throat.

Killian rested his toned shoulder against the trunk of a tree, a wicked smirk gracing his sculpted features. His hands were tucked casually into his trouser pockets, arrowhead tail held loosely along the line of his muscular thigh. The dusky purple of his skin blended with the night, until he resembled a dark god of shadow and sin, contrasting the angelic wings at his back. He shuffled his feathers, the wing-tips brushing the tree roots at his booted feet.

I gaped at the incubus, unable to move even to pick up my jaw.

Mirth swirled in his eyes, glinting with flecks of silvery light. He nodded his elegantly waved horns at the man I'd killed. "Doing some late-night gardening, are we? Your flower seems to be wilting."

A surprised chuckle slipped from my lips.

All amusement dried up in an instant as the seriousness of my situation hit me.

I chewed my lower lip, letting the sting of my fang ground me. "You're going to take me to the holding cells, aren't you?"

"Hmmm...and why would I do that, kid?" He flicked an imaginary piece of lint from the fabric wrapping his chest in a warrior's cross. It left a glimpse of his sculpted abs visible, covered in ink that almost blended with his shadowy purple skin.

I canted my head, unsure what game he was playing. "Because...you're an enforcer?"

He flashed me his pearly white fangs, viciously long. "So?"

I looked down at the body slumped at my feet, half-stuffed into some wild animal's den. Blinking hard didn't suddenly make it disappear.

Killian threw his head back and laughed, a deep sound I heard so rarely from him. For a second, I forgot all about the body and being caught and my horrifying power. Killian had always devoured my focus. Ever since he'd joined the Hybrid Kingdom six years ago as a blood-soaked teen, only a year after Rex had taken me in too.

Reality slapped me in the face as the hellcat lounging above us did her chuckling cough noise and slunk away, disappearing higher into the tree.

I scowled at the incubus, ignoring the mocking furball. "I know things are a slower pace since you've started finding grey hairs, Kill, but I'm kinda in a hurry. So if you're not going to lock me up, then get out of my way."

"Grey hairs, huh?" He mused, running a clawed hand through his wavy dark locks. "Do my white feathers bother you too?"

He was only a few years older than me, in his mid-twenties, with not a single grey in sight, but since he kept calling me kid, I'd keep calling him old.

I poked my tongue out at him like a mature adult.

His mirth simmered to an alluring chuckle, and he reached past me to lift the dead demon by his trouser leg like he weighed nothing. I barely resisted the urge to lean into him and inhale his smoky caramel scent like the creep I was.

The enforcer ran a critical eye over the demon's muddy face and followed the trail of destruction I'd left down my victim's body.

"Damn, kid." He whistled low. "You did this?"

I bit my lip, dropping his questioning gaze. How could I tell him, of all people, what I'd done?

That bloodthirsty sensation taking over... It hadn't been the first time. My breathing shallowed. It probably wouldn't be the last either.

"So vicious," he purred, breaking my guilty silence. His eyes twinkled with amusement and something I couldn't quite name. He shrugged his enormous wings, the snowy arches rising and falling gracefully. "Doesn't matter, I suppose."

I wet my lower lip, trying to stuff down the panic. "Because you're taking the evidence straight to Rex and the other enforcers?"

I didn't think they'd punish me harshly given the male had been trying to torture an animal, but I'd still *killed* someone. Questions would be asked.

Like how I'd managed to inflict hundreds of strange wounds on a fully grown pureblood male.

Killian quirked a brow in silent question, the same charcoal shade as his artfully messy hair.

I threw my hands up, whisper-shouting at the frustrating incubus, "Has my brother fired you or something? You're. An. Enforcer."

Silver lit his eyes like the flash of a blade. "And yet I'd break every rule for you."

This was why I had trouble pining after the seductive incubus. One second he was calling me "kid," reminding me just how he saw me, and the next he was borderline flirting.

It was infuriating.

"Why are you helping me?" I asked.

"I don't need a reason. If I find you with a body, I'll bury it for you."

My eyes shuttered. "So you're not going to force me to tell you what happened? *Why* I killed him?"

"I don't need to." Mischief curved his lips into a smirk. "Especially because I know a lie would spill from your pretty, pouty lips. So let's just hide the body. If it makes you feel better, you can owe me one."

I felt like a naive summoner making a deal with a hungry demon, but I was a fully grown demon-witch with blood under her claws. I lifted a hand, inspecting said glossy tips as if I hadn't a care in the world.

"Deal."

Chapter 3

The party raged around me.

A sensual beat swallowed my focus, the music pounding through the crowded living room loud enough to reverberate through my throat, up into my skull. I swore I could feel it right to the tips of my stubby horns, despite the number of demons between me and the band on their raised platform in the corner.

My hips rolled as I let the sultry pulse move me. Being part succubus had some perks, like an ingrained sense of rhythm strong enough to overcome my natural talent at making anything awkward.

I took a sip of the mystery punch in my glass as I swayed on the makeshift dance floor, savouring the fruity sweetness masking the sear of alcohol burning down my throat.

I could use all the potency to help numb my thoughts. Since killing the merchant last week, I'd been even more on edge, and not just because a certain incubus had been suspiciously quiet about it.

I'd not even had a chance to ask him *how* he'd found me that night. Had he stumbled across me in the woods by chance? Or had Rex had the stealthy enforcer keeping tabs on me?

Voices layered together as clusters of demons laughed and chatted around the hazy room, draped across the rustic dining table and huge sofas pushed to the edges.

Whooping and hollering. Drinking and dancing. Carefree.

Their easy smiles knifed through my vision. So I closed my eyes, willing the alcohol to work for once.

Everything else might be fucked, but for some reason, my body still healed itself. Alcohol was technically poison, and my innate magic couldn't let me have a single break, apparently.

I'd returned to Hell two months ago, but I couldn't seem to fit myself back into the life I'd known. The Hybrid Kingdom was exactly how I'd left it.

I was the one who'd changed.

"There you are." A masculine huff yanked me from my dim thoughts.

Joachim reached for me, all four sweaty palms gluing straight to my hips and the little cutouts slicing along the clingy material of my black dress. The blood demon pushed his fingers through the gaps, and I swallowed the rising bile at his overwhelming touch.

I'd thought dating a guy with four arms would be fun, but I supposed I had another regret to add to my list.

He grinned, slit pupils blown wide and glassy in the flickering candlelight from the bone chandelier above. "I've been looking for you."

And I've been hiding from you.

"Well...you've found me now." I stretched my lips in an approximation of a smile.

The distinct sugared-apples flavour of his lust seeped into me, strengthening my demonic side, which in turn fed my human magic.

Being only half-succubus, I found it harder than most to feed on the invisible currents of desire others gave off, but touch helped. Though, not many demons usually threw their attraction my way. Especially given my almost human looks and the misfortune that seemed to plague my exes.

Sometimes, I wondered what my life would have looked like if my father had cared that I'd been born. If he'd taken me to grow up amongst mages in the human realm instead of leaving me to my unstable mother in Hell.

Would I have fit in with them any better? Or would I have been just as much an outsider as I was now?

Too human for demons. Too demon for humans.

Joachim's sweet lust flowed stronger, sickly enough for saliva to pool in my mouth. Too many hands ran down my body. The demon leaned in close, and his wet tongue slicked a line up my neck.

I shuddered, and he huffed an amused chuckle, mistaking my reaction for want.

"Let's find somewhere private. I know you're starved for me, baby," he purred in my ear, and spiders crept down my spine. "I'm not afraid to keep roosting with the *widow-witch*."

I grimaced at the nickname.

My exes had a tendency to end up near dead, usually within days of breaking up with me or after a bad fight. None of them had said a word about what happened, no matter how hard people pressed them for answers.

Even I could admit it looked suspicious, though I was always the one to heal them afterwards. People had started calling me the widow-witch, after a bright-red bird native to the Bloodwood.

The females had a fun little tendency to eat their partners' organs if they weren't pleased with their...performance.

I pulled back, trying to hold myself together as Joachim's claws scraped over my sides, touching even more skin. "Maybe later... I..."

"Come on, Eve. I know you're not gonna be a flaming tease again." Irritation edged his tone, and I found myself trying to dislodge his many hands.

They tightened, refusing to budge. The feel of being trapped sharpened my breaths.

"Eeeeeve!" A tall demon barreled through the writhing crowd, her squeal loud enough to pierce the music. "It's our song!"

Shanlir's silver eyes were just as unfocused as Joachim's, but the shrewd demon plucked my wrist and yanked me away from the guy I was apparently dating.

His eyes narrowed, lip curling enough to bare a fang. "I'll find you later."

It sounded more like a threat. My brittle smile only stretched wider as I waved goodbye with my drink, grateful for my oldest friend tugging me through the gyrating bodies to the edge of the room.

I winced as I stepped on a white bone-kin fur rug, now stained with various colours.

At least it wasn't my house.

My friend halted right between two stuffed sofas overflowing with drunk demons.

I breathed a relieved sigh as I escaped wandering hands and a lapping tongue.

Shanlir booped me on the nose. "Silly witch, if you don't like him, why don't you just turn him into a frog?" She cackled at her own joke, clearly flying as high as a phoenix.

Under the dim lighting, her pale skin looked almost a plain ivory, but in the daylight, she'd sparkle like crushed pearls.

A snort broke through my forced grin. "He's fine. A good snack in a pinch."

Sometimes the screaming in my head was so loud, a distraction was the only thing stopping me from completely losing it.

Even if his touch could turn my stomach.

It was cheaper than therapy, I supposed. Not that we actually had a counsellor in our small kingdom, despite how many of us clearly needed mental help.

Shanlir shook her head, sending her frill-tipped antennae swaying around her waved horns. Her glazed eyes turned knowing, and I finally noticed the staining along her lower lip. It looked like she'd snaffled a whole bushel of darkberries.

"Onto the strong stuff, I see." I jerked my chin at the telltale darkness.

She grinned wide, showing off her elegant dagger-like teeth, perfect for tearing flesh. Subconsciously, my tongue ran over the two short fangs I possessed, crowded by flat human teeth.

"I'm sure your big brother won't kick me out of his kingdom for having a little fun." She reached out to twirl one of my red waves around her finger and give it a playful tug.

I couldn't help a real smile. "No, I guess not. For all I tease him for acting like a boring old uncle, he's actually pretty chill."

The hybrid demon king had taken me in when I was fifteen, practically raising me even though he was barely five years older than me. I loved Rex like a real brother. He was protective and funny, and he cared about us outcasts more than anyone.

My happy thoughts of Rex soured. He and his new witch queen had almost died trying to rescue me from the human realm a couple of months ago.

Guilt ate through my stomach like acid, mixing with the alcohol already sloshing around in there.

"Hey now, turn that frown upside down," Shanlir giggled, smushing my cheeks together with her hands. "You've been such a grump lately."

Probably because I was drowning in nightmares and committing accidental murders.

I swatted her hands away with a snort.

Someone knocked into my back, spilling my drink onto the floorboards.

The dark liquid splashing across the floor was a caged demon's blood gushing out as a madman sliced right through his throat. As I was forced to watch. Unable to help. Trapped in a cage of my own.

Knowing I was next.

A burst of laughter nearby yanked me back to the present, and I swallowed down the jagged memory before it could choke me.

Shanlir scowled over my shoulder, and I gripped my now empty glass tighter, already suspecting who was behind me.

"Oops," a smooth feminine voice drawled.

I turned to glare at Zahara. "Watch it."

The smirking demon was everything a succubus should be, alluring in a way that went beyond her stunning looks. Long, sumptuous hair fell in waves down to her thighs, the dim lighting darkening the forest-green shade until it almost looked black. It covered more of her curvy body than the lacy chemise dress masquerading as clothing.

If I wasn't careful, I'd get knocked out by a rogue tit when it popped out of the ridiculously tight push-up bra she'd squeezed into.

She was a hybrid, like nearly every demon here, except she was a cross between two closely linked sexual breeds. The snooty brat took that as her right to look down at the rest of us, like being a purer hybrid somehow made her better.

If she was the purest hybrid, I was the muttiest mutt. Only half demon, I lacked a lot of the usual traits. Sure, I had horns, claws, and fangs, but they were almost cute compared to a true demon's. I was practically a harmless chibi version.

"Sorry, love, didn't see you there," she purred, blinking long sooty lashes in feigned innocence. "What with all the *real* demons around drawing the eye."

Rake your claws over her throat. Make her bleed. A scratchy voice in my head hissed at me, begging for violence.

I ignored it with all the delusion I usually used to fantasise about me and Killian. My mental breakdown was looming larger with every passing day, but hearing voices was a fun new development to sprinkle in the with the flashbacks, panic attacks, and corrupted magic.

"B-Back off," Shanlir stuttered, barely audible over the music. Her clenched fists shook at her sides.

She'd been raised a slave to one of the fight rings in a fear demon kingdom to the north. Considered too weak to put on a good show, she'd served drinks instead, often becoming a snack herself when the guests terrified her enough.

I never wanted her anywhere near violence again.

Zahara continued, as if my friend hadn't even spoken. She raked her gaze from the points of my mini horns to the heeled sandals hugging my feet, her lips pouting in mock sympathy. "It must be hard, living amongst demons. Being away from your own kind."

Her tone was seductive even while insulting me. She'd thought herself the queen of the kingdom, since she'd set her sights on my brother, the king. But he'd mated a stunning witch from the human realm a few weeks ago, and now Zahara's mean streak was growing out of control.

"Just because I'm half-mage doesn't mean I'm not demon enough to put you on your perky arse," I hissed, my jaw aching with the need to sink my teeth into her throat and rip it out.

Anticipation weaved through me, coaxing my violent side out to play. My claws curled into the glass in my hand. An unhinged need to lash out burned through me until I felt like I'd explode if I didn't attack.

Darkness writhed, poking at my insides as it hunted for a way out.

Fear sliced through my rage as I struggled to hold myself together, for Shanlir and the sake of everyone here. The glass shaking in my hand told me I was doing a terrible job at that too.

At least scratch an eye out. Crush it in front of her.

I pretended the psychotic voice rasping in my head didn't exist.

A tittering laugh fell from Zahara's glossed lips. "I'm sure you are, honey, but that doesn't mean you're succubus enough to claim a man." Challenge flared in her sparkling eyes, and a sinking feeling weighed my gut. "I can't imagine anyone would want to touch you. Poor Eve, you'll probably die unmated."

Her condescending tone set my fangs on edge.

She turned her back on me in a big fuck-you insult, letting her smooth arrowhead tail slide up to brush my bare arm. The rich glide felt like satin, seeming to mock me for my lack of one.

Shanlir trembled beside me, lips too thin, eyes too wide.

It helped me swallow down the violent rage. Gripping her shoulder, covered in soft ridges from her mantle of aquatic scales, I searched her gaze. "Hey, why don't we go get a drink?"

"Y-Yeah, she's not worth the bloodshed. You'd only have to heal the ungrateful boar afterwards." She sniffed.

I didn't correct her. It had been weeks since my healing magic had actually worked.

"Exactly." I tried on another tight smile and stuffed down the horrifying sensation of something trying to slither out of my skin.

Like a monster of the deep, it watched and waited, lurking just below the surface.

Refusing to fit back in its cage.

Chapter 4

I led Shanlir towards the kitchen, weaving us through the crowd.

A drunken male tripped over the large rug in the centre of the room and almost impaled me on his branching antlers as we passed.

His drink splashed out of his cup and straight over the white dress hugging Shanlir's lithe frame. She gaped down at the dark stain before a strained laugh bubbled up her throat.

I hissed at the clumsy demon, a hybrid who'd joined a few years back after leaving the shadow-walker kingdom neighbouring ours. The dancers swallowed him before I could shake an apology out of the idiot.

"It's all right." Shanlir grabbed my wrist, giving it a quick squeeze right over the tooth-marks left by the hellcat a few days ago.

The bite had faded, but in the right light, I could still see a faint glimmer of red in a circle of points.

Shanlir pulled me through an ornate wooden archway and into the kitchen. Like the living room, it was packed as we edged inside.

As one of the bigger cabins in our village, the place was a regular for parties, and the drinks setup was always the same. A huge clay punch bowl dominated the wooden island in the middle, a fun red liquid sloshing inside with various fruits floating in the mix.

Instead of taking us closer, Shanlir tugged me around the edge to the corridor on the far side. The music faded slightly in the narrow space, and I let out a relieved breath. Dulled senses must be a blessing, because my ears only held a slight ache from the past hour dancing in front of the band.

She pouted down at her ruined outfit as we walked past closed doors to the staircase half-hidden at the end. "I've got a spare dress in Mikhail's room. I'll be right back."

I nodded, leaning against the wall. "I'll wait for you here."

There was no chance I'd follow her up to the bedroom of the guy she was on-and-off dating. If he was in there, she'd be on him like a succubus in heat.

I might feed on desire, but I had no interest in their lust fest.

She hurried up the wooden staircase, her frilled tail swishing gracefully behind her like it floated on an invisible current.

The second she disappeared, I let my head tip back into the wall, staring at the exposed beams above.

The door beside me swung open. Before I could react, a hand clamped my arm and yanked. I fell into the room with a startled yelp.

Three familiar demons towered over me, fang-filled grins stretched wide.

My stomach sank at the colourful glitter sparking in their pure-black eyes.

A hungry pain demon was a dangerous one.

Three was a blood-soaked nightmare.

"Get off me," I snarled, jerking my arm from a vicious hold.

Vanita, the silver-haired leader of the violent trio, dug her claws in, leaving deep red furrows as I freed myself. I refused to even wince, blocking out the pain to deny her whatever energy I could.

They'd pulled me into a bathroom, the grey-tiled walls and floor reminding me a little too much of the concrete prison I'd been held in.

"Well, well, well...," she drawled, raising her silver claws to the artificial light as her friends, Murag and Jessa, snickered beside her. "If it isn't our resident *human*." She licked my blood from her metallic claw tip, black forked tongue writhing like a dying slug.

Cut her open and spill out her soft, squishy organs.

The monster in my head snarled at me, batting imaginary claws to emphasise its point.

"What do you skinny wraiths want?" I sneered. The slender demons began circling me, matching layered dresses swishing around their legs, and I turned to keep them in sight. "If it's about a foursome, I'm not into grave-fresh."

Especially with what it meant. Their chalky complexions and the prominent veins pulsing around glittering black eyes were a side effect of indulging on unwilling pain. Most of their breed was careful not to feed on it too much for how it altered their appearance.

These living corpses blamed the temporary look on a quirk of being hybrids, but I knew better.

Which unlucky soul had they already hurt tonight?

"Even a whore witch like you couldn't summon us for that," Jessa huffed, flipping her straight raven hair over a bony shoulder. Her thick tail rose high over it, and she slid her stinger from the pale arrowhead, liquid sparkling from the sharp tip like a diamond.

Menace rolled off each of the fine-boned monsters.

They may look skeletal, but as a half-mage, I still couldn't compete physically. Over the years, it had been one of their favourite things to remind me of, their subtle taunts and "accidental" blows always carefully orchestrated for whenever they caught me alone.

Rex had trained me to fight the moment he'd taken me in, though, and I'd been crafting poisons to lace my knives with for almost as long.

I hadn't been an easy meal in years.

"I'm telling you now, you don't want to fuck with me tonight." I met Vanita's bottomless-pit eyes, holding steady.

Don't warn your prey. Just make them bleed.

I desperately pretended I wasn't being scolded by the voice in my head.

"Aww, little witchy witch spends some time with her own kind topside, and now what? You think you can take on three demons?" Vanita chuckled. "I think someone needs to be shown their place."

Pain exploded through my back, screaming down my spine. I stumbled forward with the hit, right into Vanita's waiting claws.

Silver agony pierced my upper chest. She dug deep, curled her fingertips around my collarbones, and slammed me to my knees. I choked back the scream they craved, frantically blocking out the pain radiating through my chest and hammering at my mind. Hot liquid ran down my front, streaming between my cleavage to soak my dress.

The blood. The pain.

My captivity came rushing back, until I was nothing but a battered demoness in a cell, trying not to bleed out on a filthy concrete floor.

Reach up and snap her wrists! Slit her arteries and wear her blood.

My hands lifted with the encouragement of the voice. I grabbed the thin wrists holding me, giving them a sharp jerk, but they didn't budge. The tug under my flesh only brought fresh agony, and with it dark memories took hold, freezing me in place.

It felt like a basilisk wrapped my chest, crushing my lungs until I could hardly breathe.

"Pathetic." Vanita smirked down at where I held her. "Delicious."

Pain pulsed through my front and back. The demon's eyes sparkled brighter as she fed with sick delight. My own darkness writhed beneath my flesh, slithering from the cage I tried to bury it in, dividing my attention at the worst possible time.

The stinger in my back wrenched out, and I couldn't hold back the whimper as bloodthirsty need expanded inside me.

Some of my training finally kicked in, and my hand dropped to the poisoned blade strapped to my thigh through the slit in my dress.

Heated ropes lashed my wrists, locking my arms out wide before I could even graze the handle. I hissed, uselessly struggling to free myself from Murag's tails tightening around my wrists like shackles.

Jessa stepped into view beside Vanita, wide eyes just as bright. She reached up, running the bone spikes jutting from her knuckles along my cheek. "Poor little witchy. It hurts, doesn't it?"

A gleeful cackle spilled from her chapped lips as she wound her tail around my throat, tightening her noose.

"We can make it all go away," Murag whispered behind me, her third tail edging into my peripheral vision, the spike-covered ball on the end flinging drops of my blood. "An abomination like you never deserved to live in the first place."

Her words dug into scabbed wounds buried deep inside me. My aunts had told me something similar all my life. Every day until I'd fled.

I hadn't survived so much torment to succumb to a few peckish bullies.

"Sh-Shut...u-up," I croaked, the air barely able to slip past my crushed throat. "Y-You're so b-boring."

"Insolent witch," Murag hissed at my back, fisting my hair with a vicious tug. "The entire kingdom celebrated when we found out you'd been taken."

Vanita yanked my collarbones, and my vision whited out. Bile gushed up my throat. I swallowed the bitter acid, trying not to choke on it with my head cruelly tipped back.

Reality blinked back into view with a worrying redness edging my vision like blood. It haloed the three pale faces leering down at me. Burning whips of power lashed my insides, like my broken magic tried to carve its way to freedom.

I groaned, clenching my jaw to stop it becoming a scream. My claws pierced my palms, but the roaring pain through my upper chest drowned the sensation.

"Should have stayed gone." Jessa punched her spiked knuckles into my ribs. Her tail at my neck and Vanita's cruel grip braced me to the point I barely moved, even though I felt like I'd been stomped by a unicorn.

Vanita grinned, a sinister slash of fangs as white as her bloodless lips. "We'll just have to correct your mistake."

Now! Tear them apart. Bathe in their blood. Feast on their liver while they watch.

The visceral image churned my stomach.

"H-Hate liver," I chuckled, the sound gurgling and wet.

Too late, I realised I'd spoken aloud.

They shared a look, and Vanita's smirk grew cruel. "So you've finally given in to madness?" She tapped her bloodied claw against her chin, dotting my bright blood on her chalky skin. "I can't tell if it's going to be *more* fun now or less."

The darkness writhed harder. It felt like my veins were trying to force their way out from beneath my skin. The sensation was nauseating, but what it meant was worse.

"S-Scurry back to your gra-aves...," I rasped. "Before you r-regret it."

Pain leached more than just my thoughts, the drain on my energy like someone piling weights on my limbs. I willed my eyes to flutter back open, to keep tugging on the tails binding me on my knees.

"Hold the filthy human's mouth open. I'm going to defang her for real."

I couldn't tell who'd said it. More blood spilled across my vision, but it was the agony radiating through my torso that stole my attention.

And in my distraction, hungry and dark, the monster slipped from its leash.

Chapter 5

Magic slunk from my chest. Growing and expanding, it took a deep breath.

And struck.

Whips of power hooked into the three pain demons crowding me against the floor. Their screams were beautiful, harmonious cries. Murag's tails dropped my wrists, and I yanked Jessa's from my neck, crushing the pale length of bone and muscle in my grip.

Vanita staggered back against the tiled bathroom wall.

Red smeared her ghostly skin, darkened by the bloody hue edging my vision. Slashes opened up, blooming cuts and bruises on every visible inch of her.

"Stop!" Jessa hissed. "You f-fucking freak!" She tried to swing her spiked fist at me, but the damage to her was almost as much as to Vanita. She tumbled to the floor, twitching as more and more wounds split and bruised her flesh.

I rose, feeling oddly light. High on the magic pulsing out from me.

"Killing us," Murag snarled, already prone on the tiles. "Help!"

Horror turned my stomach as I watched the three hybrids writhe in pools of their own blood. Dying on the bathroom floor, exactly how I'd found my mother.

I was a *healer*, dammit. Not this monster.

A whimper escaped me as I fought to keep myself in check. Darkness scrambled my thoughts, writing outwards as I struggled to reel it back.

But it was no use.

If I didn't get away, they'd die. Right here on the floor.

"Fires in Hell," I groaned.

I staggered to the door, flipping the lock and tumbling out into the dim corridor. I slammed into the opposite wall with a grunt.

A stocky male I recognised from classes snickered at me from the middle, blocking the way and flexing his muscles as he ran a hand over his shaved head. "Can't handle your brew, Eve?"

I hissed through clenched teeth, feeling that awful darkness surge in his direction.

He sucked in a breath. "Ow, shit!" He gaped down at a bruise purpling his ribs, peeking out from the white fabric crossing his torso.

Panic stabbed my middle as I lurched away.

"Hey, widow-witch! Wait, you need to fix this!" he yelled, but I was already stumbling down the corridor.

I ran to the furthest room, shoulder barging the door. The lock gave under my desperation, cracking through the wooden frame. Red hazed my vision like smeared blood.

I slammed the door behind me, unable to think. Chest heaving, I fought the darkness leaking from the depths of my soul into my flesh.

Hungry for violence.

A familiar demon, clad only in skimpy lingerie, whirled around in a flare of pine-coloured locks, her pouty lips parting. A bed loomed at the back of the room, a winged figure sprawled in a chair at its base, half-hidden behind Zahara's voluptuous frame and wild hair.

The sight was so unexpected, even my vicious magic paused.

Shock bled to cunning on Zahara's face as she cocked a hip, looking me up and down and finding me lacking. A single candle, atop the dresser by the wall, cast a ghoulish light across her pretty features.

"I know you're jealous, but that doesn't mean you can keep following me." She shooed me towards the door with perfectly painted golden claws. "Run along now, human. Me and your friend were in the middle of something."

I frowned, but my focus turned inwards, frantically trying to lock the monster back in its cage before I hurt anyone else. The sensation of something twisting under my skin lessened, along with the bubbles popping in my chest, making me jittery.

"We're not friends."

Hurt sliced through my middle, and I sucked in a sharp breath. I *knew* that voice.

It haunted my fucking dreams. Whispered to me in that lilting accent, teasing and seductive.

Zahara smirked, victorious. "Oh, that's right, Killian. The widow-witch has no friends."

Evil threatened to spill from my fingertips once more, writhing in my veins, polluting my blood.

Killian's chosen hookup was the exact opposite of me in appearance. Zahara was everything a succubus should be, and I was barely considered a demon most days.

"Leave," Killian snarled.

Pain hollowed me out. I turned, stomping away to do as my brother's best friend demanded. That invisible darkness thrashed harder. My heart pounded as I lurched for the door.

"Not you, kid."

I froze.

Zahara stiffened, tail snapping angrily behind her before she pasted on a sultry pout for the incubus. "But I'm about to go into heat, baby. You're gonna want to ease me through it. You won't be able to help yourself."

My insides pinched at the thought. After maturity, most sexual-type demonesses had an annual heat. Instinct could force one too, if things were dire enough that an influx of energy was needed to survive. Since your enemy could become your lover if they were willing, it was thankfully quite rare for a non-cycle heat to occur.

Partaking in someone's heat was considered quite the prize, though, and Zahara never let me forget that I wasn't demon enough to have one.

Killian chuckled, a dark sound that stroked me like one of his feathers. "You think I can't resist a succubus in heat? Your pathetic pheromones mean nothing. Scrape up what's left of your dignity, and run along. I need Eve."

His words spiked a longing deep into my chest. Whatever he meant by that statement, it wasn't what I craved in the dark corners of my battered heart.

"You're a real bastard," Zahara sniffed. She stalked past me, shoulder barging me as she left the room with a slam of the already cracked door.

I staggered, expecting pain, but the claw-marks that should have curved around my collarbone had already healed.

I frowned down at my bloodstained dress in the hazy darkness of the room. The evidence was there. It had been real and not another bloodied nightmare or break from reality.

The distinct, sweet floral scent of haze reached me, perfumed with metallic blood.

Peering through the drugging smoke lingering around the room, I sucked in a gasp as I finally got a good look at the enforcer, sprawled in a chair like it was a throne.

Scant moonlight pooled through the window at his back to cast his face in shadows that danced in the candlelight. The straight ends of his rich charcoal hair fell across his face to graze his angular cheekbones. His eyes glowed silver, seeming to pierce right through me.

Angelic wings draped on either side of him, the feathers splayed dramatically, the only light thing about the dark demon.

Red smears stained his purple-grey skin. Deep gashes lacerated his muscular chest, left bare.

Panic strangled me. A glazed look had entered his eyes. Given the stain on his lower lip and the rolled-up stick of haze perched between his knuckles, it could either be the drugs or the damage.

The monster rattled inside me, not done with me yet.

I clenched my jaw, struggling to call on the healing light in my middle and fight back the slithering evil that battled for its freedom.

Killian's handsome features creased as he watched me. I probably looked constipated, face scrunched up and fists clenching.

I lifted my hands and stepped towards him.

He looked away, voice a dark rasp of smoke. "You shouldn't touch me."

I ignored the sting of his words. He never let me heal him. It was only if he passed out from the severity of his injuries that I'd get to save the stubborn idiot's life.

No warm light lit my hands though.

If anything, a crimson shade seemed to make my fingertips glow. Like I'd dipped my claws in fluorescent blood.

My heartbeat thundered too loud in my ears.

Control slipped through my grasping fingers. The violent *thing* inside me lashed out, turning my emotional pain into a more physical one.

But not mine.

Killian quirked a brow as the wounds on his chest widened like gaping maws, spewing blood down his skin in thick torrents.

Hollow and clawing, my invisible darkness latched onto the seated demon even as I scrabbled to hold it back.

He pushed to his feet, unhurried, eyes raking me. A small crease formed between his brows, the only outward sign of emotion despite him being torn open, bleeding out on the floorboards.

Something flickered in his depthless eyes. "Eve? Are you okay?"

Only he would be bleeding to death and ask if *I* was okay.

I swayed in my heels, and he reached out his hands as if to steady me, hovering on either side of my shoulders without touching.

"I..." It was all I could garble out as the red misting my vision darkened like lifeblood.

I was vaguely aware of his lips moving in response, but the rushing in my ears drowned everything else out.

Power churned and twisted, making me dizzy with the push and pull through my chest. The world spun with the angry tide. It tunnelled until Killian's glowing eyes were the only thing I could see.

I collapsed face-first into his waiting arms.

Chapter 6

“Tell me, sweetness, what do you think about when you’re all alone in bed at night?” a familiar voice purred with an indulgent lilt.

I blinked sleepily, looking around for the source. The room sat empty apart from a king-size bed and painted furniture, messily laden with clay pots of various beauty products. A single candle flickered on the dresser, battling the shadows. Smoke drifted through the air, darkening the space and bringing the rich floral scent of haze.

The air had a dreamlike quality, softening reality like I'd smoked the drug for hours even though I'd never touched the stuff.

Music pulsed from somewhere beyond the bedroom.

I must still be at the house party. Judging by the confusion swimming through my mind, I really had drunk too much brew.

This was the room where I'd stumbled upon Zahara and Killian, but something about it looked different. I just couldn't figure out what.

As if my thoughts summoned the wicked incubus, Killian's voice came again. "Is it fluffy kittens and rainbows?" The edge of mocking in his voice skated over my skin, sinfully caressing me like the tease of claws. "Or...do you find something darker to play with?"

I turned again, this time finding him sprawled in the ornate chair at the end of the bed, just like before I'd collapsed, a smirk toying with his lips.

I could have sworn it was empty a second ago. Doubt crept in on silent paws, clawing at my sense of reality.

Killian's chest was still bare, exposing slate-purple skin and inky tattoos to my hungry gaze. Muscular pecs were unmarred by the cuts that should have been there. Defined abs carved a trim waist, leading my attention down the dips and valleys until I hit leather trousers, wrapping his lower body to hide the rest of him from view.

Enormous snowy wings spread from his back, the feathered tips spanning wide enough to block the king-size bed I knew was behind him. The tall arches jutted gracefully above his broad shoulders, adding to the overwhelming presence that was Killian.

The sight of one of my brother's enforcer's shouldn't set my pulse fluttering, but it was as if the sexy bastard called to me so strongly even the blood in my veins responded.

I guessed that was what I got for having a crush on an incubus.

He rose from his makeshift throne, all fluid grace and power. His wings flared under my attention, showing off the pure beauty of each pearly feather, impossibly bright in the candlelit room. He tucked them tight with barely a rustle, swallowed by the dull thud of music, too distant to be real.

Killian stalked me, circling me like I was prey. I widened my stance, standing my ground as I tracked him through the smoke.

I was prey that wanted to be caught. I wanted him to pounce on me and take me to the floor. I wanted his hands pinning me down with the threat of claws. His mouth on me. His fangs in my skin. His venom taking me to new heights.

I swallowed thickly, letting the drugging flavour of haze sweep away my worries before they could surface. Another taste coated my tongue, vibrant energy filling me with a burned-caramel flavour that instinct told me belonged to Killian.

This was a dream.

If the blurred quality and odd details hadn't clued me in, the apparent taste of Killian's desire did.

In real life, he treated me like a child. He called me "kid."

I'd only ever tasted his energy once, when he'd rescued me from the hunter compound, and even then I wasn't sure what had really happened, except he'd somehow given me the strength I needed to heal my critical injuries along with Rex's.

Killian would bury a body for me, but he'd never look at me with all the hunger of a starved dragon. He'd never stalk me through a darkened bedroom, radiating lust and bad intentions.

Dream-Killian stepped in close, towering over me. His wings curved around me, soft feathers stroking my exposed back through the low cut of my silky dress as he trapped me in a luxurious cage.

He tipped my chin up with a single claw. Moonlight kissed stormy waves in his eyes, a siren's song luring me into his depths.

His presence wrapped around me, overwhelming everything.

Without words, he leaned down, pressing a chaste kiss to the corner of my lips. Just missing where I craved.

Feather-light kisses trailed along my jaw until his warm breath grazed the shell of my ear.

"Sweetness... You have no idea how long I've craved this."

I licked my lips, struggling to catch my breath as he whispered words I'd longed to hear.

"And you *do* owe me that favour..." He trailed off, the forked tip of his tongue grazing my throat.

"What do you want?" My words came out husky, like I was already drunk on him.

"My silence...for your screams." His words were a tease against my skin, lighting my nerve endings with sparks of need. "Drown me in the sweet taste of you."

"What a nightmare if I didn't," I mused.

He smiled against my jaw, fangs tracing my delicate skin a second before pain stung just below. Sharp teeth bit deep into my neck. The flare of pain ceded to the most delicious warmth. Pleasure bloomed as he drank from me, venom gliding through me like silk.

A hard length pressed against my hip, making my thighs clench in anticipation. Just that vague impression was enough for me to moan at the sheer size of him. The steel. The heat.

As quick as it started, his fangs left my flesh, leaving me cold and wanting. He stepped back, wings releasing me. I stumbled a step, dizzy from his masculine intensity being ripped away.

He grinned, the startling image of a fallen angel from human myth. If there was one thing I knew about Killian, though, he'd lost whatever halo he might have had a long time ago.

Demonic sin dripped off him.

His tail whipped out, hooking behind my knees.

I yelped, falling backwards. But instead of hitting the floor, I fell on a soft bed that was somehow beneath me. If furniture was moving on a whim, I really must be in a dream.

The confirmation made me bold, and I parted my legs, inch by inch. My skimpy dress rode up my hips, exposing my satin-covered core as I dug my heels into the furs.

Dream-Killian bit his fist, a low growl spilling out as his eyes devoured me, laid out on the bed just for him. His wings flared, shivering in what I hoped was excitement.

He prowled close, looming over me like a dark god.

I'd never felt so attractive in my life.

"Eve..." His voice roughened. "Tell me you want this. Let me take care of you," he purred, and the silken tip of his mischievous tail trailed up my calf, leaving goosebumps in its wake.

I swallowed thickly. Even in my dreams, it was harder than it should have been to admit to everything I'd secretly hungered for all these years.

"Yes." The word ended in a faint moan.

A dark smirk hooked one side of his lips. He was every sinful fantasy I'd had, too tantalising to be real.

His tail flashed, the stinger slicing through my panties with deadly precision.

Before I'd even finished gasping, his hands grabbed under my knees and shoved them up to my ribs, spreading me to the limit.

A groan left his lips, and then he feasted.

I moaned as his forked tongue laved straight through my slick folds to swirl over my clit. He snarled, vibrating my lower lips with a delicious sensation that knocked another desperate sound free.

Burned caramel peppered the air, the smoky scent infusing the dream with sparks of power, like energy really was seeping into me, alongside the pleasure Killian delivered.

His tongue ghosted over my clit before faintly circling my entrance, teasing and taunting. I'd never felt so much from so little contact.

Sharp points dug into my thighs as Killian gripped me harder, pinning me to the bed beneath him. His wings clamped around me, trapping me in the softest cage.

I arched off the furs as he shoved his tongue into me, the slick thickness making me writhe.

"Killian!" I moaned, hands fisting his horns. Their feather-ridged texture grounded me even as he pushed me higher.

My hips moved of their own accord, until I was shamelessly grinding myself against his face, using his horns for leverage. He growled into my pussy like a threat, tongue vibrating deep inside me even as the base worked the needy bundle of nerves at my apex.

Rich caramel energy drowned me while he ate me like a demon starved.

His tail shot under my neck and wrapped around my throat. My lips parted as he tightened his hold and curved me up to face him, half-supporting, half-choking.

Something big loomed on the horizon, rushing towards me.

Our eyes locked, fresh blood on sharp steel.

"Pay me, sweetness," he snarled against my clit.

And smashed me apart.

I screamed just for him.

Waves of pleasure rolled through my core, spreading outwards and drenching every broken piece of me in bright ecstasy.

My hips bucked, and I was vaguely aware of the demon throwing his weight on top of me, pinning me as he continued to feast. Lips, tongue, and teeth worshipped between my thighs until I couldn't take any more.

A feeble mewling sound was spilling from my lips. My claws scraped at broad shoulders.

The vicious demon finally relented, slowing his attack. He placed a delicate kiss on my inner thigh, gaze holding mine.

My chest heaved, whole body twitching on the bed, after-shocks electrifying every inch of me. Power fizzled through my veins, like I was drunk on the energy of pleasure, even in a dream.

"So fucking delicious," Killian purred, licking his swollen, glossy lips. His warm breath peppered my sensitive core, and I shuddered beneath him. "Consider our deal...*satisfied*."

The sound of something shattering outside tugged at my attention.

He cocked his head aside even as his eyes held me prisoner. A wicked smirk, just as sharp as the peek of his fangs, was the last thing I saw before the world faded completely.

Chapter 7

I bolted upright.

Heavy covers pooled at my waist. My breath laboured in and out of my lungs in a harsh rhythm like I'd run from a pack of rabid hellhounds.

The familiar sight of my bedroom greeted me, but the sexy demon of my dreams wasn't hiding amongst my overflowing laundry pile.

Disappointment squeezed my chest. I was all alone in my bed, oddly energised like I'd been shot up with more than just the adrenaline of a rude awakening.

The sun peeked through the windows with the early rays of dawn, trying to pierce the towering darkness of the Bloodwood. My cabin rested beside the forest, much to Rex's dismay. Being close to nature had always soothed me, though, despite the dangers it held.

The sound of breaking clay yanked me fully from sleep's groggy hold. I shoved my blanket off and lurched out of bed, stuffing on my fuzzy slippers and hurrying towards the source of the noise.

Adrenaline dumped into my veins, leaving me jittery yet hyper-focused as I rushed out of my bedroom, into the short hallway.

I lived alone.

Anyone here this early in the morning, smashing the place up, was an intruder.

Or a monster.

My claws ached with the threat of oncoming violence as I swept into the kitchen, homing in on the noise.

I screeched to a halt just inside.

My mouth dried up, all moisture heading south.

Killian stood in my kitchen, topless, cuddling a vicious hellcat to his broad chest.

The lean beast reminded me of a black leopard I'd seen in a human realm zoo once, complete with black fur and almost invisible darker rosettes. She was about the same size but sleeker, with intelligence burning in familiar blood-red eyes. A darker crimson tufted her triangular ears and tail tip, the tail fluff hiding a deadly stinger loaded with venom.

Some said they'd seen hellcats with their own magic, like how hellhounds could play with fire. Given the felines were a lot more elusive than their doggy nemeses, the rumours weren't widely confirmed.

Well, they were *meant* to be elusive.

This particular hellcat, with red accents and a notch in its left ear, had been terrorising me since I'd freed her four days ago. She'd broken into my cabin a handful of times, causing havoc and stealing whatever took her fancy before sauntering back out.

"It's okay, pretty girl, I've got you," Killian cooed, stroking a clawed hand down her back.

The traitorous death kitty *purred*.

I blinked rapidly, sure I'd lost my fires-damned mind.

But the vision before me didn't change.

Not only had that stalker of a hellcat found me again, but the demon I'd just had a sex dream about...

Was. Right. Here.

"Um..." I trailed off, meeting Killian's mirthful gaze. "What are you doing here?"

"Don't you remember last night?" His voice dropped to a sinfully husky purr.

Every muscle in my body locked up. My heart was about to slam its way out of my chest.

Did he mean...?

Surely not.

Right?

Unless...?

"You fainted in my arms." His upper lip curled as if he tasted something bitter.

I tried not to let his obvious distaste get to me, but little claws of hurt scratched at my chest anyway.

"You shouldn't touch me."

His brows rose as his gaze dipped to take me in.

I blushed furiously. Apparently, I'd slept in the slinky minidress from the party, still spattered with blood, and it had ridden dangerously high up my bare legs.

Paired with fluffy pink cat slippers, it was *quite* the look.

Thoughts of what Killian had done to me in my dream flashed through my mind, offering me visions of the sexy incubus pinning me beneath him and devouring me with a fiery passion only my alcohol-fuelled subconscious could torture me with.

The worst thing was, as a sex demon, he could sense my arousal. I had a little of the ability, being only half-succubus, but like Zahara, he was a hybrid of two sexual types.

As if confirming my thoughts, he shot me a knowing grin.

My cheeks flamed as red as my hair.

I fought the urge to squirm in the tense silence, layered with that damn hellcat's purring.

If a monstrous feline could lap up drama, that was exactly what she was doing, evil mirth in her bright eyes.

Killian scratched the beast under her chin, barely missing the lethal sabre-like fangs that jutted down past it. Her purrs increased to the rumble of stampeding unicorns.

I cleared my throat, gesturing at all of him. "And now?"

"Your kitty knocked my coffee over, so I thought I'd encourage her to leave the rest of your things alone before you had to drink directly from the pot."

Broken shards of painted clay littered the island's countertop. He'd already picked them up, and the idea of Killian not only in my house, drinking my coffee, but cleaning up sent my mind into a tizzy.

Why was it so hot for a topless guy to cuddle a fluffy animal and clean for me?

I cleared my throat, trying to unstick my tongue from the roof of my mouth. "Thanks… Um, that's not *my* hellcat. She's a menace that's been breaking in and stealing my food. But I meant…what are you doing in my house, Killian?"

He smirked, but the lazy mirth didn't soften the intensity in his dark eyes. "After you passed out on me, I carried you home, but I couldn't just leave you, kid."

Kid.

The reminder of how he'd seen me was like a pail of ice water, snuffing out the lingering fantasy from my dumb dream.

A dry chuckle forced its way up my throat, just this side of bitter. "Oh. Well, um, thanks, I guess."

Yeah, real smooth, Eve.

His sinful lips twitched, and he placed the monster kitty down on the counter. She rubbed her head against his hand, as if she couldn't resist one last snuzzle, and turned to me with what I swore was a smug expression.

She sauntered to the edge of the rough-hewn marble top. Her sinuous tail smacked into the tower of mugs beside the coffee machine, rattling them ominously.

The hellcat sat back on her haunches, lifted a huge paw, and looked me dead in the eye.

"Kitty, no! Don't you do it...," I hissed, watching her from the other side of the island, too far to do anything.

Her lips peeled back to reveal a vicious maw of pointy teeth. A feline grin.

She smacked the tower of mugs, wicked glee burning in her eyes. My cups crashed to the floor with a harsh shattering.

I gaped at the destruction. "Why!?"

Her eyes seemed to scream, "You know why!"

She lifted her snooty tail, daintily picked out a cookie from the somehow lidless jar next to where the tower had been, and leaped off the counter with the silent fuck-you grace only a feline can possess. The psycho sauntered off into the living room. Probably to get crumbs and fur all over my sofa.

"Ugh, stop stealing my damn cookies, you monster!" I yelled at her retreating cat butt.

No wonder humans thought Hell was a place of tortured souls.

It was a hellcats' world. We just tried to survive it.

A husky chuckle drew my attention back to the winged incubus dominating my kitchen, and I finally allowed myself to take in the rest of him.

My jaw slackened. "What the fuck happened to you?"

Bloody gashes tore through Killian's impressive chest, slicing the avian tattoos across his torso and arms. The bleeding was down to a trickle for most of the wounds, some almost healed, but damage littered his body.

The amount of pain should have been excruciating, yet he'd had a casual chat with me about the ungrateful feline who'd been bullying me.

A sardonic grin curved lips pouty enough to make a succubus jealous. "I'm an enforcer, kid. I was enforcing. Or did you forget what I do for your uncle?"

His insistence on always calling me "kid" and referring to Rex as my "uncle" irritated me to no end. Sure, he and Rex were years older than me, but that didn't mean I was a child.

"He's more like an overbearing brother," I muttered under my breath, even though I called Rex "Uncle" to his face all the damn time to get under our king's thick skin.

I was already reaching for the light I kept inside me as I rounded the counter towards the stubborn demon. Getting close to Killian was like stepping into the shadow of a mountain: dark and awe-inspiring. Nothing could draw my attention away for long.

I met his piercing gaze, fighting not to squirm under his intensity. Especially after the dream I'd just had.

The warm light of my healing magic swelled within me, and my relief was immediate. I blew out a breath as I watched my palm glow. I hadn't been able to heal anyone properly since I'd returned. Only the occasional minor injury, if I was lucky.

A wave of tiredness washed over me, and my glow flickered.

Killian stared at my hand, a worried crease between his brows. "It's happening again, isn't it?"

"Everything's fine," I blurted, struggling to leash the monster hunting through my veins, hungry as it stalked my healing energy.

The glow at my fingertips reddened. Or maybe it was my vision, tingeing at the edges.

Killian hissed through clenched fangs, the wounds across his chest gaping wider.

My heart pounded erratically as I pulled back, stumbling away before I could hurt him any more. "Fuck!"

Guilt nipped at me as my vision cleared. Killian grabbed a tea towel from one of the cabinet drawers, somehow knowing exactly where it would be, and used it to casually staunch the bleeding across his abs.

His eyes met mine, a steady anchor in the chaos swirling around me. "It's going to be okay." His voice pitched low, like he was trying to soothe a wounded animal.

"I'm meant to be healing you, not whatever this is!" I hissed, and the fresh burn of tears pressed behind my eyes.

I was the healer of this kingdom. It was my purpose. The one thing that made me valuable.

And I couldn't even get that right.

A warm palm cupped my cheek. Killian tipped my face up to his, thumb tugging my lower lip out from where I'd been ruthlessly biting it.

"We are going to figure this out." His lilting voice burrowed down to my soul, wrapping around me. "I promise."

The way he said "we" almost had the tears spilling over.

Somehow, he had a way of making me feel safe, no matter what chaos was going on. But this wasn't his problem.

I didn't want to be another issue for the enforcer to fix.

I pulled my face from his warmth, ignoring the pang in my heart.

His cuts were healing at a rapid rate, meaning he'd fed recently. Gorged himself, in fact.

"This is how you killed that idiot the other night?" he asked, gesturing to his bloodied torso. "It's happening a lot?"

I stuffed down the truth, spitting out a lie instead. "No."

His navy eyes churned like an ocean in the moonlight, dark and dangerous. He arched a perfectly shaped brow. "Don't make me bend you over my knee."

I practically choked on my own tongue.

My desire saturated the air.

But nobody else's did.

Killian's nostrils flared as he inhaled my scent and drew a few wisps of my energy into himself. His navy eyes glinted silver.

I ruthlessly shoved the lust down, cutting him a glare. "Fine. It's happened a couple of times since I returned from my...visit topside."

"Who else knows about this?"

This time, the truth came easily, despite the tightness in my throat. "Nobody."

He nodded, looking contemplative. "It's something to do with your human magic, isn't it?"

My gaze dropped, tracing the inked feathers twitching on his throat with his steady pulse. The winged birds looked alive as if they took flight across his skin, refusing to stay as mere tattoos.

"You need to speak to the queen," he said, pushing my chin up with the sneaky tip of his tail and forcing me to meet his depthless eyes.

The "or I will" was left unspoken. My brother's most ruthless enforcer never made empty threats.

I pulled back, annoyed he was treating me like a kid. Again.

"You threatening to tattle on me, Kill?" I quirked a brow, batting aside his silken heart-tipped tail and crossing my arms.

He smirked, a deliciously dark twitch of his lips, like he found my defiance amusing. My quip felt more petulant than sassy now, and it pissed me off even more.

"I don't need to, Eve. Here I am the law, and I'll do whatever it takes to protect this kingdom."

"Stop bleeding all over my kitchen and get out," I huffed, pinning him with a stern glare. "Apparently, I've got a witch to see."

Chapter 8

I slammed the ornately carved door shut a little harder than necessary.

Killian crossed his arms, and his biceps tensed distractingly. The stubborn bastard had insisted on waiting while I'd sped through a shower and dressed.

I'd then pretended the cookie-thieving hellcat sprawled out on my sofa didn't exist, and left her snoozing peacefully.

The incubus leaned against the wood siding of my cottage like he had a right to it. A part of me hated that he sort of did.

After all, he had built it.

Last year, when my brother had finally crumbled enough to admit I did need my own space, Rex and his enforcers had built my cabin. I'd shamelessly ogled the hot enforcers while we'd worked—I was part succubus, after all—but really, I'd only ever had eyes for one infuriating incubus.

Until my brother had jokingly growled at me to focus on nailing the timber and not one of his friends.

Killian's lips twitched like he was remembering a similar thing.

The Bloodwood called to me from just behind the single-storey cabin as I avoided piercing navy eyes. The trees were like the pine forests I'd seen on Earth but with a mix of subspecies native to Hell. Towering redwoods dominated, bleeding rich crimson sap to give the forest its name, but there was a myriad of flora from black ebony hugged by lichens to colourful wildflowers brimming with poisons.

The day after construction, two trough-like planters had appeared outside my cottage, right under my shuttered front windows.

Blooming inside was my favourite flower: bloodbores.

The rich red petals brightened the dark wood façade of my home as much as warning people away, given this flower held a special kind of poison. The same flowers had also been carved into my heavy-set front door.

The flowers were similar to the hellebores I'd seen on Earth, which I supposed was how they'd got their name given demons had been visiting since ancient times. I'd been foolish enough to accept the summons from a nature mage. At first, he'd seemed sweet when he'd started by offering me a multicoloured bouquet of the pretty flowers. Too bad he'd tried to bargain for a deal that would have had me on my knees to earn them and a bland dose of his energy.

Unsurprisingly, I hadn't taken the deal, but it was still a better experience than my last summoning, which had ended up with me sold to hunters.

From what our witch queen had told me, I wasn't strictly a nature mage myself, but the healer in me had always been drawn to certain plants for their medicinal uses, as much as their beauty. The majestic creatures of Hell had always fascinated me too.

Killian watched me with an unwavering intensity.

I turned from my cabin and my scrambled thoughts, heading down the path. My throat dried as the demon fell in step beside me, in the opposite direction of his home.

I shot him a sideways glance. "Where do you think you're going?"

He shrugged his wing arches, unfazed by the blood still seeping down his front from the wounds I'd failed to heal. "With you."

I ignored the stupid little skip of my heartbeat, flattening my expression. "I don't need babysitting, Kill. I think I can walk to Rex and Zoella's on my lonesome."

It was early enough that the village was still peaceful, the sun barely cresting the vast forest to bathe the low rooftops.

He chuckled. "What if you chip a claw, sweetness? Your brother would skin me alive."

Heat flooded my cheeks. It was the nickname he'd given me in my dream. He'd never called me that before. I would have remembered. It would be scrawled all over my stupid journal with little hearts all around it.

Had I done something before blacking out last night to make him call me that? That could explain why I'd dreamt about it too.

"Such a stalker," I muttered, focusing intently on the other cabins making up the Hybrid Kingdom instead.

A hodge-podge of mismatched log cabins dotted the grass, edging the Bloodwood. The village sprawled for a mile beyond the imposing forest's border, growing every month as more and more outcasts and hybrids found their way into the safety Rex offered to all.

Unless I murdered them, of course.

I swallowed down the guilt trying to choke me.

Crop fields, small orchards, and livestock paddocks had been cultivated along one edge of the village kingdom. Most preferred to hunt for themselves in the Bloodwood, though, so any animals kept were mostly for eggs and dairy.

My recent unintentional stay on Earth had me drawing comparisons between our two realms more than before. Where they had mass farming, we tended towards smaller practices, but what I wouldn't do for a greasy fast food burger and chips salty enough to murder a snail right now.

I literally had the hangover from Hell.

My stomach grumbled, punctuating the thought, and I stifled a chuckle at my own stupid thoughts.

"Hungry, are we?" Killian's lips quirked. "Too much glowing drain your energy?"

I flipped my messy red waves over a shoulder. "I'm not the one leaking everywhere. You look fresh from a massacre. And smell like it too."

I wished that were true. Instead, his smoky-sweet scent taunted me.

He chuckled. "Not a morning person, huh?"

I rolled my eyes, but worry grazed me with its fangs. Killian might be one tough bastard, but he'd been hurt and bleeding for hours now.

And I'd only made things worse. Which seemed accurate for my life right now.

As a sexual demon like myself, Killian siphoned desire for a power boost and faster recovery.

My cheeks rouged again. According to my dreams, I had a few creative ideas for how to help without using my broken magic.

Sexual feeding didn't have to mean getting frisky with someone, but I was still struck by the idea of him with someone else.

Someone like Zahara.

She was the opposite of me in almost every way. Tall and curvy, she had an innate allure to go with her every demonic feature. Demons prized all those useful extras: horns, tails, spikes, wings, limbs, you name it.

In comparison, I was practically human.

I hurried down the stone path, squeezing between two snowberry bushes the neighbouring houses had let grow out of control, trying to outpace my babysitter in case he could sense my bubbling insecurities.

He already thought of me as an awkward kid. His best friend's sister. Nothing in the last twenty-four hours would help him take me seriously.

I swear, if he started to coo and pinch my cheeks, I'd nut him in the face. Diddly horns first.

It wasn't long before a large redwood cabin peeked out from between the thinning buildings up ahead. At one time, it had been the only building here. Rex had slowly built more, budding off the simple one he'd started with. The thought of him all alone, in a kingdom for one, always made my heart ache.

"I think I can make it from here." I shot Killian an arch look.

A wry smile answered. "You can't get rid of me that easily."

"Go lie down before you fall down," I said, shooing him with a hand. "At your age, you should take it easy."

"I'm going to ignore that because your pretty kitty stole your coffee," he drawled.

I rolled my eyes so hard I thought my headache would take me, but closed the distance to my old home. The enormous front door was a solid ebony, polished to a gleaming shine and nestled within the rich redwood logs making up the rest of the expanded cabin. It was easily big enough for someone winged and twice my height to walk through without brushing the sides.

I eyed Killian's muscular frame. Given who Rex's enforcer generals were, the door choice made sense.

I could probably roll through it, limbs akimbo.

I'd never thought so much about a door.

I may or may not have been stalling.

The thought of confessing my dangerous secret to anyone, let alone our new queen, had a nervous laugh bubbling up. I clamped down hard as the first unhinged peal burst free.

Zoella was a glowing goddess of nature magic and, courtesy of her hellhound familiar, pretty lilac hell-fire too.

I was tainted. Broken.

I swallowed down another crazed giggle, all too aware of the weight of a certain enforcer's attention on my back.

"Do you need me to knock for you, Princess? Maybe carry you inside?" he purred beside me.

His taunting gave me the push I needed to rap my knuckles against the wood, shooting him a quick scowl that was met by a wicked grin.

A banging sounded within the house, and then the door was thrown open.

A stunning witch with pale-purple hair and matching eyes beamed at me. She threw her arms around my neck in an exuberance I was grudgingly getting used to.

"Eve!" She squeezed me tight, knocking the breath from my lungs.

Since moving to Hell last month, Zoella had been getting stronger with all the training she'd been doing with her mate.

I loved having her around. Not only was she hilarious and sweet, and badass enough to keep my brother in line, but she was magekind. One of the few connections I had to that half of my heritage, since I'd never even met my father. He'd abandoned my mother before I was born.

Zoella and I had started our own grimoire, recording spells and rituals to perform together. She'd been teaching me basic witch magic, like glamouring my appearance and casting truth spells. Things that didn't rely on my healing affinity.

My eyes welled as a flood of emotions hit me all at once.

I blinked furiously, hugging her right back. If anyone was going to understand what I was going through, it was her. Even though a part of me was filled with shame for bringing even more danger to her door.

She'd almost died for me once already.

I was putting her at risk, just being around her now. That hungry darkness slithered just beneath the surface. Watching. Waiting.

I pulled back, swallowing thickly. "Hey, Queenie."

Her eyes narrowed, telling me she didn't miss the extra sad sparkle in mine, but she let it slide. For now.

"Don't start. Your brother is insisting on calling me 'Your Highness' ever since I asked the demon in charge of the orchards not to bother with titles." She waved a hand, and I knew I could count on her to lighten the mood. "Now let's head inside before your winged stalker bores a hole through the back of your head."

She gave an exaggerated wave to said stalker, and I suppressed a sigh at the knowledge that he was still lurking behind me.

Did he think I'd trip over the doorframe and bash my skull in?

The incubus really had no faith in me.

And after what I'd done to him last night and again this morning, who could blame him? He'd probably followed me here to make sure I didn't assault any unsuspecting citizens.

Zoella lifted her hand, faking a static crackle and speaking into the jumper sleeve at her wrist. "The package has been delivered. I repeat, the package has been delivered. Over."

I snorted, shaking my horns. "You are such a human sometimes."

Killian's husky chuckle reached me too, and I turned to watch him lingering at the edge of the path. His eyes raked me one last time, sending warmth spiralling through me. White feathers spread wide as he flared his wings. With enviable ease, he launched himself into the air and soared gracefully towards the far side of town.

"Yeesh, just fuck him already." Zoella slapped me on the back with a giggle.

"Oh my fires, could you have said that any louder!?" I hissed, whirling around to see if anyone had heard her, but the streets were mercifully empty, and peering past her into her house didn't reveal my overprotective brother lurking around.

"Quit your worrying. Rex is still out hunting." She slapped me on the shoulder. "Come on in. I'm guessing you're not here for saucy girl talk about why a certain feathered friend was walking you to my place in the early hours, dripping blood and bad intentions, hmm?"

I swallowed thickly. "If only."

Chapter 9

Just say it.

Say. It.

"I'm broken," I blurted the words.

Zoella's lilac brows lifted as she glanced at me over a shoulder, striding into my favourite room of the house. I followed her into the newly refurbed space, lined with floor-to-ceiling bookshelves and stuffed with exotic houseplants until it was more jungle than library.

The floral scent of poisonous flowers soothed the raw edge of my nerves.

Haunting lilac and black hell-fire crackled in the fireplace, nestled deep between tall bookshelves. Creeping red vines draped its sides, reaching towards the flames rather than away.

A monster sprawled beneath.

He lifted his boxy head from meaty front paws, watching me enter his domain with fiery purple eyes. The hellhound's head was twice the size of mine, his maw filled with more sharp teeth than I could count. Rich black fur reflected the firelight, interrupted by too many white lines scarring his flesh.

The intimidating sight was tempered by an adorable lilac sock pattern on one of his front paws, matching the shade of one ear and cresting his fluffy chest.

"Hey, Alpha." I gave him an awkward wave.

It was so much more embarrassing to have this conversation in front of the proud hellhound, but Zoella never separated from her familiar for long.

She'd reunited with him in the human realm when she'd freed him from the same hunters who'd captured me. He'd followed Zoella here, to live in the Bloodwood with his pack of pups, and like his bonded witch, he'd been healing, getting stronger and healthier with every passing day.

Giving me a peek at his vicious fangs, he rumbled a sleepy growl like he was greeting me right back, and returned his muzzle to his paws before closing his eyes. His tail swept back, the end dipping right into the fire without a care.

In a way, I felt like Alpha and I shared a bond too, enough for me to understand his meaning in my own way. It was just another strange thing I'd been experiencing lately, like I could understand a creature's intent more than I should.

I brushed off the crazy before it could add more anxiety to an already messed-up situation. Hellhounds were highly intelligent animals, and being familiar bonded to a mage meant he was more in tune with magic; that was all.

Zoella lifted a glass pot of coffee from the low table in offering, and I silently shook my head, my stomach in knots as I waited for her to say something about my blurted confession. I took a seat on the sofa opposite her, sinking into the worn leather. She topped a ceramic cup to the brim with the dark brew before returning the pot to the scratched table.

The queen plonked herself onto the other sofa beside the vast windows, her back to the fireplace, somehow not spilling a single drop of liquid joy.

Taking a delicate sip, she leaned back amongst the fuzzy cushions and crossed her legs, seeming to ponder her response until I wanted to flip the coffee table between us and run around screaming.

"And what makes you say that?" she asked.

I was grateful for the lack of judgement in her tone, even if her arced brows hinted at disbelief.

I fanged my lower lip, debating where to start. "In the hunter compound, where they held me captive...something happened." I swallowed thickly, trying to ignore the memories surging up.

It had been terrifying, but things weren't nearly as bad for me as they were for others there. One of the hunter's scientists had even tried to protect me.

And at least I'd made it out alive.

I could practically feel the rage sparking off Zoella. It wouldn't be long before I saw actual black-and-purple flames in her hands. She'd come a long way in controlling her magic, but it was still new to her.

She was handling it all with the grace of a warrior queen.

"What happened?" she asked, tone soft, but beneath it lingered enough lethal promise to put any demon to shame.

I forced down a nervous giggle. "I...reached a limit. Too battered and drained. I thought I was going to die down there. And... I couldn't watch them hurt anyone else." I swallowed thickly, refusing to give in to the dark memories of how I'd ended up in solitary confinement.

Two months had passed since Rex, Zoella, and the enforcers had freed me from the hunters' not-so-tender care. The memories still hadn't dulled.

My gaze dropped to my hands. Sometimes, I'd still catch them covered in cuts and bruises from the corner of my eye. But I barely had a single scar on the outside.

A perk of innate healing magic, I supposed.

"And then?" she prompted, voice gentle as she set her cup on the table between us.

"I broke," I said, shutting down all emotions to hold my sanity together. "My magic bled. Corrupted. It lashed out, past their suppressor spells, and clawed open every hunter in the room." The heavy scent of gore filled my nose, and I had to swallow back bile before continuing. "It was a massacre."

My eyes found her lilac ones, and she nodded slowly, nowhere near as horrified by that as she should have been.

"I'm glad they're dead." Purple flames licked her fingertips before she squeezed her hands into fists to extinguish them. "Nothing is wrong with your magic, Eve. It's just different. You're only twenty-one. Your powers are still developing."

The conviction in her tone gave me hope. I didn't believe that was true, but it sounded like a problem that could be fixed, at least.

"So... You can make it stop? I can barely heal, and it's lashed out again since. Last night... I hurt some of our own," I said, voice strangling tight.

The pain trio may be hateful bullies, but I'd almost killed them.

"It was an accident, Eve. It's going to be okay, you hear?" Her hand gripped mine, an antique silver ring glinting on her finger. "Powers are always hard to control at our age, especially while we're relatively untrained and don't have a large coven to anchor us. But we can seek a specialist coven for advice." She nodded as if to herself, brows creasing in thought. "The Sage Coven in England is famous for its skilled healers. They've probably had all kinds of fun offshoots and quirks of your affinity over the years. I bet they've seen something like this before, or they'll at least know the best way to control your power as it grows."

Fuck.

I hadn't even thought about that. My magic was still growing, so whatever *this* was, it was only going to get stronger.

Everyone around me was going to die a bloody, painful death.

I flashed her a watery smile, blinking back the moisture I refused to let fall. "Great, so I don't have to exile myself from the kingdom of exiles."

She squeezed my palm tighter, the ache in my bones grounding me. "Never. Your brother and I would never cast you aside when you needed us most." Her voice cracked at the end.

There was a reason she was a lone witch in hell, and I squeezed her hand back just as hard.

Her throat bobbed as she swallowed. "Plus, you're half of the coven here. I can't lose my only sister in magic."

A genuine smile broke through at that. Zoella was kind, and so fiercely loyal when she finally let someone in. She'd been a tough nut to crack, but now I couldn't imagine our kingdom without her.

The sound of a door banging open had us both swivelling in our seats.

"Oh, honey, I'm hoooome!" Rex called out in a sing-song voice a second before he slid through the doorway into the jungle library.

The Hybrid King looked as psychotically happy as always these days, with a huge fanged grin like a white slash through his dove-grey lips.

He'd let his fire-ombre hair grow out to his chin, the thick waves falling messily into his face before he brushed them back between his vertical pair of waved horns, knocking free a stray leaf that somehow clung to the lower pair curving around his ears.

The hulking grey demon clapped his palms together as he spotted me. "Ohhh, am I interrupting a super-secret coven meeting, hmm?"

His arrowhead tail flicked back and forth behind him with his teasing mirth.

"Yes. Actually, *Uncle*. Now be a dear and leave before we turn you into a toad." I flicked my claws, adding a snooty sniff for good measure.

Alpha backed me up by deigning to lift his head and huff at the king.

Rex chuckled and sauntered over to plant a kiss on Zoella's lips. They both grinned goofily at each other for a long moment.

"Geez, you two, can you keep it in your pants for like two seconds?" I scoffed, but just seeing them together brought me so much joy.

If anyone deserved to grin like unhinged maniacs all the time, it was them.

Rex straightened and pinned me with a mock glare. "Still no respect for your elders, I see."

I stuck my tongue out. The only appropriate response.

He huffed back.

"Why are you covered in blood?" Zoella's tone was as sharp as her gaze, narrowed on the dried flecks peppering Rex's bare shoulders.

"Kingly duties." The big oaf threw the back of his hand to his tall horns, sighing dramatically. "Someone got creative with justice. Vanita, Jessa, and Murag were left in bloody heaps up a tall tree in the Bloodwood last night. I had to send someone to fetch them down and drag the idiots to the clinic, since they refused to see a certain witchy healer." He shot me a pointed look.

My eye twitched as I fought to smother my shock.

After a tense beat, he continued, "Apparently, they fed on unwilling pain last night and someone took offence to it. Seems they've only got themselves to blame."

My heart beat rapidly. Guilt wriggled through my middle because I had the sneaking suspicion their punishment had something to do with me.

I'd always thought Rex was responsible for my nickname as the widow-witch, but either he was a great actor...or it wasn't him.

I didn't know what to do with that.

"Damn." Zoella whistled. "Demon justice is *brutal*."

"But necessary," Rex mused, and his attention swung back to me, lips pursed. "So...is there anything you want to tell me?"

I froze, trying not to squirm on the sofa as Rex pinned me with his big-brother stare. The one that had always made me confess when I was younger.

I notched my chin.

Had the pain trio tattled on me for what I'd done to them at the party? Had Rex found out about the demon I'd accidentally torn apart?

Did he already know about my corrupted magic?

Either way, I'd decided to find the coven Zoella had mentioned. I couldn't stay here as a loaded gun being tossed between innocent people.

I didn't want to drag the happy couple on another rescue-the-demoness-in-distress mission though.

It was time I faced my problems like an adult.

By running away.

"Nope." I popped the *p*, giving Rex my best bratty grin.

Zoella rolled her eyes at me. "Eve's magic has been developing in a more...aggressive way, and we're going to the Sage Coven for help. They're healer affinity focused. And from what I've heard from your enforcers, *particularly* demon friendly." She shot her mate a loaded look.

I frowned. Was she implying what I thought she was?

Rex's eyes slid to mine, a flash of hurt in them. "If you've been having problems, why haven't you come to us sooner?"

I swallowed thickly. "I...didn't know what was going on. It's only happened a few times...and I thought it might just stop now that I'm home safe."

A deeper pain pinched his features. "You *are* safe, Eve. And if heading back to the human realm to beat information out of some crusty old wizards will help, then we'll leave first thing in the morning."

"You mean politely *ask* the nice *healers*," Zoella muttered under her breath.

Rex's lips twitched in mischief, lifting some of the heaviness in his expression, but he continued like his mate hadn't huffed at his natural inclination for violence. "It will give us enough daylight to get through the worst of the Bloodwood, and I can put Briar and Grell in charge while we're gone. Maybe I'll ask a few of the guys to come with us, though Kill isn't in my good books since he offed that merchant last week without even telling me why." He trailed off before pinning me with a flat stare.

I knew that look.

I couldn't even process the fact that Killian had taken the fall for my murdery little *accident*.

"Speaking of our feathered friend... Why is he waiting outside for you like some lovesick pup?" Rex quirked a brow at me, suspicion gathering in his red eyes like storm clouds.

"Um." I bit my lower lip, thoughts scrambling for something to say. "He walked me over this morning."

Somehow, he arched his brow even higher. "It's the arse crack of dawn. Has he been following you? Was he at your house? Did he stay there last night?" His voice rose slightly with each question, hitting that incredulous warning octave that had me fighting a wince.

Zoella's gaze bounced between us, glee tugging at her lips. She was seconds from bursting into giddy applause.

Rex held up a hand as I opened my mouth to explain. "You know what? I'll go ask him. I knew I should have put a stop to his bloody hobby."

I had no idea what *bloody hobby* he meant, but if a pit of hell-fire could open up and swallow me, that would be a mercy.

I ducked my head as he sauntered out of the room, a casual pace that belied the sharpness he was ready to wield.

Zoella's wide eyes met mine.

We leaped for the window at the same time.

Pressing our faces to the glass, we watched Rex stalk up to Killian, who lounged outside the house, thick arms folded and huge wings tucked.

He eyed Rex's approach, a grim sort of acceptance on his stunning face.

"Why were you at my baby sister's house this morning?" Rex's lightly muffled voice reached us through the thin pane. He put his hands in his trouser pockets, all casual like.

I hissed at him through the closed window. We weren't actually blood relatives, but we'd always had a sort of brother-sister relationship and I loved him like family.

I usually called him my boring old uncle, but *baby sister* was laying it on a bit thick.

Zoella practically vibrated beside me, valiantly trying to hold back a laugh.

Killian stood his ground. "She got hurt at a party last night, and I carried her home, put her to bed"—Rex snarled at the word, but Killian didn't pause—"and then slept on the couch to make sure she was okay."

Rex nodded, almost a thoughtful, wise king for a second.

Then he blurred, and his fist smashed into Kilian's face. The incubus's head whipped aside.

He spat blood before straightening.

My jaw dropped, but irritation blazed in the next beat.

"Oh my goddesses." Zoella finally let her laughter out with a snort. "Men."

The insane dolts stared at each other, then wide grins replaced hard expressions. Killian had a mouthful of bloodied fangs and a split lip he was only worsening with his unhinged mirth.

Nothing was said, and yet something had passed between them regardless.

I shook my horns with a dramatic sigh. "Yup."

Chapter 10

"What in the holy fires are you doing?" Dayla frowned, a bemused expression on her matronly features.

I'd left Rex's house only an hour ago, with the urge to run straight for the portal, an itch beneath my skin. Killian had stalked me all the way to work, though, as if he could sense something was off. He'd seen me safely over the clinic's threshold before finally flying away, and I'd rewarded him with a sarcastic little wave.

A nervous titter spilled out. "Oh, um, just trying a new technique. I learned it from the human realm. Very effective." I nodded sagely, pretending I was gluing a cut closed with the medicinal paste I'd created out of choice, not horrifying necessity.

Dayla's triple set of horns and spiked shoulder might give her an intimidating look, but she was a sweet, caring pain demon. She was also one of the few purebloods in our kingdom.

She'd been exiled from her village years ago, after refusing to heal their corrupt leader, and had set up the healing clinic when she'd found us. Thankfully, she did all the boring admin needed to run it, giving me a space to work on patients and supporting my magic with her more traditional medical techniques.

I'd been too young to have magic when my mother died, but if I'd known the things Dayla had taught me since, maybe I could have saved her.

"Hmmm, well, as long as your patient is okay with that?" Dayla trailed off in question, eyeing Hubert with a frown. "You must stop going after the most dangerous prey."

The elderly blood demon seated before me blushed a bright gold against his peachy skin tone. He ducked his horns, chipped and gouged from countless battles. "Aye, you're right on that one, matron. Sometimes, I just can't resist a good challenge."

Dayla shook her horns, spiked tail ball jabbing over her shoulder to point at my patient. "And that's why we see you in here almost weekly."

With a good-natured huff, she strode down the corridor, leaving me and my regular patient to share a conspiratory smile.

"Don't worry, Hughey, I think what you're doing is brave. Though, maybe take someone with you to watch your wings next time."

He smiled, almost sheepishly. "I will, Healer Eve."

"That's all done now. Try not to get it wet today, and by the morning, it should be fully sealed," I said, eyeing my work.

It would have been quicker to heal him with magic, but for weeks now, I'd been coming up with excuses for why I'd not been using it.

Hopefully, Hubert would be the last patient I had to treat the old way.

"Thank you." He patted me on the hand. "Your healing abilities keep this kingdom from falling apart."

He'd meant it as a compliment, but the words raked claws through my middle.

"I'm going away for a few days, so try not to take on any more shadow boars alone. You're lucky you got away with a mild maiming," I replied, curter than I'd intended.

He grinned, showing off a chipped fang.

A sigh escaped me. There was no way he was staying out of trouble.

I saw him out and grabbed my healer kit, complete with all the new pastes and potions I'd created. Between treating a handful of minor injuries from dawn hunts, I'd packed anything I could get my claws on that might help me get to the Sage Coven, and shakily written a note I'd carefully folded and placed into my pocket.

Shanlir had even come to find me, making sure I was okay after I'd disappeared on her last night. Guilt bit me at how frantic she'd seemed, even with the hangover. I'd given her a tonic and broken the news that I'd be gone for a few days on a trip topside for witchy things. The poor demon had been too groggy to ask questions, and I'd promised to bring her back something incredibly human, like cheesy puffs or an adorable devil plushie.

Taking a shaky breath, I eased out of the clinic's side door, picking my way carefully through the thriving herb garden and hopping the low fence that was more decorative than anything.

The healing clinic was near the middle of the settlement, in an area with most of the other services, right beside the small market. I gave it a wide berth, creeping past the quiet leather tannery instead.

Traders from other kingdoms had only started visiting us a few months ago, and it was still a novelty to get goods we hadn't made or brought back from dangerous trips to other kingdoms and the human realm.

Hopefully, news of the merchant I'd disappeared didn't spread.

I stuck to the side paths and offshoots between cabins, sneaking the ten minutes back to my home. The single-storey cabin with neat red log siding sat at the end of a worn stone path, a healthy distance from my neighbours. Unlike me, they preferred not to get too close to the Bloodwood.

Bright sunshine highlighted the bloodbore flowers overflowing two great planters on either side of my carved front door. The dark forest loomed behind. Some people might think it was creepy living next to the most dangerous woods in Hell, but it soothed my witchy side.

Sneaking furtive glances up at the skies, I raced to the backdoor of my house and crept inside. Silence greeted me in the dim interior, punctuated by the rapid thud of my heart.

I had to leave before anyone could follow me to their doom. A journey to the human realm was no joke.

It was safer since Rex had brokered a peace deal with our shadow-walker neighbours last month, but countless other dangers lurked between here and the portal that could get Rex and Zoella killed.

Me being one of them.

Panic iced my veins at the thought, and I drew a calming breath to stop myself spiralling.

I hurried through the small mud room and into the main corridor bisecting my cabin. After grabbing a battered pack from the cupboard, I raided my bedroom for all the necessities, including tough leathers and bland clothing. It would take days for me to reach the portal, and as a lone hybrid travelling through the Bloodwood, skirting a neighbouring kingdom or two, I needed to go unnoticed.

Adding a light bedroll, gold coins for Hell and cash for the human realm, I charged into my kitchen next.

And stopped short.

A feast lay across the island counter: an enormous steaming joint of roasted boar resting on a wooden chopping block.

Along with a familiar evil hellcat, dramatically stretched out to get the maximum amount of fur on my stone surfaces. The curious feline lazily sniffed the golden meat and practically unhinged her jaw.

Wicked fangs disappeared into the plump haunch as the fuzzy wretch chomped off a bite. Her throat bobbed with the lump she swallowed lying down before she rolled to a sit and casually licked the grease from her chops.

Even the heavenly scent couldn't stop me from scowling as I noticed the glass cookie jar beside the meat was empty save a few crumbs.

"Oh, well, if it isn't the fluffy menace. Have you even left yet, *Cookie*?" I mocked, brushing my curls back between my horns.

Her tail flicked in annoyance, the cute tuft hiding a deadly stinger. It was the most emotion she'd shown.

"Cookie," I drawled again, smirking to myself when her tail puff gave another irate twitch. I jerked a claw at the food. "I'm guessing this isn't your handiwork?"

She began licking a hefty paw, somehow mocking me without words like she was saying, "Does it look like I roasted you a fucking boar?"

I shifted on my feet, watching the steaming food, now missing a sizeable chunk, like it might turn into a viper and bite me first.

Only a skilled hunter could bring down a shadow boar. I'd literally just patched up poor old Hubert for even looking at one wrong.

The more docile wild pig breeds were eaten regularly, but the type with midnight bristles and sharpened tusks was a deadly delicacy, usually reserved for special occasions like mating ceremonies.

Must have been from Rex. The old worrier was always looking after me, and he knew I'd been craving more ever since I'd tried it for the first time at his mating ceremony last month.

My brother was one of the few people in the kingdom who could hunt the creature without having to visit me afterwards.

He definitely couldn't cook it though. The poor demon was so culinarily challenged, he'd once burned water.

I snagged a neatly cut amber-hued slice from the chopping block. The scent of honey-apple cider wafted off the prime cut. Its crispy crackling passed the test as I tapped it with a claw, making a hollow noise I knew would crunch deliciously.

"Damn." I bit into the juicy piece, letting the heavenly food melt in my mouth with a low moan. "I'd literally mate the person who cooked this."

The hellcat made that weird hacking rasp I just knew was her laughing at me.

"At least you've got dinner for a few days, since you already snaffled all the cookies," I huffed back and wrapped as much of the meat as I could carry in wax paper, throwing it into my pack with a few other essentials.

I had no clue how the hellcat kept getting in, but she'd see herself out when she was good and ready, apparently.

My hands shook slightly as I placed the letter I'd written earlier on the kitchen counter. I had to get far away from the Hybrid Kingdom before Rex found out I was gone. I didn't want him to think I'd just disappeared on him again though.

He was family. He'd be worried sick if I didn't reassure him I was coming back as soon as I'd fixed myself.

I needed to do this on my own, without putting anyone else in danger, and I hoped explaining that in my note would be enough to keep him and his mate here, where they'd be safe.

With a deep breath, I snuck out the backdoor, turning to face the Bloodwood.

It loomed quiet and dark, despite the sunshine pouring over the village, pretending nothing was amiss.

Lying bastard.

There'd be dangers the second I stepped within its embrace.

With a final look back at the Hybrid Kingdom and its mismatched wonder, I strode into the Bloodwood.

Chapter 11

Crickets chirped at me as I waded through the long grass.

A fallen pine created a gap in the leafy canopy, letting colourful wildflowers run riot in the moonlit clearing. Their earthy perfume calmed me, despite the blood-like sap dripping from the dominant redwoods forming a gory backdrop.

Stars peeked here and there through the cloud cover. Moonlight pierced the canopy, but shadows owned the Bloodwood. I'd been walking for hours since I fled my home this morning, and it wouldn't be long before I'd have to set up camp for the night.

I hiked my pack higher, keeping my senses alert. The forest was eerily gorgeous, with tiny hints of colourful bioluminescence glowing from clustered petals.

Firebugs lazily buzzed through the air, helping illuminate the leaf litter. My night vision was nowhere near as good as most demons', so I couldn't help but thank the little critters for their help. As if they could feel my gratitude, a few more drifted into the path I took, creating a loose cloud of light in front of me.

Something inside me lit up too, a faint impression on the edges of my mind.

I frowned but ignored the sensation. Too many weird things were going on inside me as it was. I felt like I was going through a second puberty, and it was so unfair I wanted to hiss and stomp my foot like an actual teen.

I'd already undergone the most awkward sexual awakening for my succubus energy needs. I'd done my time.

I drew fresh air deep into my lungs. The moment I stepped into the human realm, I'd miss it. That and the balmy warmth of Hell.

A hungry energy buzzed through my chest, along with the dark undertone I'd come to fear. I chewed my lip as I walked, ignoring the nervous giggle trying to bubble up as a multitude of worries swept.

That hungry darkness was the whole reason I was traipsing through the Bloodwood. I'd do anything to keep my hybrid family safe.

A low growl rumbled through the trees.

I swallowed thickly, holding still as I scanned for the threat my instincts screamed was close.

Apparently, the "anything" might include getting eaten by one of the many beasties who called the Bloodwood home.

My magic hummed, as if it could sense the danger slinking closer.

The hungry darkness within writhed excitedly at the thought.

Through the trees, a creature appeared.

Shadows swathed its frame, hiding its true size. From this distance, I couldn't tell if it was some feral beast or Night, another of Rex's inner circle of enforcers. The brooding bastard was already topside, though, dealing with some other secretive mission.

The shadows tightened, condensing into a solid form on all fours, easily taller than I was and twice the bulk.

This was no friend of mine.

Invisible tendrils reached out from the magic inside me, tracing over the beast. The faint wisps tickled at my intuition.

"Fires." The whispered curse fell from my lips.

Apparently, this must be the karma humans loved banging on about, since what remained of the deadly shadow boar's kin was wrapped neatly in my pack.

Maybe it'd sniffed it out and come for revenge.

I held my hands out at my sides, preparing to swipe my knives from their sheathes around my hips and thighs. I'd laced half of them with beastbane, a rare poison from a pretty flower that Zoella had taken a liking to.

The other half was my own concoction from the bloodbores outside my house.

Slowly, so as not to startle the boar into attack, I unsheathed one of each type, savouring the knives' scant weight in my palms.

My special poison stained the black of my blade with red like it had already tasted blood.

The beast waited at the edge of the clearing, watching me from the darkness. I lingered in the moonlight, wishing the field of glowing wildflowers would keep the monster away.

The creature squealed in threat, the harsh pitch like a knife to my ears. Shadows flared wide, like a night viper about to strike, revealing pearlescent eyes and glinting tusks as the giant boar tossed its head.

Adrenaline pumped through my veins, but it was the darkness hunting after it that had my heart pounding. It felt eager, desperate for an outlet.

"I don't want to hurt you!" I called out, hoping to scare it off. "So trot along now, before you become crackling."

It snorted, pawing the ground, ready to charge.

Claw open its tender underbelly. Feast on its flesh while it's still hot.

I swallowed hard, gripping my knives tighter and pretending I wasn't having psychotic thoughts.

The poison on both my blades might end up killing it. I'd designed mine to paralyse the average demon, and we were a tough lot. The queen's one would drop the boar with a single nick.

The nightmare boar charged.

Hooves thundered against the dirt as the beast raced towards me.

I widened my stance, holding my ground.

Vile magic lashed my insides, but I had no time to worry about what it might do, only raise my blades and see which one of us would walk away.

My heart drummed faster with each pounding step it took as the distance between us narrowed to the width of the fallen tree.

Spill its lifeblood before it takes yours!

I hissed, baring my fangs and brandishing my blade in warning at both the beast and the crazy voice in my head.

The boar's eyes flashed silver, and it screeched to a halt, its tufted tail shooting up behind it. Squealing like a dying animal, it bolted back the way it had come, its shadows writhing around it in a smoky mess.

Shock gave way to a sense of triumph, and a grin stretched my lips. "Pffft, and they thought I needed babysitting."

An odd hush cocooned the space, like the clearing had detached itself from the rest of the forest.

I frowned at the boar's retreating form as logic seeped in. The thing was bigger than I was, and my diddly little fangs weren't particularly fearsome compared to its sharpened tusks.

Dark foreboding clawed down my spine.

No way would a shadow boar run off, tail between its legs, for a demon-mage half its size.

Something more monstrous had scared it away.

As if the thought conjured my fears, those odd magical tendrils grazed something living, breathing.

And lurking right behind me.

Warm breath met the shell of my ear.

Chapter 12

I sucked in a gasp to scream, but a palm covered my mouth, trapping the sound.

My brain engaged, and I stabbed back with my poisoned blades. Before they could taste blood, a thick tail lashed one of my wrists, and a firm hand caught the other.

A hard body pressed against my back, shaking with a low chuckle. "Now, now, sweetness, is that any way to greet your saviour?"

The suave voice, layered with a sexy lilting accent, finally penetrated my panic.

My body responded without my command, melting into his embrace as he held me close to his muscular chest. His wings curved around me, caressing my bare arms. The scent of sweet, drugging smoke clung to him, cocooning me in bad intentions and wicked promises.

"Killian," I mumbled into his palm, lips brushing his skin.

He held me for a long moment, body hard with tension at my back. It was so at odds with my instinctual reaction that I finally found the sense to pull away, giving myself a single moment to get composed, sheathing my blades, before facing him.

"What are you doing here?" I pinned him with my best glare, like I hadn't just swooned in his arms.

His lips twitched as he drank me in, a slow once-over from the tips of my stubby horns down to my leather boots, snagging on the blades strapped around my hips that I'd tried to stab him with.

Apparently, whatever he saw was *amusing*.

Just what every girl wanted a man to think about her body.

"I could ask you the same question," he drawled.

"I asked first." I crossed my arms, arching a brow at the incubus.

He smirked, and I hated how much it made my lips ache to taste that wicked expression. "I'm here to make sure you're not doing something reckless."

I rolled my eyes. "So Rex sent you, huh? I don't need a babysitter."

He quirked a brow. "You were being charged by dinner."

"I had it under control." My fingers twitched to grab my knives again and show him just how well I could look after myself.

He chuckled. "Sure, sweetness. Your cute little blades were definitely not going to get your pretty face gouged."

My scowl deepened, and I furiously ignored the dumb, girly part of me that preened because he'd called me pretty. He'd also called that feline menace who'd broken into my house pretty, so I guessed it didn't mean much.

"They're laced." I swiped one of my red-lined blades and threw it up. It completed its arc, tumbling end over end, and I plucked it from the air, pointing it towards Killian. "I would have had dinner roasting over a fire by now if not for you startling it with a flash of your weird pigeon wings."

He smirked, flexing said wings so the edge feathers fluttered. They were stunning, almost glowing under the moonlight.

"What was your plan, kid? You're just going to run off to the human realm on your own and find mages who might be as likely to hurt you as help you?" Rage simmered in his silvered eyes, his usual bad boy charm turning deadly serious. Darkness bled through his wings, a slow ombre starting from the arches like he'd spilled ink down their angelic innocence. "What about the hunters on Earth? They already took you once."

My claws pricked my palms as I squeezed the hilt of my poisoned blade.

Memories assaulted me. Of fists hitting my flesh. Of my claws dulling on the bars as I tried to fight my way free. The constant screaming. Mine and the other captives'.

"You think I could forget?" I hissed. "Why do you think I need to go alone?"

"Stop being ridiculous." He scowled, but the blackness only reached the top few inches of his wings.

If they'd turned fully, someone would be about to die. Painfully.

And since I was the only person around, I kinda wanted to avoid triggering the psycho enforcer.

"You wouldn't understand," I bit out through clenched fangs. "I can't see anyone else get hurt again. Not for me."

Softness dulled his hard expression, and I looked away, unable to face his pity. Slow trails of crimson sap bled down the dark trees surrounding us, oddly mesmerising.

Pitying looks and sad smiles were all I'd been seeing for weeks. Everyone treated me like I was fragile.

They didn't know it was more than just my body and mind that had been fractured. I shoved my blade roughly back into its sheath.

"Eve..." The enforcer trailed off.

"Go home, Killian," I muttered, unable to meet his piercing eyes. "I have to do this. And I'm not dragging anyone else into my mess this time."

"You're being a brat."

My lips popped open. Irritation licked my insides as I glared. "Excuse me?"

His smirk returned, a fraction of his usual dark charm seeping back in. "I'm coming with you, kid, no matter how much you pout."

"No. You're going back. I'm sure Zahara misses you." The last bit slipped out with a little more bitterness than I'd intended, and I fought not to cringe at how blatantly jealous I sounded.

I had no right to feel jealousy over a demon I'd exchanged nothing more than sass and sarcasm with.

His lips twitched. "Perhaps. But I have more important matters to attend to."

I swallowed thickly, reading too deep into his words. Did he mean the orders from his king?

Or did he mean *me*?

"So, unless you're going to stab me with those adorable little knives again—which I would love to see—we should get moving." He jerked a wing in the direction I'd been heading before the shadow boar had charged me.

I hesitated, toying with the hilts of my sheathed weapons. I didn't want Killian getting hurt following me around on Rex's orders, but I also knew I couldn't exactly stab the infuriating demon.

Not when my healing magic was on the fritz, anyway.

I'd just have to bide my time for a better way to get rid of the stubborn enforcer.

"Do you even know where we're going either?" I arched a brow. Hopefully, Rex had at least given him the details I hadn't stuck around for.

His gaze darted aside before returning to mine with a shrug of his broad shoulders and wing arches.

"Fine," I huffed, eyeing his enormous frame packed with cut muscle. "But if you insist on stalking me, you'd better stop scaring off our food."

<h1 style="text-align:center">Chapter 13</h1>

Killian and I weaved through the trees, beneath the darkened canopy high above. Twigs and dried leaves crunched beneath my boots.

The incubus might as well be floating with those pretty wings for all the noise he made, just a ghost of temptation gliding along beside me in the night.

I peered at him through my lashes, trying to process the fact that the most bloodthirsty and unhinged enforcer of the Hybrid Kingdom was apparently following me to the human realm.

I didn't know what to do about it.

I'd never spent so much time alone with him. Maybe because he didn't have much interest in getting to know me, or maybe because he just saw me as his best friend's annoying little sister.

Either way, it was going to be a long trip.

But I had to get my magic fixed. I couldn't go around hurting people. I was meant to help them.

If I wasn't a healer, then who was I?

"I can hear your inner monologue from here," Killian drawled, knocking me from my thoughts.

I scowled at the side of his stupidly carved face, picking my feet up over a fallen branch laden with glowing mushrooms the colour of rust.

"At least I have deep thoughts," I said. "What's going on between those horns, hmm? Just saucy images of Zahara naked?"

Gah. Why was I bringing her up again!?

I glanced around as if I was scanning our dangerous surroundings like a competent warrior, not avoiding his gaze so I didn't die of embarrassment.

"You've got a real issue with her, huh?" he asked, wry tone laced with amusement.

I supposed he wouldn't understand why seeing her practically naked and salivating over him would be a problem for me.

"Me? An issue with *her*? I don't know what you're talking about." My voice came out a little too high-pitched to be convincing.

I wanted to swipe my claws at him in annoyance.

He chuckled, letting me know he'd seen right through my not-so-convincing act.

"Sweetness... This wouldn't have anything to do with what she was planning to do to me, would it?" His low purr was somehow so suave, I almost missed what he'd actually said.

Heat singed my cheeks. "What? No. I..."

He waved me off, and the chain tattoo wrapping his forearm winked at me. "I'm just teasing. You're a succubus. I know you're not afraid of a little sexual tension. If anything, I'm sure you were snacking on her lust like I was."

"Right. So tasty." I forced a wide smile onto my face, like I could totally just skim energy from anyone feeling intense lust.

Another oddity that I kept to myself.

Most demons fed on heightened emotions. They tuned in to the specific frequencies they gave out. Sexual demon types, like Zahara and Killian, fed on the energy of someone feeling lust, no matter who it was they desired.

Me, I could only strengthen myself with powerful desire aimed right at me, and even then, for demons, I had to be touching them to feel it.

It was no wonder I was barely stronger than a human. My demonic side was practically malnourished.

His brows drew closer. "Eve... You *do* feed on lust, right?"

I nodded quickly. "Oh yeah, big lust eater right here." I pointed both crimson-clawed thumbs at myself and turned up the brightness on my fake smile.

His textured horns canted aside. "What aren't you telling me?"

I tucked a stray blood-red wave behind my ear. "I usually need direct touch to feed."

"What?" He stilled, regarding me with a shocked intensity that made me squirm.

He'd found me with a dead body last week and shown less emotion.

Warmth lit my cheeks like a blast of hell-fire. "It's not that big a deal."

"Maybe not to you…," he murmured, something unreadable yet strangely intense swirling through the stormy depths in his eyes.

Before I could question the cagey incubus, a low snarl ripped through the woods. It echoed oddly, bouncing from random points between the trees.

My magic pulsed. Multiple glowing points dotted around in my mind's eye. Surrounding us.

It wasn't an echo.

It was an ambush.

My gaze slammed into Killian's.

His wings blackened, aura darkening with violence. "Eve, run."

"You run." I drew my poisoned daggers, eyes narrowing as I scanned the trees.

"Stubborn witch," he muttered, unsheathing the sword strapped between his wings. "It's bone-kin."

Somehow, I already knew that, even though the bright-white beasts had cloaked themselves. Now they hinted at their presence in order to terrify their prey. Us.

More snarls ricocheted through the forest, every patch of darkness heavy with the monsters hiding within.

Between two thick redwoods, an unnatural group of shadows parted like a curtain. A furred beast stepped out on all fours. An external skull protected the outside of its face like a mask. Long fangs greeted us as bloodless lips peeled back in a silent snarl. A whole mouth full of blades dripped a violet liquid that glowed eerily, brighter for being the only colour to paint the beast.

"There're too many," Killian growled low, eyes tracing the heavy shadows creeping towards us. "On my signal, we run past the beast for the river. I can fly us from there. Stay close."

Barely a day from home, and I was already in over my head.

"You can't just flap us to safety now?" I muttered under my breath, edging closer to Killian and gripping my blades tighter.

He shot a bemused look over a wing arch. "They're very good at jumping."

Right. Shit. Given the dense canopy and wide trees, they'd be tearing us out of the air before we got more than a few spans up.

"Okay," I breathed, trusting Killian's judgement like the wingless peasant I was.

Killian eased his sword aside, ready. "On three."

Stand your ground and show them the meaning of fear. Carve your name into their dumb skulls.

I furiously ignored the voice in my head. The adrenaline must be making me jittery.

"One... Two... Now!" Killian hissed.

He surged towards the single visible beast, and I was right on his heels.

It roared at our approach, and chaos erupted.

All at once, the beasts dropped their shadowed cloaks.

A sea of bright-white monsters surrounded us, skulls gleaming in the moonlight. Reinforced ribs curved along their sides like armour between dense fur. They looked like the biologically challenged love-children of a snow bear and an anaemic hellhound.

They descended on us in the next breath, and my world narrowed to the pale creatures charging after me on all fours.

I was a hybrid in Hell. I'd had to learn to defend myself by any means, but I was not a trained warrior.

Not like Killian.

He swept forward to meet the danger in our path, slicing his broadsword right through a bone-kin's throat in an arc of dark blood, ending his swing through the eye of another as he streamed past.

He eyed me over his shoulder, and his tail wrapped around my wrist, urging me in front of him.

My poisoned dagger nicked a bone-kin between its ribs as I dashed past, leaping to stay ahead of snapping jaws. I heard the creature thud to the ground behind us a second after.

Killian and I darted between the bleeding trees, bone-kin howling too close for comfort. My thighs burned as I pushed myself to match Killian's speed, to not be the reason he got mauled to death.

Pale moonlight appeared between the thick trunks ahead. The rushing of a river was barely audible over my pounding heart and the scrape of my boots against the leaf litter.

"Almost there!" Killian yelled, upping his pace and pulling me onwards.

One of the pale beasts snarled, gaining on us with a thunderous gait.

It drew level.

Darkness writhed in my chest, an angry pit of snakes hissing and snapping at me.

I stumbled, fighting to hold back the vile hunger.

"Eve!" Killian roared, righting me with his tail and swinging me out of the way.

Death arced through the air. Killian stepped between me and the leaping beast, obsidian blade flashing.

Heat splashed my back as momentum carried me forward. The beast's skull severed from its body before it hit the ground.

Killian hissed as another monster clawed him, and I slid to a stop, turning back.

"Go!" he snarled, sword ripping through another bone-kin's throat and lurching towards me. "I'm right behind you."

I had barely a second to take in the claw-marks gouging his chest before I sprinted for the river, taking the threat of my vicious magic with me. I burst through the tree-line, the river a pink serpent winding before me.

Something slammed into my back.

I hissed, tumbling to the grass. The heavy thing landed on top of me, crushing the air from my lungs, and we rolled.

Right over the bank.

I hit the water with a splash. Pink liquid closed over my head, drowning out the monster's snarling. A bone-kin raked claws through my side as I struggled to untangle myself from it. Boned jaws snapped inches from my face in a burst of bubbles. I turned in the dark water, kicking my boots into its middle.

My head broke the surface, and I gulped in air, swimming towards the riverbank. Mud sucked at my feet as I hit the shallows, stumbling for the grassy verge.

An enraged roar shook the night.

A dark blur soared overhead, landing with a splash behind me. I spun, gaping as Killian tackled the beast hunting me through the water.

His fist smashed into the creature's skull, shattering the protective mask. Its pained whine sliced my eardrums. Killian swatted away its claws and buried his own in its throat, ripping through flesh with a vicious growl.

Blood spilled into the river, eddying darkness into the dusky pink.

Killian's chest heaved. He'd lost his sword at some point while I'd been trying not to drown. He bled in too many places, the crimson diluted by drops of water streaming down his front. His eyes locked onto mine, silvered like a blade.

They flicked to something above me and hardened. "Get behind me. Now."

He was already reaching for me. His tail caught my wrist and yanked me into deeper waters. The river tugged at my body, urging me downstream as it swallowed my torso, but Killian anchored me to him.

He raised his claws to face the threat, shielding me with his body.

Bone-kin lined up along the riverbank, low growls rumbling like thunder.

Chapter 14

My heart fluttered as I stared down the pack of hungry bone-kin.

We were fucked.

Even a wingless mutt like me knew Killian couldn't take off with wet feathers in dead air carrying my dead weight before we became dinner.

"Kill...go," I whispered, voice cracking. "Leave me."

"Never." His voice was soft, barely audible over the bone-kin, snapping and snarling only a few paces away on the grassy bank.

Any second, they'd go fishing for their meal.

A yowling roar pierced the low snarls.

Blood and darkness collided with the pale monsters, tumbling in a ball of flashing fangs and fur, knocking three bone-kin aside before they could escape.

My mouth popped open.

A familiar hellcat tore into the bone-kin like one of the chocolate chip cookies she'd stolen from me.

Growls layered over the pained keening, and I sucked in a breath as several of the pale beasts finally took the plunge. Killian roared, surging to meet the creatures in the water head-on with nothing but his claws and fangs.

A hair-raising howl added to the chaos, and Alpha tore into the melee, his paws of lilac flame bright in the gloom. The hellhound snarled, snapping sharp teeth at bone-kin before they could reach the hellcat. The two fearsome creatures fought on the raised verge, blood and fur flying in their wake.

Killian didn't even flinch as a bone-kin bit down on his forearm. He angled his head and rammed a horn right through the monster's glowing eye socket. The beast screeched, releasing the incubus and rearing to get away.

I staggered in the water, fighting my own battle.

Tendrils of violence coiled through me. I gritted my teeth, stuffing the ravenous darkness as deep as I could, willing it to leave me alone. There were even more allies to protect from myself now.

The last beast slid off Killian's claws, collapsing into the water with a splash. It bobbed lazily as the river carried it off downstream, a wet ball of white fur stained with inky blood.

A hush descended over the night, broken only by the gentle rush of water.

The hellcat yanked her tail stinger out of a downed beast with a squelch and bared her fangs in a smug feline grin. A deep gouge through her foreleg closed before my eyes, her ability to heal herself as unexpected as her appearance.

"Thank you," I said, unsure what to do with the fact that two near-mythical creatures had saved me and Killian. "I'll give you both all the cookies and belly rubs you want."

What was the proper etiquette to thank near-mythical creatures?

Killian inclined his horns at our unlikely rescuers onshore. The ends of his wings glided through the water as he turned to me, silvered eyes sharp as they trailed over me, checking for injuries.

I returned the favour.

My gasp drowned out his relieved breath.

"Fires, Kill. You're tenderised meat!" I hurried towards him, wading into shallower water until only a pace separated us.

The shadows in Killian's wings dissipated, retreating like smoke to leave behind white feathers stained red. They were scratched deep, oozing blood in places where the water hadn't yet reached.

Claw-marks and fang holes pierced his muscular arms. His inked chest rose and fell in a steady rhythm, despite the pain from multiple lacerations criss-crossing his skin beneath the shreds of his top.

Unlike at last night's party, none of his wounds appeared too deep. At least I'd not caused them all this time either.

My hand shook as I ran it through my damp hair, pushing the slick strands back between my stubby horns. "That was close," I muttered. "Too close."

Killian smirked, too unfazed by his brush with death. "You're right. I was about three seconds from shoving you downriver. You're lucky your furry friends were here to save you the swim."

I cast him a sour look. "You wouldn't have dared."

He shrugged his wings, feigning innocence. "I would have fished you out after I'd dealt with the bone-kin. Your safety is my priority."

Right. Of course it was.

Because he'd been sent to babysit me by my overprotective brother/uncle/king.

I eyed the hellhound waiting regally onshore. Killian wasn't the only one on babysitting duty.

"I'm going to heal you," I whispered, throat tight. I lifted my palm to hover over Killian's chest, shooting him a questioning look.

The darkness inside me writhed, scenting fresh blood. I swallowed thickly, trying not to panic as saliva pooled on my tongue until I wanted to gag.

"They barely scratched me." Killian shrugged, the tips of his wings dipping lower in the pink water.

Of course he'd tough it out as usual. The stubborn boar never let me heal him.

No part of me wanted to battle the hungry beast that lived inside me, but for Killian, I would. This wasn't the first time he'd stepped between me and danger. I owed him more than I could ever repay.

Steeling my nerves, I reached for my magic. Slowly. Tentatively. I felt down for the well of light in my chest. My warm, cosy magic. The one good thing my father had given me.

Darkness reached back.

I slammed the connection closed, breathing hard, and wrenched back from Killian. I shook my horns fast enough to make myself dizzy, clutching my chest where something evil lurked.

Killian watched me with a quiet understanding I didn't deserve. I swallowed the lump in my throat, unable to face his intensity.

"It's okay, Eve. Really. This is nothing. You've seen me more battered just this week. I'm barely even bleeding," he murmured, edging closer.

I edged back. But he was right. Killian was no stranger to pain. And I hated it.

"You shouldn't have to suffer. Not for anyone, and especially not for me," I muttered, running a hand through the pink water, like it could wash away the sensation of something crawling beneath my skin.

His eyes bored into me, silvery flecks through the stormy blue, some intensity I couldn't name filling them.

I looked away first. "At least I didn't rip you apart any further."

He chuckled. "At least you'd be touching me."

"Really, Kill?" I levelled a flat look his way. "What happened to 'you shouldn't touch me'?" I did my best impression of his raspy, lilting voice.

He smirked, unapologetic and incessantly flirty. A true incubus. "That was *before*."

"Before what?"

His lips split into a wide grin, showing off wicked fangs and more than a hint of crazy.

"Fine, be all cryptic and weird." I barely suppressed an eye-roll. "There's a salve in my pack that should kill off any nasties from those bone-kin claws. We just need to find it back in the woods."

His smile turned wry. "Sure, kid. If you insist."

My eyes narrowed on the infuriatingly calm demon.

Alpha yipped, drawing my attention back to the hellcat and hellhound watching us. They stared like we'd been putting on quite the show.

Alpha's canine features pinched like a disapproving parent. His fiery eyes bored into me, seeming to judge my reckless behaviour. Somehow, the hellhound was both stern and sarcastic, all in one look.

Cookie just grinned, loaded with pointy fangs and smugness. I couldn't tell if the stalker cat was mocking me or not.

Probably safe to assume she was.

Killian grabbed the black cloth wrapping his torso and ripped the shredded remains free, chucking the material onto the bank.

Thick muscular pectorals and carved abs revealed themselves in my periphery. I did everything in my power not to react.

Inky tattoos graced his slate-purple skin, flowing into stunning predatory birds in flight, their feathers wrapping his ribs and up over his chest to grace his neck and shoulders. Scars accented the feathers, adding a texture that only made them more realistic. Silvery chains of ink wrapped around his forearms, a reminder of his past.

I'd seen him topless before.

It never failed to floor me.

I battled to hold back my attraction to him, but desire wisped through my mental grasp, an intangible pull on my reserves as I unintentionally fed Killian my desire. His eyes glowed brighter, the silver so piercing it stabbed my heart.

He moistened his lower lip, forked tongue tracing it erotically slow. I swallowed thickly, battling to think unsexy thoughts as I greedily drank in his powerful frame and sinful features caressed by moonlight.

Just when I thought I'd combust from need, he dipped below the surface, the pink river swallowing him entirely.

My cheeks flamed as reality bitch-slapped me. He knew how much I craved him. He could literally taste my desire for him. There was no doubt about how I felt.

But I'd never once sensed his desire leak towards me.

Except for the one time he'd given me energy when he rescued me from the hunters, I'd never fed from Killian.

Because he clearly didn't think of me in that way. I was just too stupid to learn the lesson repeatedly smacking me over the head.

The demon's unique white horns broke the surface of the water, followed by his pearly wing arches and the arrogant smirk of a sinful incubus.

"Get cleaned up, Eve. I'll grab your bag, and we can set up camp for a few hours to rest," Killian said. He eyed the dead bone-kin on the grassy bank. "Upstream."

He eased to the edge, hauling himself out with a fluid grace that shouldn't be possible with the weight of hundreds of soaked feathers at his back. The pretty water seemed reluctant to let him leave.

He straightened to his full imposing height on the grass, raining heavy droplets.

I raised a brow, ignoring the way my need for him spiked as I traced the wet tendrils snaking their way over his broad shoulders and down his chest. His white horns gleamed under the moonlight with more droplets, like pink diamonds studded their patterned rippling lengths. He should look like a soggy pigeon. Instead, he was dipped in crystalline drops with that sexy wet look that made zero sense.

He turned his wings on me, passing the watching creatures with a respectful nod, and the shadows between the trees welcomed him into their embrace.

Chapter 15

I ducked beneath the water, scrubbing my hands over my clothes and through my hair. Dark blood swirled through the pale liquid, barely visible even with the penetrating moonlight. I surfaced quickly, drawing in a deep breath.

The cool river left me shivering as my adrenaline waned, but at least I was clean.

My sodden boots squished in the soft mud as I dragged my carcass to the high bank and hauled myself up.

Bloodied bone-kin corpses littered the grass, leading right into the bleeding tree-line set several paces back from the river's edge. Tufts of once white fur dotted the sparse trunks, thick grass pushing between creeping roots. Glowing wildflowers bloomed in patches between the bodies, already soaking up the nectar of their lifeblood.

Squeezing the excess water from my hair, I finger-combed it out as best I could, knowing full well it was going to dry into frizzy curls rather than the smooth waves I preferred, even though the humidity was still low this time of year.

I peeled up my wet shirt, inspecting my side where the bone-kin had caught me. The wounds were nothing but shallow scratches of red against my pale skin. At least my magic still healed my own wounds.

I let the soggy material slap back down, stifling a cringe because I was meant to be a competent demoness.

My attention drifted to the two creatures I'd almost hurt with my magic.

Alpha sat patiently on the bank, scanning the surrounding forest. Cookie, on the other hand, radiated smug aloofness as she sat on her haunches, licking a paw clean. I stifled a grimace at the dark blood she lapped up.

The feline may trash my cabin like a mischievous pet, but things like this reminded me of what a vicious predator she was. Not only had she clawed several bone-kin to death, biting through their defensive bones like they were twigs, but she didn't have a single scratch on her.

Just the blood of her victims.

That she was now sipping.

She eyed me, pausing mid-lick just to taunt me. Her dagger-like fangs framed her pink tongue, smeared with inky blood.

"What are you two doing here?" I murmured before offering a sheepish smile. "Not that I'm not grateful for your help."

Alpha barked, tossing his huge head in the direction he'd come before staring at me pointedly.

I frowned, convinced I could understand the gist of what he was trying to tell me.

But I'd also thought I could take on the Bloodwood alone in the dead of night.

I snorted. "You can go home and tell Zoella one vicious guard dog is enough."

At least Rex and Zoella hadn't turned up themselves though.

Cookie let out a rasping purr that was definitely a mocking laugh. I shot her a glare. She stared right back, unblinking.

Shifting towards the hellhound, she flicked her tail, swiping it through the blood soaking Alpha's wide jaw.

The hellhound snapped at her, but she didn't even flinch, letting his fangs snap closed a hair from the furred tuft. She stared the great beast down, blood-red eyes swirling ominously bright in the gloom.

Alpha turned his back on her in clear dismissal. He yipped at me, shaking his head sharp enough for his long ears to sway adorably.

"I know, and I'm grateful for your help, and Cookie's... But I need to do this alone," I said, my voice dropping to a quiet whisper.

Alpha cocked his head, and jerked his muzzle at the hellcat in question as if to say, "What about her?"

I frowned. "Isn't she with you?"

A chuffing laugh rumbled from the hellhound.

"Chatting with the beasties of the Bloodwood, kid?" Killian's amused rasp had me startling.

He stalked from the bleeding trees with a wicked smirk and my pack in hand, the hilt of his dark sword peeking above his shoulder.

I swallowed thickly.

Could I actually understand the furry pair like they were saying things? Maybe some part of my mutt self had an animal affinity. Like Zoella.

I hoped so. Because if not, I was going crazy.

And my fractured psyche was too fragile for another blow.

I grinned wide, baring my fangs. "They're less irritating than the alternative."

"Hmmm, if only that were true." He jerked his chin further along the exposed riverbank, and I followed, pulling a face behind his wings.

Picking my way past the fallen creatures, I tried not to trip on logs at the distracting sight of Killian's back, the heavy muscles bunching and flexing under the weight of his neatly folded wings with each step, half-hidden by the broadsword resting along his spine.

The wind picked up, the breeze chilling my damp skin. Or at least, that was what I told myself the shiver was for.

The incubus set down my pack beside a fallen log and made quick work of dragging over a bunch of dry branches to stack together.

Alpha prowled over and slammed his dark paw on the ground. Lilac flames burst to life around the black fur. He pressed his paw to the wood, and his hell-fire swallowed the logs, casting an eerie purple glow.

"Thanks, Alpha." With a relieved smile, I hurried closer to the demonic bonfire, right beside the huge log Killian rested on, my pack by his booted feet.

The hellcat sauntered over too, ignoring us all. She flicked her tail, and the tuft caught alight, stealing the lilac flames from the logs in an impressive trick.

Cookie looked at me and blinked slowly, as if to say, "I am impressive."

She sat beside Alpha and lifted a paw, licking the enormous claws she'd unsheathed, as if her tail wasn't softly crackling with deadly fire.

Her red eyes blazed with power, cut through with vertical pupils of the darkest night. Her fur absorbed the light until she was more shadow than creature. Long fangs threatened to rip out the throat of anyone stupid enough to get close to the beast.

I dug around inside my battered pack until my fingers closed around a small wax-lined pouch. I pulled it free, holding my leathery prize aloft. "Ah, here it is!"

Killian quirked a brow, kicking one ankle over the other as he leaned back on the log. His wings hadn't been dunked in the river long enough to become fully waterlogged, but they'd still dried a little fluffier than usual, warmed by the pretty lilac flames before us.

The incubus looked like a demon at one with nature, relaxing in the great outdoors like he hadn't almost died half an hour ago. Some of the deeper claw-marks still wept blood, but most had stopped.

I made my way over, gripping my salve bag tight. A frisson of nerves cascaded through me at the thought of laying my hands on Killian.

He barely looked up at my approach but widened his thighs as if I were going to stand between his muscular legs. At the last second, I chickened out, plonking myself down on the bark next to him. I fumbled with the pouch, dunking two fingers in and scooping out the cool paste. It tingled against my fingertips as I brought it to the first gash on Killian's forearm, trying not to let the silver chains wrapping his forearms in ink mesmerise me beyond concentration.

It didn't work. And all I could think about was how much they'd flexed when he held me down in my dream.

Every second crawled by as I desperately clung to the most unsexy thoughts I could summon while rubbing in the medicine.

The pus that came out of Hubert's crusty horn after a nasty infection.

The hunter that tried to seduce me while I was in captivity.

That furball Cookie coughed up in my sink.

Rex in big frilly knickers.

"I know what you're doing, sweetness," he murmured, his attention on the side of my face like a warm palm cupping my cheek.

I swallowed thickly, fighting a one-sided blush. "I'm putting a salve on your open wounds so you don't get necrosis. You already smell bad enough."

His lips twitched, kicking up into a smirk with his unshakeable confidence. "You don't have to keep giving me handouts."

I stilled, and some of the chalky paste dropped from my hovering finger to splat against the log beside his hip.

He cocked a brow, that infuriating smirk still gracing his lips. "What?"

"You're throwing off enough sexual energy that I'd almost think it was more than just a healer helping her patient." His eyes glinted with a dangerous edge. His forked tongue swiped his lower lip as if he were wondering how I'd taste if he ever got his teeth into me. "But I know you're just being nice. Good girls don't tease monsters. Do they, sweetness?"

Even my heart stopped. For a single moment, reality suspended and I could have sworn there was an invitation in his words. A hunger in his demonic eyes.

The faintest hint of burned caramel traced my tongue. Energy teased through me with the lightest charge in the air.

Heavy silence dragged on, and the stormy oceans shuttered a breath later, averting from me.

Whatever madness gripped me shattered.

He was giving me an out. A way for us both to shrug off my embarrassing crush.

A forced laugh spilled from my lips, the sound raking my skin like claws. "Well, I can't help you heal in my usual way..."

I could have choked on my own bitterness. I just hoped it hadn't leaked into my tone. My cheeks probably rouged enough to match my hair though.

He was literally telling me to stop salivating over him like the prime cut he was. Despite how it was strengthening him with every sip he took.

Even for me, that was a new level of embarrassment.

I pressed the salve a little harder than necessary into the next set of fang marks on his bicep, ignoring the way his muscles flexed under my touch.

"There." I swiped one final smear on the top of his forearm before peering around his wing to check his back. I'd noticed it was unscathed when I was ogling him earlier, but I was meant to be a professional healer, dammit, and he already thought my crush was pathetic. "All done."

"Not going to kiss it all better?" he purred.

I pulled a sour face at his taunting. "In your dreams."

"And yours." He smirked.

I rolled my eyes so hard I almost fell off the log.

He leaned back on his palms, showing off his toned abs like that was meant to help me stop doing his energy levels a favour. "We need to talk about your new gifts."

I fumbled with the ties to the leather pouch, stowing it in my bag to give myself a second to get composed before meeting his intense stare. "What *gifts*?"

The word tasted foul in my mouth. I knew exactly what he was referring to, and you'd have to be an unhinged lunatic like Killian to consider it anything close to a blessing.

Killian levelled me with his "stern" look, brow furrowing ever so slightly and the faintest tightening at his mouth.

I eyed the hellcat and hellhound lounging on the other side of the fire, seemingly uninterested in our conversation. But I had the strangest certainty that they were, in fact, lapping up every word.

I huffed. "More like a curse."

"I'm going to ignore that because you're having a rough day," he said. "What does it feel like when it rises?"

Only Killian would call almost getting mauled to death and drowned by a pack of monsters as a "rough day."

I fanged my lower lip, trying to put the foreign sensation into words. "It's...like there's something dark inside me. Something vicious and...*hungry.*"

A shudder crawled down my spine, and I dug my claws into my forearms, hugging my middle like I could physically hold the evil inside me.

Instead of looking horrified like a sane person, Killian canted his horns, the feather-patterned waves as stunning as the rest of him. He seemed to mull over my words. "Maybe it is."

I frowned. "Maybe it's what?"

"Hungry." His voice dropped an octave, low and husky.

My lips pressed together, preventing anything stupid from falling out.

"Do you feel stronger afterwards?" he asked.

I threw him a sour look. "You mean when I fainted in your arms last night? Not particularly."

"Such a brat," he tutted with a roll of his storm-blue eyes. "I meant *after*. What about when you killed that merchant? Did you have more witchy magic then?"

Unease dripped down my spine like ice water. Because I *had* felt stronger in a way, my magic fuller, wilder.

"But my magic and demonic energy are linked. I'm like a glitch in nature because one side of me can feed the other."

"And have you been feeding your demonic half lately?" That same whisky purr rumbled his throat.

Suddenly, I was parched. My tongue swiped my dry lips. "That's none of your business."

Especially not after he'd told me to stop throwing myself at him.

His eyes narrowed the smallest fraction. "Everything about you is my business."

"Right. Because Rex clicked his claws, and you came running."

His narrowed stare held, but his tail reached for something in his pocket. The familiar sound of scraping metal had me frowning. Somehow, he pulled a rolled-up stick of haze from the tiny case he always had on him, using the coils of his elegant slate-purple tail. He dipped the end into the fire and brought the dark drug to his lips.

Killian took a long drag, the haze tip glowing hot. His cut chest flared wide a second before he blew shadowy smoke into the air, blending into the night.

The gesture reminded me how bland and human he must see me as. I had no tail to casually help me smoke. No wings to lift me into the night sky. Barely any length of horns or claws to defend myself with.

No. My one gift was healing magic. And that was going about as well for me as being a succubus.

A weight crushed my chest until I struggled to take a full breath.

Was this why my birth father had abandoned me? Long before I'd found my mother in a pool of her own blood, too useless to save her. Why my aunts had beaten me for years before they got bored enough to throw me to a brothel for a few silvers? Why the mage I'd been infatuated with had sold me out to hunters?

Even my own magic turned on me.

"Hey." Killian's voice yanked me from my spiral. "What's going on between those cute horns of yours?"

He sucked in another smoky lungful.

I gave him a rueful smile. "Nothing. They're too small. What could fit?"

He chuckled, and smoke trickled from between his lips like a dragon. "You're the smartest person in our kingdom."

"What realm do you live in?" I scoffed. "I'm our useless *human*," I muttered, scratching at the bark on my seat, half-hoping he wouldn't hear my embarrassing self-pity.

A low snarl ripped from Killian's lips. He pointed a claw at my face. "Don't ever say anything like that again."

I blinked rapidly, taken aback by his sudden intensity.

"Why the fuck not?" I snapped, irrational anger igniting like hell-fire. "My magic is twisted," I hissed. "Broken. Just like the rest of me."

To my horror, angry tears blurred the edges of my vision.

Killian leaned over, forcing me to bend back on the log, or that salve I'd carefully applied to his chest would smear mine.

"Fires burn it, Eve." Killian snarled, gripping his precious drug tighter with his tail. "You're not *broken*."

I glared at him, blinking rapidly as my stupid emotions churned like a dark ocean. "How can you say that after all I've done?"

Guilt rose up to tug me down into its murky depths.

The incubus straightened, one vertebra at a time, lethal precision in every slight movement. "Because."

I huffed a bitter laugh. "Because what?"

His eyes pinned me with the sharpest focus, slit pupils like blades. "Because you're perfect. Every damn inch of you. Inside and out."

He might as well have roared the words. His measured intensity was overwhelming and all the more captivating for it.

Because I felt every syllable like he spoke them against my skin.

He puffed a lungful of blackness into my face. Fragrant haze muddied my senses, and when the smoke cleared, he was gone.

Chapter 16

Cookie lifted her head, cocking a tufted ear to the lightening sky. For the past half an hour since Killian had disappeared, she'd been lurking within the hell-fire Alpha had lit, much to his irritation.

I never knew a hellhound could pout.

Something pulsed through the tendrils of my magic that snaked around me, like a disturbance in the currents of power. I followed the ripples overhead and squinted out at the winding pink river, bathed in the first rays of dawn.

Killian dropped to the grassy riverbank on silent wings. His white feathers still held a damp sheen, painting them almost silver like the flecks in his eyes when he felt particularly violent. He folded his wings and strode towards our makeshift camp.

A small brace of spear quails, already plucked of their sharp feathers, dangled from his raised hand.

I quirked a brow, but my stomach rumbled, betraying me.

Killian's eyes ran over me, some tightness around them easing a fraction.

I hadn't moved from the log where he'd left me, throwing out his confusing words and vanishing like a cloaked bone-kin. I was exhausted, both physically and mentally, and when I'd tried to grab the wrapped boar from my pack, it was no longer there, even though I'd seen it when I'd fished out the salve earlier.

I hadn't seen the hellcat take it, but I just knew it was her. I didn't call her *Cookie* because she baked.

Killian busied himself setting a spit over the hell-fire, shooing the hellcat like a misbehaving kitten. Within minutes, he had the four game birds roasting nicely.

The scent of cooking meat filled the area, ridding the last of the bloody tang leftover from the bone-kin massacre.

I was half-surprised he hadn't just hauled one of them over to cook up, but then again, just because I was immune to most poisons with my healing abilities didn't mean anyone else was safe.

The incubus cleared his throat, sitting beside me while he watched the flames dance. Given the extreme heat of hell-fire, it was only a few minutes before Killian was pulling the roasted birds out. He handed me one with a small smile. "Here. I didn't bring any seasoning when I came after you, but they're pretty good plain, anyway."

I smiled back, accepting his offering with a grateful nod. I gripped the base of the stick, still warm from the fire, eyeing the golden-coloured delight it held. Crispy skin and a pleasant aroma reminded me of the deep-fried chicken I'd had in the human realm once.

"Do your pets want a snack too?" His lips twitched, and he raised the last two cooked birds to Alpha and Cookie in offering.

With a grouchy huff, Alpha stalked over, muzzle extended to sniff at the meat in Killian's outstretched hand.

Cookie leaped through the fire with an excited yowl, snagged both birds between her giant fangs, and darted off into the bushes. Alpha barked and raced after her.

A small chuckle fell from my lips.

Killian peered after them. "Should we be worried?"

They might annoy each other as only a hellcat and a hell-hound could, but they weren't actually out to hurt each other. They'd fought the bone-kin together, and whatever uneasy truce they'd forged seemed intact.

I shook my head. "They're just playing. Besides, your feline admirer can fend for herself."

A light frown formed between his brows, and I could almost feel his curiosity around my new understanding of animals.

Before he could question me further, I bit into dinner. The warm poultry was delicious, with a lick of smoke from the hell-fire, and I took another bite with a pleased hum.

A hush descended as we finished our quails to the crackle of burning wood and the faint symphony of insects.

Killian chucked the speared remains into the fire, the lilac flames devouring the bones with a loud pop. "You need to learn to block before I take you to bed."

"What are you talking about?" I almost choked on my last bite of food, but Killian didn't seem to notice his word choice might give a girl a heart attack. I copied his movements, pushing my leftovers into the hungry bonfire that warmed us.

He rested his inked forearms on the scuffed leather at his knees. "If your magic is lashing out because you're underfed, you can't afford to leak so much, even to help me heal. It's probably more potent than your other emotions because of your heritage."

"It's fine." I pointedly ignored the squeaky quality to my voice, swiping back the scarlet curls determined to get into my mouth. "I always give off energy. Must be a mage thing."

Killian shot me a knowing smirk, half his features cast into shadow by the eerie fire.

I wanted to punch his pretty face in.

Of course the stunning incubus found this amusing. He was used to demons lusting after him. Every unmated person in the kingdom wanted to fuck the guy.

I'd even seen a racist of pure blood linger a heated gaze on him.

He shrugged, shoulders and wings rising and falling as one. "Let's try blocking anyway. More energy left to satisfy your hungry magic, then."

The enforcer was always trying to look after me. It would be cute, but I knew he saw me as more of a kid in need of protection. To him, I was just his best friend's bratty little sister.

"And how will you teach me to block?" I arched a brow, crossing my legs as I shifted on the bark, pricking me even through the drying fabric of my trousers.

He grinned, a heart-stopping smile that could liquefy the robes off a priest. "I'm going to seduce you, sweetness. And you're going to shut that door in your mind until I can't taste your drugging need on my tongue."

Flaming. Hell-fires.

I somehow managed to unstick my mouth to cough out a word. "What?"

"A man could get lost in your big, innocent eyes. So eager to be corrupted, aren't you? My pretty princess," he purred, watching me with all the intensity of a predator cornering prey.

Yet his voice was like being wrapped in silk and stroked by claws.

The shiver that ran through me was nothing to do with the light breeze across my skin.

He cleared his throat, forked tongue tracing his lower lip. "Picture the front door of your house and slam it closed."

I frowned, but the image he painted came to me. The sturdy dark wood of my cottage wouldn't close fully, though, like something invisible wedged it open.

Killian leaned close, planting a palm on the trunk, grazing my thigh. His eyes dropped to my lips, slit pupils dilating, and then trailed down the rest of me, like feathers caressing my flesh.

I blinked at him, hyperaware of the scant distance between us. "What?"

Apparently, that word was all I could manage.

He grinned wider, sharp fangs giving his beauty its vicious edge. "You heard me, sweet witch." He stole more of my personal space and reached for me, tucking a damp strand of my hair behind my rounded ear, so different from the demonic points of his. "Close that door for me."

I tried to imagine my house again, that wooden door he'd built for me. Strong and solid from the dark timber of the bleeding trees this forest was notorious for. Poisonous bloodbores and scattered feathers had been carved around the door's edges, grander than any simple door had a right to display.

His smile turned wicked. "Unless you want me to come inside..."

My fang sank into my lower lip, the slight drain on my energy letting me know I wasn't winning the battle for concentration.

Killian inhaled deep, leaning closer as if he were going to scent me properly before stilling, his face mere inches away. My pulse thundered too loud in my ears.

Stormy eyes glittered silver as they locked with mine.

"I...can't," I rasped. His smoky sweetness drugged me, and wetness slicked between my thighs as I breathed him in. "You're such an incubus." I tried to brush it off, like it was a normal reaction.

And, I supposed, it was. Killian was designed for sex. For seduction.

He'd have any demoness panting for him now. I had nothing to feel embarrassed about. Having a high sex drive was literally in my blood.

As well as his.

For a moment, fantasies ran rampant through my thoughts.

What would it feel like? To have him shove me down onto the grass and fuck me by the eerie light of the hell-fire like I was his to possess.

I tried to slam the door in my mind, but it wouldn't budge. Everything about Killian was intoxicating. Seductive.

Who cared about losing energy when he was the prize I'd win?

His claws trailed a path down my arm. Even that innocent touch had me stifling a moan that tried to work its way up my throat.

"Push harder for me, sweetness. Shut that door in my face before I drink you down and swallow you whole. You shouldn't be devoured by a dark creature like me. You're too good for that."

Beneath the wicked fantasy running through my mind, frustration licked my insides. He had no right to decide what was good enough for me or not.

I slammed the door.

The relief was instant. The drain on my energy ceased. I'd been losing so much power, and my cheeks heated as I realised how obvious my longing for him was.

A smirk broke across Killian's lips even as the flecks in his eyes dimmed. "That's my good girl."

His seductive voice shouldn't be doing the things it was. Especially after he'd just used dirty talk as a lesson like he was a professor and I the unruly pupil.

My schoolgirl crush was making a lot more sense.

He was a few years older than me, twenty-six where I was just turning twenty-two.

Tomorrow, in fact.

I huffed. "I'm hardly a *good girl*. The other night, you caught me with a dead body." I inspected my scarlet claws like I was checking for blood.

Killian's chuckle was a dark, rich sound as he straightened, giving me space to breathe. "No, I suppose you're not...unless it's for me."

This new flirty side to him was giving me heart palpitations.

I cleared my throat, steering well clear of that dangerous territory.

"You never cashed in that favour for your disposal services." I shot a pointed look at the smirking incubus. "And this whole stalking thing you're doing does not get you another."

A slow smile bloomed across his features. "You really don't know. Do you?"

I stilled. "Know what?"

His vicious grin widened, a small chuckle seeping out. "I already called in my favour. Last night, in fact. Your screams still echo in my ears when I taste your sweet essence in the air."

My lips parted with dawning horror. "What?" I squeaked. "You...how?"

His forked tongue ran the length of his fangs. "How what? How did I get into your dreams?" he purred. "You summoned me into them, naughty witch. Your need dragged my slumbering consciousness the short distance to yours. I was sleeping in your house that night, after all."

My jaw stubbornly refused to close.

How could anyone process something this embarrassing?

It. Was. Real.

Killian, my first crush, off-limits best friend of my brother...had made me scream for him.

And. It. Had. Been. Real.

I finally closed my mouth with a snick of my dainty fangs.

Shuffling on the log, I crossed my ankles in a forced display of feminine grace. "Well, I guess that settles that, then." I lifted my nose and sniffed like a snooty pureblood. "You're still not getting another favour."

"Are you sure? That wasn't the first body I've buried for you. If anything, you owe me quite a few now." He tapped a claw against his chin. "And does it count if I've just left them begging for a burial?"

"What?!" My voice hit a dangerously high pitch.

Alpha was probably wincing somewhere off in the woods.

Silver lightning illuminated the storm in his eyes. "Nobody gets to hurt you, sweetness."

Realisation gripped me by the horns and back-handed me in the face.

The *bloody* hobby Rex had mentioned. Why none of my exes had ever confessed to who'd almost killed them. Why nobody had looked for the ones who'd disappeared.

I'd bet my last gold coin I knew who'd punished the pain trio too.

"Holy hell-fires," I gasped. "You're the reason they call me the widow-witch."

His grin was as lethal as a poison-tipped blade.

Chapter 17

"**S**weetness," a lilting rasp called to me, echoing strangely in my ears.

Pine and wood smoke mixed with the scent of something rich and sweet, tempting me to seek its source. Warmth bathed my lower body, and a fire crackled nearby.

Soft material covered my eyes, shrouding me in darkness.

I tried to reach for it, but the same softness coiled around my wrists, trapping my arms above my head. It tightened as I pulled against it.

My ankles were similarly bound, spread wide to lay me out, arched over a curved surface. The angle gave me the faintest rush of blood to the head.

Roughness scraped at my back through a thin material as I tried to wriggle out of my restraints. A silken fabric draped my body, cinching in at my waist like a dress.

I'd been blindfolded and bound.

I sucked in a deep breath, trying to figure out what was going on, but the instinctual panic I'd have expected was missing.

Something soothed my nerves, cocooning me in a detached sense of safety I had no right to feel.

Why? Had I been drugged?

I twisted my hand, grazing the surface I lay on. Cool, rough grooves met my fingertips—the bark of a tree, but I was at the wrong angle for it to be upright.

The melodious hum of firebugs seeped in.

I was still in the forest. It must still be night-time.

But why was I trussed to a fallen tree like some sacrificial offering?

"Sweetness," the familiar voice purred again, right by my ear.

I jolted in my restraints. "Kill?"

Sharp points traced down my neck, causing me to shudder. My nipples peaked against the soft fabric, teasing me with each sharp inhale.

"You summoned, my witch?" His rich voice washed over me.

My fangs found my lower lip as his meaning sank in.

I was dreaming and had somehow drawn him here. Just like before.

Warmth that had nothing to do with the fire bathed my cheeks.

After the evening's surprise revelations, the furry duo had returned, giving me an excuse to hurry off to feign sleep on my flimsy bedroll, trusting they'd keep watch. Clearly, I'd actually fallen into sleep's clutches, and the psychotic incubus had followed me into them.

"You can go," I rasped, moistening my dry lips and feigning casual, like I wasn't strapped to a tree. "We don't need a repeat of last time."

Wood creaked on either side of my head. Something brushed my hair, sharpness faintly scraping my temples. Warmth hovered over my front.

"Don't we?" His words whispered against my lips with the faintest tease of air. "And what would you know about what I need?"

Darkness wrapped around me like feathered wings.

The lack of sight heightened every feeling, yet nothing felt quite real, because I couldn't see the incubus above me.

Like maybe this could just be a dream after all.

"Maybe I *need* to feed you. Maybe I *need* your taste on my tongue again. Your screams echoing oh so prettily in my ears."

Warm and damp, his forked tongue flicked over my lips in the barest trace.

My breathing roughened until my chest grazed him with every harsh inhale, taunting the stiff peaks of my nipples through the material separating us.

Something silken traced up my calf, running along the inside of my leg. I shivered at the feel of his tail on me. Already knowing if he inched higher, he'd find out just how much I wanted him.

"Tell me what you need, sweetness." His voice dropped to that husky, low octave that had me craving him even more. "You wouldn't have summoned me here with you laid out like a beautiful offering if there wasn't something you wanted."

The smoky caramel scent of his was drugging. I knew he was just above me, taunting and teasing, but there was nothing I could do to reach for him. Or stop him.

My fang found my lower lip again.

Words were impossible.

Warm, rough skin gripped my jaw. His other palm stroked down my throat, over my collarbone, ending in sharp points across my heaving chest.

The slight sting was so at odds with the delicate graze of his silky tail up and down my thighs. Every touch sent ripples of sensation through my body. Even his teasing was merciless.

He withdrew all at once, and cool air rushed over me, leaving me bereft.

"Sweetness...," he rasped. "Tell me what you want, or I leave. I'm not a good demon. I can't promise I won't have to pleasure myself, all alone, to the image of your sweet body tied up like a gift just for me."

"Stay." The word slipped past my lips before I could think it through.

The forest seemed to hold its breath along with me.

I could practically feel his devious smirk. Feel his gaze caressing my body, offered up for him to claim like some dark god.

I licked my lips, fantasies running riot. I was unable to see a thing, my nerves wound so tight I thought I'd snap.

"Please, Kill." The words slipped out on a breathy moan, and I yanked on my restraints.

A growl rumbled above me. I had a single moment to brace as warmth swamped my front without touching.

Sharp heat sliced into my throat.

My back arched off the rough bark at the sting delivered between Killian's soft lips.

Pleasure drowned the pain in the next breath. Heat rushed through my bloodstream, pulsing outwards as his venom slid through my veins. It pooled low in my body, sparking through my core in the most delicious way I'd never felt before. Hot but so achingly empty.

A low whine slipped from my lips, and Killian growled into my throat, sending another rush of heat slicking my core.

I ached to rub my thighs together, to do anything to ease the throb between them, but the restraints held me in place. I was unable to do anything but thrash and moan as Killian toyed with me.

His fangs released me, and the incubus laved my throat, his forked tongue almost as hot as the venom lighting me up.

"Even the nectar in your veins is sweet," he growled. "So fucking addictive."

Soft tips traced both my arms, igniting the venom everywhere it touched until it fizzed beneath my skin. His feathers continued their path, teasing over the tops of my breasts. They slipped under the material covering me, brushing my nipples.

I moaned as the sensation peaked with his taunting caress.

The feathers dipped to my legs, dragging along my sensitive inner thighs and slowly pushing the fabric up, baring me to the warm night.

A sharp inhale sliced the tension, followed by a masculine groan. "You're dripping for me. Such a needy little witch, aren't you?" Killian purred, his voice as teasing as his wings on my body and his venom in my blood.

My chest heaved, heart pounding hard enough to rush his drugging essence through my entire body. A part of Killian was already inside me, and the thought made me dizzy until I floated adrift in the soft darkness.

"Kill," I moaned, aching for him to really touch me. "Please."

A dark chuckle rumbled from above. "Oh, sweetness. I like you moaning my name just a little too much."

Silken steel traced through my slick folds. It reached the sensitive bundle of nerves at my apex, and I bucked in my restraints on a desperate gasp.

"Say it again," he demanded.

My lips parted on a moan instead, my cheeks on fire.

This was *Killian*.

The tantalising venom in my system blurred how real this was, but nerves crept in at the edges.

His tail descended with a wet slap.

I gasped, arching off the tree. The lewd sound jolted through me as much as the shock of sensation through my clit.

"Say. My. Fucking. Name," he snarled.

But he didn't wait.

His arrowhead plunged into me, eclipsing the emptiness in one punishing thrust. I writhed, biting my lip until I tasted blood, scraping my back through the material trapped under me, but not a single part of me could care.

The ruthless demon dragged his tail out and thrust back in. The stretch was sinful, but I was already soaked from his unique venom, rushing liquid pleasure through my bloodstream.

Hands skimmed down my sides and pinned my hips to the tree. My heart pounded in anticipation, laced with nervous energy.

A low growl rumbled from him. "If you won't say it, sweetness, I'll make you scream it while you come on my tail like my good girl."

His tail drew back and slammed home. Only Killian's hands kept my body in place as I thrashed. He tail-fucked me like a demon possessed, my whole body jerking with every rough thrust filling me.

Something warm and wet lashed my clit.

"Oh fires!" I yanked on my restraints, but my wrists were locked in place. "Please," I whined, almost sobbing at the overwhelming sensations assaulting my core.

I couldn't see him, but knowing it was Killian playing with me, choosing how he wanted to touch me, to take me...

It drove me right to the edge.

His forked tongue laved my clit, rough yet wet, hard, sloppy lashes that gave me everything I needed and forced me to take even more.

He snarled, the dangerous sound raising the hair on my nape even as the sensation drugged me.

Vibrations quaked my lower lips as he growled low, "The sweetest thing I've ever tasted."

He upped the ferocity until his silken tail attacked my fluttering channel. My inner walls squeezed the wide intrusion, struggling to take the delicious onslaught.

The fire in my blood roared, lighting me up from the inside as pleasure crashed through me, exploding like fireworks in the darkness.

"Killian!" The scream finally burst free, shattering me from the inside out.

Everything hazed as I writhed and thrashed, trapped on Killian's tail as he drew out every ounce of my pleasure, fucking me through wave after wave of bliss, wringing it from my aching core until I whimpered at the overstimulation.

His arrow eased from between my thighs, and I twitched with the aftershocks.

A low groan washed over me, a wet sound snagging my attention through the dark. "Sweeter than candied petals."

My core clenched at the mental image of him tasting my pleasure off his tail.

Heat covered me, and soft, moist lips pressed to mine. I gasped into the gentle kiss, my lips trying to follow after his, but the tricky demon pulled back.

The fabric was tugged from my eyes, and I blinked rapidly as light flooded my vision.

A bonfire crackled and popped in the centre of a shadowy forest. The smokeless fire was an unnatural ruby shade, like blood set aflame—the colour of my dark magic rather than the hell-fire's lilac shade outside the dreamscape. Wildflowers, painted with a rainbow of bioluminescence, swayed in an invisible breeze before the huge fallen redwood I was draped over. More trees bordered the cocooned space. Colourful firebugs dotted the air like stars brought within reach, their low humming a lazy melody.

It looked like the Bloodwood clearing where Killian had snuck up on me but with the magic dial cranked way up.

The dream world filtered in with each hazy blink.

And Killian was at its centre, a sinful smirk on glistening lips.

Chapter 18

"Shhh." Killian held up a hand, stopping along the grassy riverbank and cocking his pale horns aside.

I immediately swallowed the inane small talk I'd been making for the last hour as we'd trekked along the river. It hadn't done a thing to ease the tense awareness between us since last night's fiery dream and all the mind-blowing revelations that had come before it.

This morning, I'd blushed just looking in his direction, and that was before we'd bathed in the river and I'd reapplied salve to his wounds. Though, they'd mostly healed from the energy we'd shared in my dream.

He'd not said a peep about it, and I sure as hell-fires were hot wasn't going to bring it up first. I still couldn't process that for years he'd been beating up any exes who'd hurt me. Pretty much everyone in our kingdom had a rejection complex from being born an unwanted hybrid, so most break-ups ended up as vicious things.

Did that mean they deserved to be beaten bloody for insulting me? Probably not.

Now that I thought about it, it was only the handful who'd been truly cruel, or physical, that had actually disappeared.

Which I now knew meant Killian had *murdered* them.

My brother clearly knew about it too and hadn't interfered.

It was enough to make any sane demoness start hissing and clawing the faces off such psychotic, overprotective males.

I scanned the forest for whatever had triggered the incubus, struggling to stomp my inner turmoil into submission.

I might not have the senses of a full-blooded demon, but lately, *other* senses had been sharpening. Ones I didn't quite know how to define. Like the odd awareness of creatures around me when I couldn't see, hear, or scent them.

I shuddered, stuffing the feeling away with the hungry wisps of darkness lingering inside me, even though it seemed tamed this morning. Possibly because of the things Killian had done in my sleep.

Alpha stilled beside the incubus, lifting his nose to the air. Like a summoned demon, the hellcat slunk from the tree-line, winding silently closer to us as she, too, scanned the river and the trees.

Anticipation sang through me. That was the danger of following the river; life needed to drink to survive, and we were right in their way.

We'd already spotted several animals sipping from the riverbank as we'd passed by, most baring their fangs in threat or stomping hooves aggressively. Some I could feel waited in hiding for us to pass before they revealed themselves. My weird senses latched on to them to deliver odd instinctual knowings—like that one of the delicate vine dragons was pregnant, and a hornless deer was looking for a mate. A phoenix had even swooped through the sky like a comet, blazing past as it scooped a mouthful of pink river water on the fly.

I heard it then. The rustle of bushes and crack of twigs. The squeak of a wheel.

The chatter of voices.

Killian planted himself between me and the sound. "Whatever happens this time, if I tell you to run, you'd better listen." His voice was quiet, but the command rang clear.

Too bad for him, I was absolutely going to ignore it.

Glimpses of green and grey demons preceded a dark wooden cart pulled along by a scarred unicorn. The magnificent creature should have shone with a brilliant silvery glow in the patches of dappled sunlight. Instead, angry red lines cut through its once white coat, now tinted a filthy yellow and smeared with mud.

To see a unicorn mistreated was a crime against nature.

My heart squeezed as the procession drew closer through the trees. A small travelling band of merchants from the looks of the laden carts.

In the cities, demons used mechanical vehicles that were basically monster trucks. Out here in the wilderness between kingdoms, though, the landscape wasn't kind to such tech. Using beasts was still the best way to travel, especially when transporting goods.

The travelling party slowed to a halt as they spotted us. We were in a weird standoff, the river at our backs as we faced the demons emerging from the forest, half blocking our way forward along the bank.

Killian's eyes narrowed on the unicorn, and he stalked towards the merchants. My brows shot up at his recklessness, but I hurried along behind him, heart pounding with each step closer.

Maybe we could have slipped past them without incident, but the sight of the abused creature wouldn't have let me either. I reached out with my magic, a foreign stretching sensation jumbling my mind. It brushed over the unicorn, and the old male tossed his head, tugging at the chains restraining his face. The thin golden links wrapped around his muzzle so he couldn't open his mouth to bare his dagger-sharp teeth.

I traced the length of his restraints, which tied him to the front of the convoy of three heavy carts.

Killian halted a few feet from the waiting demons—all pure-bred orcs, by the looks of it.

They sized him up, with his countless scars, half-healed wounds slathered with cracked paste, and most prominent of all, his mixed heritage.

Thin lips curled in contempt. Brows lowered. Eyes tightened. Hands strayed to weapon hilts.

"Unhitch the unicorn, and be on your way," Killian said, voice deadly neutral.

Silence answered before a rasping chuckle broke from the largest orc of the group.

The towering male puffed out his chest, a sneer carving his heavy features. "Why? You going to take its place, beast?"

Sniggering rippled the group of orcs at his back. The males focused their mocking stares on us, filtering closer. Tension hummed through the air, the oncoming bloodshed contrasting the sunny morning scene beside the pretty pink river.

Killian joined in with the orcs, his laughter harsh enough for theirs to die on their lips. "Actually, I was going to set him free and give you quick, clean deaths because we've got places to be. But now I think I'll take my time. Let him gorge on your bloated carcasses instead."

The lead orc scoffed, snorting like a shadow boar. "A battered mutt like you? Your frail body would give out before I even raised a fist."

I winced at his assessment. Layers of damage etched Killian's chest, despite the salve I'd packed into his cuts.

Voices murmured from within the carts.

The six visible demons already outnumbered us. I frowned, easing a few steps aside to glimpse the others.

A blood-smeared arm poked through the bars of a cage. Thin and scarred.

Horror choked me.

My gaze raked across the orcs bristling around the cart.

They were all purebloods, and I knew that shouldn't make me jump to conclusions, but life had taught me too many lessons for me to assume they were transporting prisoners for bounty.

Killian caught sight of the arm hanging limply from the cart. His eyes cut to the demon at the front. "What's back there?"

The hulking orc took a menacing step closer. "Nothing that concerns you. But if you want, you can join the rest of your worthless kind in there. Even a weakling like you can fetch a good price in certain kingdoms."

Killian chuckled, and the sound scraped like the edge of a blade. "Be careful, this slave isn't collared anymore."

The orc ran his gaze more fully over Killian, then moved onto me. His dull green skin rippled with disgust, and I saw the exact moment he realised what I must be, his face puckering like a dried berry.

My insides pinched as his judgement washed over me.

I had been born in one of the more purist succubus kingdoms. Sneers and mocking were nothing new, from strangers or my own kin. It shouldn't bother me anymore.

But something about this orc was a little too familiar.

After I'd failed to save my mother, her two sisters raised me. They'd got bored after a few years of beating me, and so the cruel succubae pushed me towards one of the pleasure houses to "earn my keep."

I'd been fourteen.

Other demon breeds flocked to my old kingdom for a good time, despite the drain on their energy that came with seeking pleasure.

I barely remembered killing my first customer: an orc just like this male sneering at me. All I knew was that I'd run for days, clutching a bloodstained knife in my hand, until I collapsed in this very forest. Rex had found me, half-clothed and coated in dried blood that wasn't mine.

He'd brought me home and nursed me back to health like I was a baby phoenix with a broken wing.

Seeing this demon brought back a surge of toxic memories. Ones I'd blocked out long ago for my own sanity.

A sharp smile stretched Killian's lips. Shadow bled through his feathers.

"Hybrid scum." The orc spat on the floor at his boots. "We're going to take you and your human whore abomination." His sneer turned on me as he jabbed a dull claw towards my face.

Killian blurred, sword flashing in a gleam of obsidian.

The orc screamed, black blood spurting from the stump of his arm.

Killian had sliced off his hand.

But he didn't stop there.

The psycho speared his weapon into the grass and launched himself at the squealing male, slashing chunks of flesh off with his bare claws. An unhinged laugh spilled from Killian's lips, soaked in darkness.

He kicked the orc's knee out, sending him screaming to the floor, and pounced.

I couldn't breathe. Killian straddled the giant male and punched his hand through the orc's heaving chest, reaching in and scrambling organs until the thick scent of gore perfumed the air.

The unicorn beside them whinnied in excitement, stomping his pointy hooves like he wanted the orc beneath them.

Killian bared his fangs at his victim. "You're not fit to be in her presence, let alone speak about her."

Violence danced in his glowing eyes. He removed his dripping hands from the chest cavity he'd cracked open like a crab shell. He pried open the orc's mouth, reaching his fist in and yanking at something.

I gagged the second Killian ripped the forked tongue free, cackling like a madman. "Now you can never address her again. She's above you. My fucking princess."

The light dimmed from the orc's eyes, their yellow glow dying to a putrid pus colour.

Silence blanketed the forest.

None of the orc's comrades dared move. Not a leaf dared rustle, nor an insect dared chirp.

"Ohhhhkaayyyy..." I drew out the word, struggling to process the brutality I'd just witnessed.

I mean, I knew Killian was a little unhinged. He was a lead enforcer for a brutal kingdom constantly under threat. The things he did to protect us involved bloody fangs and stringy flesh under his claws.

But this was a whole new level of crazy.

Killian had the gall to look up at me, raise the slippery grey tongue in offering, and *smirk*. "A gift, sweetness."

My birthday wasn't until tomorrow, but I doubted he knew that.

He'd just dismembered a demon and cackled while doing it. And then was trying to give me a piece of his victim.

Like a complete psychopath.

I couldn't help the snort of disbelief that escaped me. "No wonder people avoid our kingdom."

He grinned manically. "It's called a show of excessive force."

I coughed. "Isn't it just."

One slaver at the back of the group gagged, a fine leather-gloved hand coming up to cover his tusks, and the shocked stupor holding the others broke.

"Throw them in with the rest!" A wrinkled orc beside the carts stamped a crooked staff with a booming thud.

The orcs moved as one, a surge of violence bristling towards us.

Killian leaped to his feet and threw his black wings wide, intimidating enough to make a few hesitate. The rest plunged towards us.

I wouldn't be caged. Not ever again.

My magic surged. A desperate dark thing. It clasped me by the throat and tore from its cage.

Everyone flinched, and time stilled.

Bones snapped, and screams answered. Cuts and bruises ruptured through the crowd.

Green skin. Purple. Black fur. White hide. All began to split and gush blood.

Only the hellcat seemed unaffected.

Power writhed through me in a torrent, choking me.

Killian was the first to react, grunting as he swiped up his sword and began chopping off heads like a macabre logger, the black blood of his kills wetting his skin along with the red of his own.

And I couldn't do a thing except stand there and wage an internal war against the evil I carried.

I really was an abomination.

The moans of the dying filled me with horror. And a strange bubbly energy that made me want to vomit.

I groaned along with my victims, dropping forward. A thud reverberated up my knees, quaking my thigh bones.

My purpose was to heal people. Not...not this.

"Eve...," Killian spluttered, coughing up blood as he reached for me. Black wings drooped at his sides, coated in wetness.

The horrifying sight burned into my retinas, and I willed something to stop me.

Anything.

I'd rather die than hurt Killian like this.

Cookie leaped for me, clawless paws looming large in my vision.

They slammed into my face.

And the black void caught me.

Chapter 19

Darkness clung to me like a jealous ex.

Something warm wrapped around me, and a rhythmic whooshing sound filtered in. Motion gripped me, like I was being yanked downwards.

I cracked my eyes open with horrendous effort. A lush canopy hung in the distance.

Getting closer.

Movement in my periphery stole my hazy focus. Ink-dipped feathers fluttered with powerful wing-beats.

"Killian," I breathed.

The arms holding me adjusted their grip, cradling my head closer against a firm chest. I tipped my face up to meet Killian's frantic gaze.

"Sweetness," he whispered, voice hoarse.

Enough brain function returned to have me jolting in his arms as reality hit.

We burst through the greenery, which spit us out high above.

I sucked in a scream.

Killian hovered us for a moment, and I tore my eyes from him to marvel at the sea of dark green spreading for miles in all directions. Far in the distance, mountains pierced the landscape, sharp peaks capped in snow that protected this region from the constant infighting of the larger kingdoms beyond.

I had barely a second to take it in before Killian angled his wings. Gravity called, and we swooped towards the canopy before the demon's wings flared, catching the breeze to level us out above the leaves reaching for us.

Nerves tried to choke me, despite the sluggish weight to my body.

I didn't have wings. In fact, I barely had any demonic traits.

I'd never flown before, despite the number of times I'd fantasised about Killian wrapping me in his arms and making me see stars.

His strong arms held me now as we soared. The only sound was the rushing of the wind in my ears, whipping my hair into a tornado of blood-red curls.

It was definitely smacking Killian in the face, but the demon didn't say a thing as he flew me away.

My body shook as I thought about what had happened. What I'd *done*.

"Kill." My voice cracked with the anguish. "Drop me. Drop me right fucking now. Before I hurt you even more."

Killian stared down at me, jaw clenched, with a wildness in his demonic eyes I'd rarely seen. He blinked rapidly, seeming unstable.

Well, more so than usual.

"Never," he snarled. "I'd take any pain, just to be near you."

My throat closed off with panic at his words. I couldn't think straight. Was I hurting him, even now?

But that horrifying darkness seemed satiated. Almost like it had taken its fill and slumbered happily while I was left with the fallout.

"Alpha and Cookie? And those captives…" I had to swallow thickly, my mouth dry from the wicking wind. "Did I…?"

I couldn't finish that sentence.

"No," he rasped. "They're fine. But I hadn't hurt some of the slaver scum enough for your magic to finish them off though."

Relief flooded me, but it was short-lived.

"What…happened?" I asked slowly, voice barely audible over the breeze.

"Your magic… It was…unstable," he began.

Understatement.

His jaw clenched for a moment, lashed by my red strands, but he didn't seem to notice. He finally gritted out words: "That damn cat hit you."

My last memory before waking up in his arms was the giant furball launching herself at me. But I wasn't annoyed.

I was relieved.

"Thank fires," I murmured.

Killian's scowl deepened, carving furrows between his brows.

Those hybrids were safe from me, and free. Hopefully Alpha would head back to Zoella now too, and that crazy hellcat would stop stalking me.

Everyone was fine and far away from me.

Except the stubborn enforcer, clutching a monster to his chest.

He folded his wings around me, their soothing feel immediately overshadowed by the lurch in my middle as we plummeted.

"Kill!" I squealed, clinging to him as tight as my trembling arms could.

I caught his wicked grin from the corner of my eye. The falling sensation left my organs up in the clouds, and all I could do was squirm.

Even though that was a *really* bad idea.

Killian's rich chuckle smoothed over me. "Relax, Princess, I'll never let you go."

You knew your obsession was bad when innocent words like that were enough to snap you out of a panic spiral while literally falling from the sky.

His wings shot out, revealing the rich colours of the forest as he turned our death tumble into a smooth glide. I took a deep, shaky breath and twisted a little to get a better look.

We soared over the pink river, winding towards a rustic inn perched on the riverbank. The redwood structure blended with the tree trunks beyond and was complete with a water wheel for old-school power and a stone chimney coughing smoke.

I'd been to the inn a few times, but Rex, in his classic overprotective brother mode, had banned me from it when I was younger. Apparently, it was a bad place for good girls.

My lips twitched at the memory.

I was a hated combination of demon and mage, with the curses of both. A hybrid raised in a cruel succubus kingdom.

I'd never been a "good girl."

Killian angled his wings, taking us down to the tavern with a few light wing-beats. I marvelled at the idea of flying. Sure, my stomach wasn't a huge fan of being scrambled, but it would have taken me a whole day of hiking to get here.

Killian just jumped into the sky, flapped his pretty wings a few times, and dived right back down to where we needed to be.

Lucky bastard.

Killian landed in front of the battered structure with barely a thud in the grass. Like carrying me around was nothing.

I levelled him with a stern look even as a wave of dizziness tried to sweep me under. "You can put me down now."

An odd sort of weakness seemed to hunt through my limbs, like I was drunk on too much power, but it had tipped straight into the hangover phase.

"Can I? After what just happened, I'm not sure you can stand." He eyed me with that concerned look I'd always hated.

Like he saw me as a wayward child in need of protecting.

"Kill," I warned.

He sighed and released my legs, gently lowering me to the ground. I hated how much my knees wobbled, forcing me to grip his muscular arm for support as I tried to lock them in place.

A gasp burst free as I got a real look at the incubus.

Blood, bruising, and split skin covered every inch of his exposed chest and arms. No doubt the damage extended to his back and lower body too.

Once again, Killian was a fucking state.

"Fires-dammit, Kill. When were you going to tell me you were hurt? That *I'd* hurt you?" I hissed.

The unspoken "again" stabbed right through my heart.

Killian shrugged, and his huge wings, now back to their usual pearly white beneath the splattered red and black, followed the rise and fall of his broad shoulders. "It didn't seem important."

My eye twitched. "Didn't seem...?" I blew out a breath, fighting for control and the will not to pass out. I held up a hand. "You know what? Doesn't matter. Come here."

I tried to grab him and stopped short. No pale glow wreathed my fingertips, my hand as inert as my healing powers.

The stubborn demon leaned out of reach anyway, eyes flashing. "No."

Of course he wouldn't want my magic anywhere near him. That was twice now I'd maimed him with the dark beast lurking inside me.

I swallowed thickly, dull hand dropping back to my side. "Sorry."

He shook his horns. "It's not what you think. Let's get inside. You need to rest, not to drain yourself further."

I let him lead me to the inn, feeling the crushing weight of disappointment with every open wound I mapped across Killian's toned back. Even his wings had little tears in them, reddening the white feathers.

I'd done that.

I'd killed most of those orcs too. Not that I harboured much guilt over them, given they'd abused a magical creature and caged living beings to sell.

Killian pushed inside the enormous double doors of the inn. Chatter spilled out to greet us.

Groups of demons clustered around worn tables, laden with clay platters of steaming food and countless drinks. A few fruity-looking cocktails in sophisticated martini glasses dotted amongst the tankards of frothy ale and honeyed mead, the mismatch in tune with the patrons inside.

Hell was a stunning mix of new and old. Of traditional demon customs, interspersed with modern human technology and culture.

An orc, like the ones I'd just slaughtered, even wore a Nirvana band tee from the human realm, bringing a smile to my lips even as exhaustion dragged me down.

A few other hybrids lingered inside, their mismatches of features and downtrodden auras an obvious tell.

I hoped they were on their way to our kingdom, where freedom and safety waited for them under Rex's rule.

Unless they dated me, apparently.

A hush descended over the tavern as the patrons caught sight of who darkened their doorway. Killian ignored the tension, striding right up to the worn bar along the far side. Most demons scowled at us, but given the gore coating us both, and Killian's impressive brawn, nobody said a thing.

Killian leaned his muscled forearms on the wooden countertop and addressed the blood demon behind it with one of his signature grins, loaded with dark charm. "Your best room please, Darya."

That he knew her name set my fangs on edge.

She beamed, showing off her shiny onyx fangs, longer and sharper than mine. The demon coyly batted her spiky horned lashes and placed the glass jug she was cleaning behind the counter. "Anything for you, Kill."

I couldn't help the squirm of something ugly that ran through me as I joined Killian.

Did he find her attractive? Was he planning to feed on her while we were here? Had he slept with her already?

I gave her a brief once-over, trying to be subtle. Long sable hair ran to her thighs in an impractical but luscious waterfall of stunning locks. Bright eyes glowed gold, slashed through with vertical pupils and framed by spiny weaponry. Long horns spiralled into a curl around each of her tapered ears, capped with hammered gold to emphasise their points. Dusky pink skin gave her a warm blush of colour, mixing beautifully with her golden accents.

I didn't want to be a jealous bitch, but I was half-tempted to see which way my magic wanted to swing with her, and she'd only *smiled* at him.

I forced a brittle stretch to my lips.

Stab your claws through her eyes for daring to look at what's yours. Throw them at the other females in warning!

"Two rooms, actually," I bit out, keeping my manic grin fixed in place to cling to denial. I *definitely* wasn't hearing bloodthirsty voices in my head.

She returned a small dip of her pointed chin.

Killian cut her a hard look. "One."

Chapter 20

I scowled at the side of Killian's stupidly pretty face. "What do you think you're doing? I'm not sharing a bed with you."

Not that the idea didn't bring to life too many fantasies to count.

He ignored me, taking the offered key from the pouty demon behind the bar in exchange for a handful of gold coins. You paid half upfront and half on leaving in a place like this.

Part of the inn's vague claim to "safety" was that they only got full payment if you made it out alive.

Though, if another patron killed you, they charged your murderer an extra cleaning fee. All in all, I was not reassured by their monetary investment in my survival.

Killian turned his wings on the barmaid, who stared dreamily after the demon enforcer, hearts in her eyes. I huffed under my breath, following the stubborn bastard as he made his way for the stairs in the far corner, dripping blood onto their floorboards like it was mere rain.

We climbed the creaking stairs, and I tried not to ogle his firm arse, lovingly hugged by his battered leather trousers.

Instead, I stared at the sinuous joints of his upper back where white wing met slate-purple flesh. A sheathed blade nestled between, running the length of his spine.

The enforcer had sexy back muscles, even bruised and cut up as he was. Given the weight and power of his feathered wings, his toned back was a fires-damned masterpiece.

He reached the top of the stairs, head swivelling as if he expected an attack from any closed door we passed along the corridor.

To be fair to him, it wouldn't be the first time someone had popped out from a room and tried to stab me for no reason.

Since the inn edged the Bloodwood, hordes of passing travellers and merchants frequented the place. Many were as bloodthirsty as they were prejudiced. At least most knew the Hybrid Kingdom was close by and that we would defend and avenge our own with brutal force.

It made it far safer for our kind.

We walked to our room in silence, and Killian unlocked the simple blackwood door, raked through with claw-marks in another show of how safe the inn was.

He stepped in first, flaring his wings like a barrier. Shielding me, as always.

I huffed at the feathered wall. It only highlighted his overprotectiveness, or my apparent lack of defensive skill.

Or both.

"How many assassins are lying in wait this time? Ten? Twenty?" I drawled.

He folded his feathered beauties tight to his back, shooting me a wry smirk over an arched joint. "Such a brat," he tutted. "Come on, let's get you to bed."

My cheeks flamed.

Of course, he didn't mean it like that, but my stupid hormones were always up for a little delusion.

The room was a simple affair of redwood flooring and dark timber furniture, all courtesy of the Bloodwood. A dresser leaned against one scratched wall, a broken mirror resting atop it, shards littering the surface like pulled fangs.

A low bed lurked in the corner beneath a shuttered window. It gave us a peek at the dusky sky between towering, blood-drenched trees. At least a healthy number of furs layered the bed, in all shades and shapes, to ward off the chill prickling the air with night's approach.

The bedside table held a plastic box with a faded red cross painted on top. A discarded med kit from the human realm was just the kind of reassuring thing you wanted to come as standard with your room.

For once, I was grateful though. Apparently, all I had now were the clothes on my back and the poisoned knives strapped to my thighs, my pack lost somewhere amongst the bodies of my victims.

"At least let me dress your wounds," I said, holding up a hand to cut him off as he spun to face me with a protest on his lips. "Nope."

His features hardened into what I thought of as his serious look, like an angry statue. "You need rest."

"And you need to stop bleeding all over the floor." I glanced pointedly at the worn flooring, already stained with various shades of blood, now decorated with an extra trail of bright red.

How did he have anything left inside him? All he'd done since I'd walked in on him in the bedroom at that party was bleed out.

He chuckled, the stupid, sexy sound I hated to love. "Why, sweetness, who knew you were so concerned about little old me?"

"Old is right. Little, not so much." I stalked towards him, trying not to blush as my eyes dropped to the obvious bulge at his crotch.

I'd meant his frame in general, but of course, that wasn't how it sounded. I was the queen of making things awkward.

He raised his hands in mock surrender, that damn smirk tugging up one corner of his mouth as he backed up. "So eager to get me into bed?"

I hissed and shoved the one uninjured part of his chest, forcing him to sit back heavily on the furs.

The sight of him on a bed threatened to distract me from my mission, but I managed to scramble enough sense together and grabbed the kit off the nightstand. Rifling through the contents, I found an expired antiseptic cream from the human realm, thread with no needle, and gauze pads that may or may not have already been opened.

I sighed. "It won't be as effective as healing magic, but it's better than tearing you apart further." I pinned him with my stern healer glare. "Wait here."

An indulgent smirk curved his lips, and I turned away before he could draw another hiss from me, stepping into the tiny attached bathroom. Ignoring the cracked tiles and cloudy mirror above the rough-hewn basin, I filled a small bucket of pale-pink liquid from the tap. At least the inn had running water, piped in and filtered from the river flowing alongside it.

After fishing a threadbare cloth from the wicker basket beside the sink, I hurried back out.

The enforcer remained exactly how I'd left him, ankles crossed, leaned back on forearms propped on the bed beneath him, wings splayed over the fur blankets.

Countless wounds trickled bright blood down his plum skin, smearing the predatory birds decorating his torso.

I longed to study his tattoos in more detail. I'd never really let myself look at him too closely, instinctively knowing it would only make me feel worse.

Plus, it was kinda rude to salivate over your patients. I may not have exactly been a trained doctor, but even I knew being a pervert was a no-no.

His eyes tracked my every move, but they lacked their usual mischievous gleam. All the fighting and constant injuries were finally catching up to him.

Guilt nipped me with sharp fangs. I was the one who kept hurting him.

Setting the bucket on the creaky bedside table, I dunked the cloth and leaned over his wide frame, gently dabbing the blood from the worst cuts before replacing each one with a gauze pad taped to his skin.

I frantically ignored the way he shivered at my almost touch, goosebumps rising on his skin where I stroked him with the damp linen.

With a shaky inhale, I finally scrounged up the courage to speak. "Thank you for carrying me out of there. You saved our furred friends and those hybrids."

From me.

His gaze felt hot on my face, but I couldn't meet it with my own.

"I didn't do it for them," he rasped.

Long minutes slunk by as I worked in silence, unable to answer him. The familiar process of tending to a patient lulled me instead. I ran out of questionable gauze before he ran out of wounds, though the worst of them were now patched up with the stark bandaging.

"Thanks, kid," the incubus murmured, and a small smile emerged, a genuine expression that showed faint dimples.

What kind of blood-soaked killer had *dimples*?

I straightened with a huff, inspecting my work. "At least you won't bleed all over me, since you insisted on sharing a bed."

He stood, bringing our bodies flush. Warmth lit my cheeks. His wing arced out to shepherd me onto the bed, taking his place.

A yawn cracked my jaw, taking me by surprise as I settled onto the firm mattress, scooting back when Killian peeled the covers aside for me, gently helping me in. My eyes blinked heavily.

The incubus paused, fisting the covers and staring at the sliver of bare mattress beside my prone form. A debate played out across his severe features.

"I don't bite," I muttered, trying not to look too much into his hesitation at climbing into bed with me, even though I'd been the one insisting on two rooms.

And they said we succubae were natural temptresses.

His lips twitched. "It's not your fangs I'm worried about."

I quirked a brow and let the weight of my head finally hit the pillow. I had no clue what he was nattering on about, but a bone-deep exhaustion robbed me of the ability to overthink that too.

"Just get in, Killian."

On the next blink, my lids didn't reopen.

Instead, I let the burned-caramel scent of Killian wrap around me, sweet enough to make my mouth water but with that edge of smoky darkness that was all him.

The covers rustled, and he slid in beside me. Somehow, he avoided touching me despite his size.

"Get some rest, Eve. I'll keep you safe."

Chapter 21

My eyes snapped open, heart racing as I took in the unfamiliar room.

"Killian?" I gasped, sitting upright and searching for the demon amongst the shadows.

A bright cherry lit the tip of a smoke stick, drawing my focus to the incubus.

He leaned out the open window, horns almost scraping the shutters. He'd removed the gauze from his chest, but it had been long enough now that the wounds had mostly closed.

"Sweetness," he rasped, exhaling a stream of dark smoke. "It's only been a few hours. Go back to sleep."

I shuffled up the bed until my back hit the wall, drawing my legs up to hug under the furs. I still felt tired, but it wasn't something sleep could fix. This was an energy drain, leaving me hollow and oddly deflated.

Really, what I needed was to feed.

The thought had me blushing as I realised *who* I wanted to feed from.

I cleared my throat, awkward in the lingering silence. "I can't sleep."

One side of his smirk slashed through the moonlight that bathed him. "In that case, wait here."

He turned, balancing the roll-up between his lips as he made his way to the door. The lock clicked behind him, and my eyes narrowed on the scarred wood sealing me in.

In seconds, he was back, though, not even a creaking floorboard outside to announce his return. The door clicked again as he turned the key, entering on silent steps.

My brows leaped up.

Killian—bloodthirsty, unhinged enforcer of the most hated kingdom in hell—was holding a cake.

I arched a brow. "First a tongue and now this?" I drawled. "Aren't you just the gift that keeps on giving?"

"Well, it *is* after midnight. You think I'd have forgotten your birthday?" he mused, a sardonic smirk on his face.

My mind struggled to process that Killian, of all people, was holding a tall cake slathered in pink frosting. It was even on a fancy gold-rimmed plate and topped with candied blood drops. He brought it over, resting it on the shoddy nightstand.

He perched on the edge of the bed. Even folded tightly, one wing-tip brushed the back of my hand where it lay over the fur blanket.

Killian tipped his head back, eyes on the starry sky through the open window. "You know... You were the first person to get me a cake, or anything sweet, actually."

I frowned at him. "I was?"

He inclined his horns with a wry quirk of his lips. "In my old kingdom, they called us *Ra Na Tha'an*." Silvered eyes pierced mine. "Child of Fate."

My brows furrowed. "That doesn't sound like a bad thing."

He held my gaze steady. "Nobody would choose to create us. We're the cruel burdens that fate delivers."

An ache fissured through my heart. I would never forget the first time I'd seen Killian. Battered. Bruised. But not broken. Never broken.

He'd staggered between kingdoms for weeks until finding ours. The rumoured safe haven for hybrids.

He was only a teenager when he'd arrived but had already lived lifetimes' worth of cruelty.

Like all of us.

"You could never be a burden," I whispered, feeling something burn in my chest. "Not to anyone who matters."

His lips twitched, but it didn't reach his eyes. "Anyway, slaves don't have birthdays." A hard look entered his eyes, almost as if he turned so brittle he might shatter. "But when I first arrived in the Hybrid Kingdom and was staying at the cabin you and Rex shared, you asked my age. I was roughly nineteen, if the other slaves were to be believed, but I knew then it was the start of my new life. I claimed that day as my birthday." He leaned toward me, giving me his full attention. Eyes unflinching in their directness, some hidden emotion churned in their endless depths. "You came back a few hours later with a giant cake, layered in bright-pink frosting, with poisoned flowers decorating the top."

The memory brought a blush to my cheeks. "Bloodbores."

He grinned, a genuine expression I didn't see often enough on his features. "The same stunning colour as your hair and eyes."

It was also the flower I used as a base for my most vicious poisons and a few healing salves. Huge planters of them sat under the front windows outside my house. But I hadn't been the one to plant my favourite flower there.

I'd always assumed the present was from Rex, a brotherly housewarming gift, but now that I thought about it... Rex was more likely to gift me weapons than flowers.

I ducked my head, unable to bear the intensity as I battled the realisation sinking in. "Sorry I tried to poison you on your birthday. Some healer, huh?"

"It was perfect." He shook his horns. "I set the sugared flowers aside and pressed them in a book," he whispered.

The words were so quiet, I could have almost imagined them.

I didn't know what to do with that information.

Was this attraction more than one-sided? I was a succubus though; wouldn't I have felt his desire before this cursed trip if that were true? Why would he flip between flirting and treating me like a kid? I knew he charmed all women. He was pure seduction, even for an incubus.

My heart beat too fast, frantically trying to pump blood to my brain to fuel my confused thoughts.

"Killian..." I trailed off, unsure what to say.

He cleared his throat, looking almost pained before donning his usual sinful mask. "Anyway, kid, here's me returning the favour."

He swiped another rolled stick of haze from somewhere and pressed it between his lips. Leaning over, he lit the end using the birthday candle and drew a deep inhale before blowing out a puff of sweet smoke. A dark stream poured from his lips, leaving behind a sharp smirk on shadowed lips.

I frowned. He didn't always smoke the numbing drug, but I suspected he'd been using it as a crutch over the years, when things got too heavy.

"Well?" He quirked a brow. "Blow out your candle, sweetness."

I rolled my eyes, lips twitching. "Yes, sir."

He jolted as if I'd struck him. Lips tightened around the drug perched between them.

I swallowed, and hurried to blow out the candle.

Everything was so damned messy when it came to Killian.

I met his gaze, the pale wisps of the extinguished candle rising between us. I was hyperaware that we were in a bed, alone, and hunger thrived inside us both.

He was a carnal being, sin and seduction made flesh.

In theory, so was I. Even though I'd never felt all that alluring.

My fangs ached to sink into something, and I darted my tongue out to wet my lower lip.

Killian's stormy gaze followed the movement, predator quick. I swallowed again, and his eyes dropped to my throat.

I couldn't help tilting my head, stretching the column of my throat in a silent invitation.

"Princess...," he breathed, voice as smoky as the drug he'd been inhaling. "I can feel how much you need to feed."

The words punched into me, slamming into my heart until my chest resounded like a drum with every pulsing beat.

He was right though. Hunger clawed at my insides, phantom aches in my chest letting me know the cake alone wouldn't satisfy me.

I needed more.

"I... You're right," I whispered, afraid to break the hushed cocoon the night had created for us. "I'll go down to the bar. See if anyone is willing to feed me."

His white wings bled darkness. His eyes hard, his lips peeled back to bare lethal fangs. "You're not going anywhere."

Before my brain could process his words, his hand wrapped around my throat and yanked me down the bed. He pinned me against the mattress with a single hand, silver eyes boring down into my very soul as he leaned over me.

"I'm only going to say this once, sweetness." His voice was a harsh rasp, his grip branding hot against my vulnerable throat. "Tell me to leave."

Did I want this?

My chest heaved with each panting breath that sawed in and out of my lungs.

I wanted this with every fibre of my fucking being.

"No."

Chapter 22

Victory flared in Killian's glowing eyes.

A slow smile crept across his lips, vicious and hungry. Dangerous.

"Oh, sweetness, you're going to feast until I've stuffed you full," he purred, hand tightening around my throat, just enough to make breathing his choice, not mine.

His dirty talk from before had nothing on this now. The full intensity of him bearing down on me, with the thrill of knowing he meant every single word.

With a deep breath that flared his rib cage, he unleashed pure bliss.

Sweetness burned my tongue in the most delicious way, his taste coating the inside of my mouth with the flavour promised by his intoxicating scent.

I'd never tasted his desire before. Not in real life, anyway.

But it wasn't just his taste; it was a fires-damned flood of *power.*

So much energy rushed to greet me, and a part of me marvelled at the preternatural control he had over his power. To unleash that much sexual energy on command was unheard of.

But I wasn't going to question it.

Right now, I could barely breathe through the onslaught.

"How do I taste, sweetness?" His wicked smile turned deviant. "I already crave your flavour on my tongue. Like candied bloodbores, did you know? Just like that fucking cake you baked me. You're the sweetest thing I've ever tasted, laced with a deadly edge that I'd gladly swallow down."

My body arched on the bed, delirious with need as silken ribbons of his desire caressed me from the inside. My core was almost embarrassingly wet, slicking my inner thighs as I rubbed them together to try to create the friction I craved.

He tutted, darkness saturating his handsome features almost as much as his shadowed wings. "Now, now, Princess. You're not allowed to ease that ache yourself. It's your birthday, after all. You should get the orgasm of your fucking life, even if you're too good to have my bloodstained lips on you."

I moaned at the bite of anticipation.

With one hand, he peeled my leather trousers down my legs in a smooth glide, letting his claws scrape my inner thighs just enough to have me stilling on the bed.

A wicked smirk carved his features. "You're soaked." His eyes locked onto my panties-covered core, wings shuddering at his back. He inhaled like he was scenting the air, and his pale horns tipped back with a groan. "Fuck. You're more succubus than you give yourself credit for."

I didn't know what he meant, but I was beyond caring.

"Kill," I moaned, his sexual energy filling me up in the most teasing way. I reached for his wrist, sinking my short red claws into his forearm as his grip tightened on my throat.

This bastard was going to make me beg; I just knew it.

His lips pursed into a wry smile. "Yes, sweetness? Something you wanted?" Mirth danced in his eyes, that wicked incubus with his dark intentions.

Taking things too far in my dreams was one thing… Having him touch me in real life was entirely different.

He reached for the cake on the nightstand, swiping a claw through it. My eyes became riveted to his hand as he dragged the frosting along my exposed inner thigh, the faint scrape winding me tighter.

I'd never felt so small compared to him, but he easily gripped my throat in one hand, curving me up a fraction, forcing me to witness him lean his face between my legs.

Warm breath fanned my panties, and the coolness rushing in on each of his inhales only highlighted how damp they were.

His tongue flickered out, the forked tip following the trail of icing he'd painted me with. Bliss hummed from deep within his throat.

"You're everything sweet to me," he purred, tracing another line of frosting, ending just short of where I ached for him.

He swiped his tongue across my thigh again, lapping up the sugar from my skin with a decadent groan, hand tightening on my throat for a thrilling second, cutting off my inhale. Silver eyes burned bright as they watched mine widen in a brief panic before he eased just enough for me to breathe again.

The forked tip of his tongue ghosted my panties in the most frustrating tease.

I bared my fangs and hissed. "This had better not be just a creative way to eat cake."

Shadowed wings shook with the rumble of his sultry laugh. "Nothing could be sweeter than your pussy on my tongue, but it's cute when you hiss at me, Princess. Do it again."

He skated another sugar-laden claw tip along my core. The most delicate threat. I hissed on command, unable to stop the harsh sound rushing out through gritted fangs.

"Fuck. Please don't be another dream," I muttered, hips rolling.

He grinned. "*Another*, hmm? Have you been dreaming about me a lot?"

He released my throat, yanked my trousers off fully, and settled himself on his knees before the bed, forcing my thighs wide open.

I whimpered at the erotic sight of the incubus, mouth hovering just inches above my core, like in my dreams.

"Answer me, sweetness." His wicked tongue flicked out to lash the crease of my inner thigh.

I sucked in a gasp at the hot sensation.

My thoughts scrambled as I tried to remember his question. "...No?"

His rich chuckle peppered the air, glowing eyes locking to mine. "Liar."

He closed the gap, and then his mouth was finally on me. He sucked the frosting from my soaked panties, teasing my lower lips with maddening friction and heat and pressure.

I writhed, gasping, and his tongue hooked the edge of my underwear and slid over my clit, lavishing sensation through me as he feasted between my thighs.

A flood of energy washed over me, drowning me in his smoky-sweet taste, feeding me even as he ate me like a demon starved.

"Killian," I moaned, unable to keep still as he laved at my core with a possessive growl. "Please!"

What mercy I begged for, I had no clue, but it was all too much. His energy seemed to stroke everywhere at once, running ghostly fingers over my neck, breathing warmth across my nipples, and teasing my inner thighs.

"That's it, sweetness, scream my name while I give you more than anyone else could." His words were a gravelly rasp against my core, drawing out the pleasure. "So fires-damned sweet, drown me in your pleasure."

His thick tongue dipped inside me with a wet stretch before retreating to suckle over my clit.

Already, I neared that sparkling peak. That delicious sensation of something looming. Big and realm-shattering.

He purred against my core, tongue vibrating against my clit, the forked tip hugging the greedy bundle of nerves with expert precision.

A scream tore from my lips as I bucked against the incubus's wicked mouth, unravelling for him.

It was an out-of-body experience. I could feel myself writhing on the soft furs, but I had no control.

Pleasure smashed me apart, and Killian rebuilt me just for him.

Chapter 23

The incubus pulled his tongue from my pussy as I watched on in a daze.

"It wouldn't be your birthday if you didn't have some of your cake," Killian purred.

The wicked demon turned to the nightstand and swiped more pink frosting from the destroyed cake, licking it straight off of his claws. Mischief blazed in his silver eyes as he leaned up and forced his thick tongue between my lips, sealing his mouth against mine.

The taste of candied petals bloomed on my tongue, along with a sweet musk I knew was the forbidden bliss he'd wrung from me. I groaned into the kiss as he half choked me with his monstrous, sugar-coated tongue. He laughed into my mouth, the sound edging cruelty as I gagged for an alarming breath.

With a vicious grin, he pulled back, licking his lips as I gasped on the bed, blinking up at him.

I bit my sweetened lips as he straightened, dipping from view as I struggled to lift my heavy head. Clothes rustled, and a second later, Killian loomed over me again.

Something wet and warm dripped between my thighs. It tingled with power. Thick droplets of heat continued to rain against my pussy, slicking me deliciously.

I moaned at the heady sensation and scraped together the strength to sit up enough to stare down between our bodies despite the boneless feel to my limbs.

A monster leered back.

My throat worked as I stared at Killian's proud length, lurking just above the apex of my thighs, beading with pearls of power.

In the dim room, his thick length looked a deep purple, richer than the slate shade of his skin. Like his horns, a feathered pattern ribbed his long length. Black edged it in a stunning pattern I knew would drive any demoness wild with every thrust. The shadowed edges matched the smooth bulbous tip that tapered into a wicked point, mimicking his arrowhead tail.

But what really caught my eye was how the feathered pattern changed as it reached his base. It became larger and thicker, like a dragon's scales. The pattern's shapes swelled as I watched.

Like a knot.

Not all incubi had them, but Killian was extreme in all things.

His sinuous tail wrapped around it and squeezed.

The wet splash of his pre-cum was indecent and so fucking sexy I couldn't breathe. As if my attention only turned him on, more tingling liquid blossomed from his pointed tip. It fizzed against my lower lips like sparkling mead, each drop driving me right to the edge again.

I breathed hard as I teetered on the edge of madness.

He was so close that all I had to do was hook a leg around his hips and I could impale myself on his throbbing, slick textured length. I could finally know what it felt like to have Killian.

A sexy growl rumbled between us, and my gaze locked with the demon's above me.

"If you keep looking at me like that, I'm going to have to fuck you," he murmured, pupils blown wide with his hunger.

I let my legs fall wider, welcoming the thought.

He snarled. "Grab my cock and cover yourself in my cum, sweetness."

He didn't wait for me to oblige, his wings scooping under my back to lean me close enough to grab him.

I reached out on instinct, my hands strangling the textured heat of him as much as his girth would allow. My claws didn't even touch.

He groaned, half-growl, half-moan, and it was the hottest sound I'd ever heard.

Silken liquid smoothed over his feathered length until my hands glided up and down, the texture scraping teasingly between my palms. I squeezed, working him faster, my breaths turning harsh and loud between us. More and more fluid seeped from his pointed tip, covering me in his mess.

It tingled hard enough that I throbbed beneath the slick coating me.

I'd never been with another sexual demon, and I didn't know quite what to expect despite the rumours.

It was pure fucking bliss.

"Faster, sweetness. Work that cock like you own it," he growled.

His hips bucked as I added a little twist to the motions, bouncing my hands up and down him fast enough to make my tits jiggle, even squeezed between my biceps.

Something thick stroked my pussy, and I gasped, losing my rhythm.

His tail slid through my folds, the arrowhead coating itself in his magical slick. The lubed head bore down at my entrance, bullying his way inside me. I moaned and writhed, trapped in his wings.

He pushed in slow enough for me to dance on the cusp of oblivion but tortured me right at the edge.

"Kill," I whined. "Please, I need you."

He shoved his tail all the way in, the arrow lodging deep and swelling. The pressure and stretch were too much in all the right ways.

I strangled his steely cock, battling to focus on pleasuring his throbbing length. The deep fullness of his tail had me moaning, everything in me tightening in anticipation. Before I knew what was happening, I lunged up, sinking my fangs into the meat of his chest and letting my venom wreak havoc through his body. The most divine sweetness hit my tongue as I finally tasted his blood.

The overwhelming taste of his nectar, the tail filling me, his needy cock in my hands—it shoved me over the edge, and I screamed through my fangs.

I pumped his cock with my hands in a punishing rhythm, and I released my bite right as he started to thrash above me.

He roared my name, coming in a fierce torrent.

Hot liquid splashed my chin and coated my breasts. It lashed my upper body and poured down my front. My nipples lit up with sensation, and even more so, my drenched pussy felt slapped with a tingling heat so hard it stung through my endless orgasm.

His tail kicked inside me, vibrating as he lost control. I writhed even harder, blackness trying to sweep me away as I broke for him over and over. Waves of pleasure crashed into me until I could hardly gasp enough air to survive the onslaught.

Minutes or hours or days passed as I writhed on a bed of wings, Killian coming over me as I shattered just for him.

Eventually, I managed to breathe again, blinking hazily up at the demon through the darkness, holding the room captive.

"Fires in Hell. That was...good," I croaked. My voice sounded like I licked sandpaper for a living.

Killian chuckled, and his tail shook inside me. I groaned, jerking on the bed beneath his impressive body. His wings held me in a soft cradle of feathers, and he looked down at me with something soft, like adoration, lighting his handsome features.

"I think it was a little more than that." A lopsided grin tugged up one side of his swollen lips.

A trickle of blood trailed from my fang marks in his chest, and I couldn't help the feminine satisfaction at seeing my mark on him.

Even with the feast of sexual energy, the bite would remain for a few days because of my venom. A perk of my succubus side.

Killian traced a finger through the mixture of thick fluids between my thighs, making me shudder at the overstimulation. He held the glistening concoction up to the moonlight and licked it clean.

He groaned, and my pussy clenched on his tail. "Gods, that combination is addictive. I want to cover you with my seed every night. I want it dripping from this tight cunt as you go about your day, blushing at how it soaks your panties while you work."

Even through the haze of pleasure, his words threw fuel onto the silly hope I tried to hide away in my heart.

He fisted his hand in my hair and pulled me up for a kiss that scorched me from the inside. I moaned into his mouth, tasting the power of us both on his wicked, forked tongue. Bliss simmered through every fibre of my being, somehow heightening every sensation even as I felt like I'd chain-smoked haze for hours.

He broke the kiss, chest heaving and eyes wild. "Now you're going to clean up every drop of this cum for me, and take my power into you like the good girl you are."

He yanked my hair, angling my head up as his other hand scooped hard between my legs, and I writhed on his wings. His fingers dripped cum across my lips and into my mouth a second before he shoved them between my lips.

I groaned at the addictive taste of him. The invasion of his smoky-sweet flavour in my mouth was everything the mouth-watering scent of his burned-caramel desire promised.

It tingled on my tongue, already working to strengthen me even as it drugged me with a high that rivalled any drug in the realms. He pushed in further, and I gagged, no choice but to swallow the sweetness he forced down my throat.

He pulled back with a vicious smirk, and I had a single second to breathe, pussy clenching hard on his throbbing tail, swollen and thick inside me—like it was lodged in deep and too wide to pull out.

Stuck.

"Fuck," I panted. "Is your tail..." I trailed off, unsure how to ask what my jumbled thoughts were hinting at.

He loomed over me, a sinister grin on his lips. "Is my tail what, sweetness? Is it knotting your tight pussy so you can't get away from me?" A dark chuckle rumbled his chest, glimpsing the unhinged psycho I knew him to be. "Just wait until it's my cock. I know you'll squeeze my knots so beautifully. That perfect pussy of mine, desperate for all my cum."

I whined, out of breath from his words as much as the aftershocks of bliss lighting me up and the tingle of power dripping down my throat, bathing my skin.

He grinned, all sharp teeth and bad intentions.

Something slapped against my pussy, a sharp sting of pleasure. I screamed, another orgasm ripping through me like venomous fangs. I writhed in a bed of feathers, trapped in Killian's dark fantasy.

A sinful chuckle met my low moans as I came back down from the shocked high, inner walls pulsing around the swollen tail knotted inside me. My clit throbbed from his rough attention.

I blinked up at Killian, his storm-blue eyes glowing with silver streaks like the flash of blades.

"Open wide, pretty girl." The demon lifted sharp claws, dripping pearly liquid onto my lips. "You still have a mess to clean up."

Chapter 24

The softest silk draped me, rubbing lightly against my bare skin with every breath I took.

A heated band wrapped around my waist. It pulled me into a firm heat at my back, and everything in me melted.

"Mmm." A contented sigh escaped as I snuggled closer to the delicious warmth cocooning me. I reached up and pulled the silky blanket tighter.

My fingers brushed wispy layers, and I frowned at the ticklish glide.

"Happy birthday, sweetness," a husky voice whispered in my ear. "If you keep fondling my wings, though, I'm going to think you want another present."

My eyes almost bugged out of my head. Harsh sunlight blinded me, and I hissed, slamming my lids closed.

A low chuckle rumbled the muscular chest at my back. "I've never had someone hiss at me for suggesting morning-after fun."

My cheeks blazed. "No... I...uh...was hissing at the sun." I finished lamely, wincing at how dumb that sounded.

Killian's warm laughter soothed my embarrassment. He nuzzled into my neck, his mirth tickling my skin as much as the messy strands of his inky hair.

My grin put the rude sun to shame. I'd dreamt of this moment for years. In more ways than one.

It was finally happening.

After making me come over and over last night, between feeding me mouthfuls of sweetness, rich with power, his tail had finally deflated enough to slide out from inside me. He'd carried me to the shower in the tiny adjoining bathroom, and we'd both cleaned off under the weak spray of tepid pink water.

Sleepily washing each other in the early hours had been strangely more intimate than what we'd done in the bed. I'd been left speechless as the playboy incubus tended to my every need, drying me off and tucking me into bed before cuddling up next to me without a word.

After the realm-shattering pleasure and the tender way he'd treated me afterwards, hope sank its claws deep into my heart, even though I knew it was a terrible idea.

Killian pressed a gentle kiss against my neck. Fangs brushed the delicate skin, and I shivered in sleepy delight.

"Clearly, it's not helped your love of early mornings," he rasped. "But at least last night should keep you topped up for a while."

I jolted like he'd stabbed me.

My chest cracked open, all that dumb hope draining out in a rush.

The embarrassment he'd staved off seconds ago came flooding back with a vengeance.

It was all about *feeding*.

Of course it was.

He was the one to suggest my dark magic might be lashing out because it was hungry.

I'd lost control of my powers, and it had drained me. I must have looked terrible after killing those orcs and hurting those hybrids, since he'd put me straight to bed before deciding I needed energy too.

Last night didn't mean a thing.

He was doing me a favour.

That stupid hope I'd been nursing for years seared to ash.

All the signs had been there from the start. I'd just been too stupid to heed them.

"I'll do whatever it takes to protect this kingdom."

"You shouldn't touch me."

"I'm here to make sure you're not doing something reckless."

"We're not friends."

I took every emotion rattling inside me and crumpled them into a tiny painful ball I could stuff deep, deep down. "You didn't have to feed me last night," I said, battling to keep my tone even.

He stilled, every muscle taut against my back. "I'd do anything for you, Eve." He cleared his throat, shifting away from me and letting the cold air rush between us. "I have to."

He *had* to.

A man had made me a fool. Again.

When would I learn?

Nobody actually wanted me. Not like that. Especially not him.

To my horror, moisture blurred my vision. I clenched my jaw against the sob building behind my fangs and carefully slipped out of Killian's arms, rising from the bed without looking at him, and padding to the en suite.

"Eve?" Confusion saturated his lilting tone. "What's wrong?"

I closed the flimsy door behind me with a soft click. "Nothing...Just...cleaning up." My voice came out steady, and I mentally applauded myself for getting something right when it came to the incubus.

One thing was clear though.

Nothing like this could happen again.

An awareness pulsed in my mind, pulling me to a stop. The odd sensation lit up with the flickering sense of *something* moving closer. Two of them. Both dangerous but not out for blood.

Not yet.

My brow scrunched up as I puzzled out the weird intuition. It pulsed with the static evidence of magic.

Though, how could I just *know* something like that?

Killian halted beside me, watching my face with a carefully neutral mask.

We'd left the inn after a tense breakfast in the main tavern area and hiked all day in an awkward silence since. The Bloodwood stretched for miles as we followed the pretty river towards the forest's edge.

The inn was only a day's hike from the portal, but you never knew what dangers lurked around it. Crossing in either direction was risky. We'd planned to camp just inside the forest's questionable safety tonight and then cross the open plains to the portal at first light when it should be quietest.

A faint growl rumbled through the woods.

Killian cocked his head, eyes pinned the direction the noise came from, but I already knew who it was.

Death stalked towards us on four paws and a bad attitude.

Cookie's eyes glowed her eerie blood-red, and she flickered her tufted tail in the air like a literal red flag.

Alpha padded between a pair of darkwood oaks behind her, easily twice the size of the slender hellcat.

A relieved breath escaped me. I was grateful to see them both in one piece, but for some reason, the sight of the hellcat eased something inside me. Some twisted knot that had tangled my insides without me knowing.

"What are you both doing here? Are you okay?" I asked, shaking out the ache in my hand. I'd been clenching hard enough for my short claws to puncture my palm.

Cookie slunk gracefully closer, a being of shadow and deception more than happy to ignore my frantic questioning. She perched in the centre of the worn path, cracking twigs and fallen leaves beneath her weight, and started grooming herself without a care in the realm.

I tensed as Alpha continued past her, worried she might take the opportunity to pounce while his back was turned.

He yipped, the sound almost like an affirmative.

I managed a tight smile back, some of my anxiety lessening with the distance between them. "I'm glad you're both okay, but you shouldn't be here. It's too dangerous, even for a fierce predator like yourself."

Alpha preened under the compliment, wagging his tail like a puppy rather than a fully grown hellhound capable of tearing me to shreds with massive paws of hell-fire.

He stepped close, bringing the tops of his triangular ears level with my chin, and nudged my palm with his damp nose. I obliged with a small smile, stroking the immense beast. Ragged scars interrupted the smooth perfection of his glossy fur, but they didn't detract from his beauty.

"Your coat is looking so shiny today," I cooed.

An irritable hiss broke the peace, and I frowned at the death kitty.

She arched her back, hissing again at the pair of us, eyes flashing the colour of freshly spilled blood.

Hellcats and hellhounds weren't known for being overly friendly. With anyone. But especially each other.

Tension froze me in place.

Alpha assessed the angry hellcat, her tail tuft with its hidden stinger snaking side to side in aggression. Her eyes narrowed on us, and her claws unsheathed to full razor-sharp daggers.

At a head smaller than Alpha, she was sleek beside his intimidating bulk but no less dangerous.

"Cookie..." I trailed off. "What are you doing?"

She swiped a paw in my direction, as if to say, "Defending what's mine."

I arched a brow, sure I was misreading her intent. This connection with animals was strange, but a part of me felt I truly understood the evil fluff ball.

That didn't mean the psycho made sense.

I shifted on my feet, fighting the urge to laugh nervously, and tried to distract the beasts. "Anyway... What happened after I...left?"

What other way could I describe being knocked unconscious and airlifted out for everyone's safety?

I was also asking a hellhound a complex question.

Even I was side-eyeing myself.

Killian held his brooding silence, oddly unfazed by me having another conversation with animals.

Alpha looked at Cookie, then back at me. He barked low a few times, tossing his head in the direction they'd emerged from.

"So...all those captives are back in our kingdom? And the unicorn too?" I asked, trying to puzzle out if I'd understood him right. "They're safe?"

He yipped like he agreed.

Relief swam through my middle, short-lived as another thought snuck in. By now, the story of what happened would have spread through the kingdom. That something was horrifically wrong with me. That I attacked innocents. People who'd already suffered so much.

I swallowed the lump in my throat, pushing the words past it. "Good. That's really good."

Guilt strangled me, along with the fear of how different things would be when I returned.

If I returned.

"And Rex and Zoella... They're not mad?" I asked.

Alpha shot me a stern look.

"Right. Right, of course they are." I held up my hands in surrender. "But they found my letter? They're staying home?"

He gave the barest nod, and I blew out a steady breath.

I'd set out on my own a few days ago to protect others. Now I just had to figure out how to ditch the furry duo and my reluctant babysitter.

After last night, it was more important than ever to get away from Killian.

His sense of loyalty to my brother was unbreakable. I knew he felt he owed Rex for saving his life and taking him in all those years ago.

But the things he was willing to do for his twisted sense of duty were too much.

He'd only just stopped bleeding this morning after *days* of constant pain and injury. Most inflicted by me.

He'd even pleasured me to keep me safe.

The reminder burned. My pride stung, but also the guilt of forcing him to do something he might not have really wanted to cut deep.

Was that why he hadn't actually fucked me? Even though I'd made it clear I wanted everything he had to give.

I'd hurt the enforcer again and again.

Enough was enough.

Alpha and Cookie wouldn't cross the portal to Earth. They were creatures of Hell. What reason would they have to hop realms? Alpha's place was by Zoella's side, with his growing pack in the Bloodwood, not getting closer to the hunters who'd hurt him for years, and who knew what that mercurial hellcat was thinking, even following me this far.

"Let's keep moving," Killian grunted, jerking a snowy wing down the path. "You can chat with your furred friends while I set up camp. We're going to need all the rest we can get to cross those blood-soaked plains."

I fingered the hilt of the knives strapped to my hips, an idea percolating in my brain as I stepped in front of Killian.

The noble bastard would continue to follow me.

Unless I forced him not to.

Chapter 25

The soft breathing beside me finally evened out. I waited a few more minutes until it deepened to a soothing, slow rhythm. Killian was asleep.

I cracked my eyes, peeking at him through my lashes. He rested on nothing but a bed of fallen leaves, since he'd insisted I take all the blankets we'd purchased from the inn. He clutched his sheathed onyx sword even in sleep, half-hidden beneath his wings, draping him like a blanket.

My stomach churned at the thought of what I was about to do.

Cookie was nowhere in sight, but I swore I could feel her, like a bright blip of energy, way up in a nearby tree. No doubt surveying her domain like the queen she thought she was.

Alpha's signature was a little murkier, but there was a rippling disturbance only a few metres beyond the small clearing Killian and I had bedded down in. His trace seemed to circle us in a slow patrol.

My plan was crazy.

I knew it.

But that didn't mean it wasn't my best option. The only way I knew to keep everyone I cared about safe.

With a steadying breath, silent as a shadow-walker, I rose from my nest of blankets.

Pulling my knife free, I winced at the light scrape of metal. When the incubus didn't stir, I leaned over his sleeping form.

I hovered there, knife poised in my shaking hand for a single second.

There was no undoing this.

His words from this morning hit me all over again.

I have to.

I struck.

Stormy eyes flashed open as my blade descended, but it was too late. The tip sliced through the meat of his forearm, opening a thin line through the chains inking his skin.

Confusion furrowed his brows a second before betrayal flooded silver-flecked eyes.

He tried to sit up but barely rose an inch.

My special poison was fast-acting. Already racing through his bloodstream, paralysing his nervous system in a numbing wave.

"Why?" he rasped through clenched fangs.

Moisture wavered my vision. I sheathed the blade at my hip and notched my chin. "I won't let your loyalty to Rex get you killed."

A growl rumbled his chest, but the sound was faint. Only a few more seconds and unconsciousness would drag him under.

Alpha padded from the shadows, moonlight bathing him as he entered the clearing. His head cocked as his hell-fire gaze jumped from me to Killian.

"Keep him safe," I pleaded but I could already sense the denial from the hellhound before he even made a sound. "Please, Alpha. He needs you more than I do. The Bloodwood is no place for the unconscious. He's free meat otherwise."

The hellhound snapped his fangs at the air, but I knew he'd do what was necessary. Zoella and Rex would be devastated if Killian died. I'd left the familiar with no choice. I wasn't the one defenceless and unable to protect myself in a place filled with hungry predators.

I was just the witch who'd left him like that.

My heart ached as I took one last look into Killian's eyes, sparking with silver like the flash of lightning. Anyone else would have been unconscious minutes ago.

"Goodbye, Killian," I whispered.

I gently pulled his wing back over him to keep him warm, resisting the urge to give his soft feathers one final caress.

I might never see him again.

Before I lost my nerve, I turned my back on the demon I'd cared more about than I should and hurried away from the clearing, plunging into the darkness of the forest proper.

Any stupid fantasies I'd had about us lay in ashes. We were never going to be together. Never going to become mates. Never have a family together.

I let it all go.

We wouldn't have worked out, anyway.

He was a blood-soaked enforcer, and I was a healer. He was an incubus who loved to feed. He'd never give up sleeping around to settle down with one person. He was my brother's closest comrade. They were practically brothers.

We weren't even friends.

But a small voice in the back of my mind screamed at me to return to his side. He'd doled out brutal justice to anyone who'd hurt me. He'd buried a body for me, no questions asked. He'd carried me home and stayed to make sure I was okay. He'd visited me in my dreams. Ripped a man's tongue out for insulting me. Remembered my birthday. Made me a cake in the middle of the Bloodwood.

He'd always protected me. No matter what it cost him.

If I'd just told him how I'd felt all these years, could we have made it work? Maybe he felt something for me too.

But how could he?

I was barely even his kind. I most certainly wasn't his type. And he'd never tried anything with me before this cursed trip, despite the countless times he'd have felt my desire for him over the years.

My chest heaved. Tears fled down my cheeks. I furiously swiped them away as I hurried amongst the sea of trees, angling towards the border of the dark forest. I needed to focus, or I was going to end up as dead as my dumb dreams of being with Killian.

The bleeding bark suited my mood as I swept between the slender redwoods in the heavy night. This close to the edge, they were getting fewer, some of the smaller trees taking their place in sparse copses.

Undulating plains opened in the gaps, spreading far into the distance. Short grasses had dried out to a crisp wheat with the warmth of summer, but some patches of green still hid near the edges, the colours barely visible under the light of the full moon.

A flat swirl of colour, the size of a small cabin, smudged the air about half a mile beyond the last tree. It glowed with ribbons of pinks, blues and golds, all merging in a beautiful eddy that called out like a siren's song.

I ducked behind a trunk just wide enough to conceal myself and scanned the dangerous territory between the forest and the portal.

The pretty smear tearing between realms sat in a hundred-metre radius of nothing. Just bare earth surrounded it on all sides until it met the dead grass beyond the barren circle, swaying lightly in the breeze.

It may seem abandoned, but it was a blood-soaked graveyard. There were always demons watching this place.

The shadow-walker kingdom lay beyond the plains, a dark beast crouched on the horizon, visible only in the red flames guarding their walls. They were our closest neighbours, and we'd only just brokered a trade agreement to allow safe passage for all hybrids crossing past their lands or using the portal.

Ironically, we traded life for death. Each month, we delivered a cart-load of our finest poisons from the Bloodwood. Half of which I'd designed myself.

Everything was quiet now though. I'd run out of reasons to stall, but the last I'd been to Earth, it hadn't exactly gone well for me.

Taking a deep breath, I rechecked my poisoned daggers, securely sheathed at my hips and down my outer thighs, and took the plunge.

The grass gave way beneath my pounding boots as I sprinted from the trees, thuds echoing through the night. Wind whipped my crimson hair behind me as I ran.

The portal loomed closer.

Silver flashed on my right.

Instinct had me ducking into a roll. Something thumped into my shoulder blade, knocking me askew. Pain throbbed down my back as I caught sight of the feathered shaft sticking out behind me.

Yank it free and stab out your enemies' eyes!

I sprang to my feet with gritted fangs, ignoring the arrow embedded in my flesh as much as the violent voice, and focused on survival. I weaved as I ran, trying to shake the archer's aim.

I wasn't too keen on getting a second arrow I'd have to rip from my flesh, even if I should be able to heal the damage.

Unless I was dead before I knew it.

I ran faster.

The portal loomed closer, pretty colours beckoning me. The air buzzed with power, even with the long metres between me and the dead zone.

Green streaked through my peripherals. A troop of orcs flowed across the plains, further along the tree-line.

My heart stuttered as it pumped liquid panic through my veins. I put on a burst of speed, ignoring the screaming pain in my torso. A few orcs in the group shot more arrows in my direction, barely pausing their loping strides.

I ducked and swerved to avoid the deadly missiles. It slowed my pace dramatically, though, and with the ground they were eating up, they'd beat me to the portal.

There was no way I could fight off this many demons. Not alone.

I reached for my dark power, pleading with the hungry beast to lash out as the group loomed closer.

Nothing happened.

"That's the magic bitch!" the orc in front crowed, lifting his sword overhead with a victorious roar. "Take her alive."

He must be one of the slavers that had escaped my massacre.

Terror made me miss a step, and my ankle rolled painfully in an unseen dip. Another spike of pain thudded into my upper back, hitting close enough to my spine for my nerves to spasm. Hissing a ragged breath, I stuffed the pain deep and shoved myself on.

Even if it came to a fight, I might be able to slip through before they could actually get their claws on me.

The logical voice in the back of my head called me a liar, but what choice did I have? If I didn't get through now, Killian would catch up to me.

He'd get hurt fighting these brutes, or my magic would take him down.

Determination pushed my legs that bit faster despite the agony ricocheting through my body with every jarring step.

Shadows materialised around the portal, dark wisps almost impossible to see in the gloom.

They condensed until a group of shadow-walkers emerged, wreathed in smoke. Their eyes glowed like molten metal. I sucked in a ragged gasp but didn't stop.

"Hey!" I screamed, breathless. "I'm a hybrid!"

We were allies, dammit. They might not take on an orc horde for me, but they'd at least let me past while they glared with glowy eyes at the orcs trying to murder me.

Another arrow whizzed by my head, nicking my ear.

I just had to get there.

The orcs loomed closer until I could see the bright-white tusks of the male in charge. He leered at me, arms pumping as his thundering steps shook the ground.

I crossed into the dead zone, smothered by a blanket of crackling power. Barely a hundred metres separated me and the shadow-walkers.

But I wasn't going to make it.

The demons guarding the portal drew onyx swords, angling them towards the oncoming horde.

The female shadow-walker in the front roared, "Defend the hybrid!"

The slaver leaped towards me, his hand lashing out. I ducked, and his claws passed overhead, yanking out a few strands of hair instead of tearing my face off.

He snarled, sprinting behind me, and reached out again. In my periphery, an arrow sailed towards my head at the same time.

I made the split-second decision to lurch away from the arrow rather than the claws.

They sank beneath my ribs.

I hissed at the pain but managed to stay upright, momentum propelling me forwards. The orc tugged back, and my hiss ended in a scream as he pulled me to a halt with a handful of flesh in my side.

He snarled in my ear, "You're going to regret killing my fucking brother, you filthy abomin–"

His claws yanked free in a flare of agony as he was knocked aside, his words cut off.

The overwhelming pain finally triggered the monster inside me.

That starved power burst free. It lashed outwards, invisible whips striking into friend and foe alike.

I cried out, blood pouring down my side. Darkness bled everyone on the plains.

Shock gripped me as I took in the downed orc. An enormous hellcat pinned him to the dirt, her claws mauling his chest as the demon screamed.

Narrowed blood-red eyes met mine. *Go, before your power knocks you out. I'll hold them off.*

The sound of a familiar raspy voice snapped me out of the shock, my power stuttering right along with it.

"Thank you," I choked out, unable to process that the violent voice in my head this past week had actually been *her*.

And what it must mean.

I lurched towards the portal before the darkness inside me could surge with a vengeance. Or the rapid blood loss could take me down.

The shadow-walkers swayed back to their feet as I staggered past, too many wounds cracking open their flesh.

A few of the stronger orcs recovered too, growling aggressively as they snatched up their weapons and faced off with Cookie and the injured shadow-walkers.

Guilt strangled me as I limped up to the pane of swirling colours, its magic already tugging me closer. Reeling me in like a fish on a hook.

I clutched my side, trying to stem the bleeding. Pain bit chunks out of my energy as my body frantically tried to repair itself.

My vision swam dangerously, but I managed a final glimpse of the proud hellcat baring her fangs at the advancing horde, and stepped back into the portal. "I'll see you again...my familiar."

Chapter 26

The world dissolved in a fizz of inexplicable sensation. Every part of me disintegrated, nothing but ash for a disorienting second before I was slapped back together and spat out.

I stumbled out of the portal, gasping for air.

Tiny needles stung my skin, and my limbs failed to respond for a few sluggish beats while my body remembered how to be a functioning whole.

Pain throbbed through my side and down my back. Warmth pulsed through my middle, contrasting the icy breeze whipping my hair into a frenzy around my face.

Sounds and scents overwhelmed me: the honking of cars, the acrid burn of exhaust smoke, and the tang of old piss. A colourless moon hung heavy in the night sky, devoid of stars and suffocated by clouds.

The human realm was just as intense as I remembered.

I reached over my shoulder, gripped the first arrow's shaft, and *pulled*.

Agony sucked at my shoulder blade as I wrenched the metal tip out, causing more damage than when it had gone in. I screamed against clenched fangs, ignoring the wet heat rushing down my back, sticking my top to my skin.

My ragged panting layered the night, and I dropped the arrow, its clatter on the paving stones echoing around the alley.

I reached for the second with a shaky hand, this time closer to my spine. The angle meant I couldn't pull it out straight.

This would not be fun.

I sucked in a breath and yanked before I lost the nerve.

Another rush of wetness preceded agony, like being jabbed with a hot poker.

I would know.

"Dragon dicks!" I snarled, throwing down the second arrow, drenched in my blood.

My back ached as fiercely as my scratched ribs, peeking through my ripped top. Magic tingled the wounds, repairing the damage in a soothing wave.

Heat pulsed through my insides, warming me with an uncomfortable sensation like heartburn that had spread beyond my stomach.

For a second, I eyed the two arrows on the dirty paving slabs, debating taking them with me, but carrying them unsheathed was a recipe for getting myself stabbed again. My poisoned blades would have to be enough.

Guilt bit at me as I felt my energy drain into healing the damage to my back and side. I'd left Cookie and those shadow-walkers to fight off an orc horde while I fled to safety. But my presence would have only put them in more danger.

I hoped my familiar was okay though.

A sense of wonder filtered through the heavy shame.

A real life mage's *familiar*.

My familiar.

An animal to help strengthen and channel my magic. To guide me in times of need through our mental bond.

And she was a psychotic, cookie-stealing hellcat.

I couldn't have wished for a better gift though. Given the few-hour time difference between England of the human realm and the Hybrid Kingdom of Hell, it was probably still my birthday here.

I shook my head. I'd never thought such a blessing could be possible. Not for me.

It explained why she'd been able to heal herself. Or maybe why I could. Zoella and Alpha controlled a gorgeous lilac hell-fire, a power they shared.

Could all hellcats heal? I wouldn't put it past the rare felines to have the ability to help others and turn their snooty whiskers up at the idea.

If I wanted to see that crazy death kitty again, I had to get myself fixed and back to Hell. I couldn't sense her presence down any mental connection, so apparently, whatever magic was involved didn't span realms. The thought left me feeling hollow, lonely despite only just discovering the bond.

I set off towards the mouth of the alley, boots splashing through puddles from a recent rainfall.

Warmth simmered in my middle as I walked, helping to stave off the chill of the human realm.

The sensation was oddly distracting, combining with the exhaustion from all the running and fighting and healing to sap my focus when I should be on high alert.

The portal topside was almost as dangerous as back in Hell. Most demons who lived here knew where it was, and some were enterprising enough to take advantage of those coming through.

But luck must be on my side for once, because nobody assaulted me as I stumbled down the lane, pushing my body towards the flickering neon sign on the far side of the street. Some mage had been paid handsomely to craft a magic signal only demons could see.

It guided those fresh from Hell towards its unassuming doors. Behind them lurked a den of demonic sin—a nightclub.

Because the first thing most of us needed when we crossed was a stiff drink.

And a good feed.

What I needed was information.

And if most of the demons topside got their glamour from the coven I sought, they'd know exactly where I needed to go.

More warmth pulsed through my body until sweat beaded my brow. I drew a deep breath, filling my lungs with cool air, but it did nothing to ease the growing heat low in my middle.

I felt every brush of fabric against my skin as I moved, my own clothes irritating me with their teasing caresses. Wetness gathered between my thighs, the material of my panties rubbing maddeningly against me with every stumbling step I took.

I didn't know what was happening to me, but I shoved down the strange feelings and focused on getting help.

Though, the kind of help I wanted right now didn't involve talking.

My thoughts swirled back to Killian. To the feel of his hands on my body.

His lips on my skin.

His forked tongue lashing my clit.

I moaned, swiping the moisture dewing my forehead as I hit the wider road, hurrying across it to the next dark alley, beneath the glowing sign. The brick walls blurred slightly, but before I knew it, I was standing outside an unassuming steel door, struggling to catch my breath like I'd been chased by hungry bone-kin. Again.

Banging on the metal, I braced to pretend everything was fine. Just a regular demon-witch on a night out. No big deal.

Not burning up from a hunger hot enough to liquefy my bones.

The door opened a crack, revealing a surly pain demon with crimson skin, just a shade brighter than my hair, and black horns twice the length of my stubby ones.

I pasted on the brightest smile I could manage. "Hello, good sir!"

I even gave him a little wave.

Totally.

Normal.

He grimaced, pinching his wide nose like he smelled something awful. "Errr, you're leaking pheromones everywhere, succubus. What are you doing?" His voice came out comically nasal, but the heat unfurling through my body made it hard to focus on anything.

I kept on waving. "Um...clubbing?"

Even through the haze of lust, his words made sense. Most sexual demons could release pheromones to heighten desire. They didn't create it, only encouraged what was already there. Usually, most could only affect a handful of demons close by, and it faded quickly.

Some powerful demons could turn a nun's convent into an orgy though.

I'd never been able to release even a whiff of the stuff.

Now was a terrible time to find out there was another power I couldn't control.

He eyed me in stony silence, the hard-man effect ruined by the way his clawed fingers pinched his nostrils.

After a long second, a honking titter left his lips. "Sure. Whatever. Fuck rooms are up the stairs at the back, succubus."

At least he hadn't sneered at me for being a hybrid.

Keeping his nose blocked, he stepped aside and waved me through the doorway. I caught sight of the bulge of his crotch, a hard length outlined beneath his jeans.

I swallowed, the furnace inside my middle burning hotter, even though logically I knew I wasn't into the guy.

"Thanks," I murmured, my voice coming out low and husky.

I fought to back away from him, a haze of lusty thoughts assaulting my mind. A whimper left my lips as I staggered back before I could do anything I'd regret.

I hurried off, barely noticing the cloakroom piled high with coats and bags as I passed. It held packs even bigger than the one I'd lost.

Apparently, I wasn't the only person fresh from the portal.

I stepped through the dark atrium and into the club proper. A wall of bassy music hit me the second I pushed opened the studded double doors.

What looked like a hundred demons and humans writhed on a sunken dance floor, bathed in flares of strobe lighting and colourful smoke. The sinuous movement of their bodies called to me, reeling me in harder than standing right next to a portal.

Saliva pooled in my mouth at the thought of feeding on all of them.

This was a terrible idea.

Chapter 27

I flung myself into the nightclub, pushing past wings and tails and limbs in a chaotic mass of revellers. Every touch pushed me higher, like a drug transferred through skin contact.

A giggle escaped my lips as my heart matched the thumping bass, vibrating me from the inside out. I was burning alive, and I *needed* the cool touch of those around me before I turned to ash.

"Fires...," I cursed, pushing faster through the crowd.

Heat licked my insides as I hurried towards the bar.

It burned and burned, growing hotter by the second, spreading liquid heat to my limbs.

I doubled over with a groan, clutching my stomach and bracing against the nearest sticky table. Hunger followed on its heels.

But not for more of the quails Killian had caught.

Need curled through me, an ache pulsing between my legs in time with the flares of heat that echoed the club's bass.

"Fuck…," I groaned, trying to edge my way off the table. "What's happening to me?"

Unsurprisingly, nobody answered.

Panic tried to set its fangs into me, sinking through the haze that made me too needy to think. I was probably still healing the wounds on my back and side, but the thought slipped away like blood through claws.

"You smell divine," a deep voice rumbled in my ear.

I blinked. My chest was pressed against a cold body. Without conscious thought, I buried my face in the male's damp shirt and inhaled his scent.

An incubus.

Another body pressed in behind me, the cool relief at their contact making my knees weak.

"She really does," the man at my back called out above the music. "Even I can smell her ripe sweetness."

I caught sight of peachy pale skin and turned enough to confirm he was human.

"Ss-cuse me…" My voice came out slurred as I tried to push past them.

I'd come here to do…something.

I just wasn't sure what.

To feed? Was that why I needed to be touched so badly?

"Hey, where are you trying to run off to, pretty thing?" the incubus purred, forked tongue darting out to slather over his plump lips. "I can smell your need. You're in heat, aren't you?"

I couldn't even form a response. A sinking terror tried to claw through the high, but it couldn't find purchase in my mind. I'd heard that term before. *Heat*. I just couldn't remember why it had panic spiralling through me.

"What's a heat?" the man behind me yelled over the music.

The incubus leaned closer, practically squishing my lungs between him and the human. "It's when a horny succubus lures in all the eager people nearby to satisfy her. Usually it's yearly, but judging by the roughed-up state of this one, she's so desperate for a feed she's early."

"Oh my god, so she's literally a bitch in heat like some animal?" The human laughed, grinding his underwhelming length against my arse. "What a slut."

The demon thrust his hips to keep us steady, and I could feel his hardness dig into my belly. "Yeah, a stupid one too, coming to a busy club in heat."

A whimper escaped me, part need, part fear. There was no way I was letting these arseholes even attempt to *satisfy* me.

I couldn't think about the fact that I'd never gone into heat before and this was the absolute worst place to do so. I could hardly think at all.

"Fuck off. I'm fine." I batted at the incubus's chest, and my fingers met the sticky fabric of his button-down shirt.

It felt good to have them rub against me like this, and I hated it. Some crazed part of me craved touch badly enough that it didn't matter who they were.

The know-it-all incubus grinned. "It's your first, isn't it?" He tipped his head back and laughed. "They're always the strongest. You're going to be so much fun." He angled to one side, revealing a table of demons lounging in a booth beside us. "Lads, we've got ourselves a party! Let's take this little thing up to one of the rooms."

Wait.

No.

I didn't want to go anywhere with a group of strangers.

Oh fires. This couldn't be happening.

Their combined energy slunk into me, their desire a cool whisper through my chest as I drank them down. But it wasn't enough.

I blinked, dazed, as the incubus tugged me towards the stairs wrapping behind their booth. I stumbled, and the human scooped me up into his icy arms, squeezing around my tits and thighs.

I could hardly breathe.

"Ssstop!" I hissed, thrashing in his hold. "Put me down!"

But the friction of my clothes and his cold skin was too much. I'd burn alive if I didn't get more though.

I kept squirming to get free, ignoring the insane need to reach between my legs so I could satisfy the incessant desire.

But it was no use. I was trapped.

More flavours and sensations added to the jumbled energy filling me as a group of demons followed behind us.

That impending sense of doom grew before the fire inside me burned it away.

We hit the top of the stairs, and the human marched me towards the first door with a green vacant sign on the oversize lock.

Another bouncer lounged at the top, giving us a once-over. His nostrils flared, and I could feel his desire spike, the taste of bitter hazelnuts coating my tongue.

"Help," I croaked, my voice barely audible even to my own ears.

"Wait," he called, holding a palm up to stop the group.

Relief surged. The bouncer was going to put a stop to this. He'd save me.

"I'll let you take your needy toy into a room, but you have to use the glass one so everyone can watch the show." Desperate glee slashed a wide grin through his narrow face. "And I'm having a turn."

The incubus cackled, gesturing for him to lead the way.

Panic stabbed through the mind-numbing need. My claws grazed the arms caging me. The male's hold tightened before I could do any actual damage, and he shook me in warning, sending my head lolling and thoughts scattering.

We were ushered into a vast room with a glass floor, showcasing the partiers below. Huge internal windows dominated the walls, with sofas facing us from the other side in the rooms beyond, mirrors lining the columns in between.

The human dropped me, and I slammed into the clear floor, my head thumping hard enough to see stars. I barely felt the pain before the heat devoured it. It ate through sensation, somehow using it to fuel the burning beneath my skin.

A whimper escaped my lips as the horror of the situation pierced my muddled thoughts. I needed to be touched. But I didn't want these men anywhere near me.

"Back off," I hissed. The usual feral sound came out like a drunken slur.

I fought not to welcome the incubus as he closed in on me, baring my fangs instead.

He crouched before me, pinching my chin between his claws. "Listen up. You're a succubus in heat. And since you clearly don't understand what that means, I'm going to do you a favour and help you out."

His thumb point punctured my skin, releasing a wet bead to trickle down the front of my throat. His cruel smile loomed too large in my vision.

Menace leaked from his pores, along with the heady energy of desire. I could feel how excited he was, and it both drove me higher and turned my stomach.

"Go fuck yourself," I snarled, jerking from his grip.

The movement caused a slice of pain along my jaw, but it was nothing compared to the agony of losing his cool touch. Like it had somehow been keeping the heat to a simmer.

Now it roared.

Flames lashed at my middle, searing and singeing my insides, and I curled up in a ball on the floor. Sweat slicked my skin. The glass room blurred as hot tears streamed down my cheeks. I could only just make out the rest of the club through the clear floor.

A bartender looked up from behind the long counter, not far below. Her glowing pink eyes locked onto me.

"Help." I could barely make my lips move, but I tried to mouth out my plea anyway.

The lithe demon vaulted the bar, getting lost in the churning crowd below.

"Oh, don't worry, slut, I've got something to help you," the human sneered, grabbing his crotch in a lewd gesture.

Demonic sniggers bounced around the room, making it hard to tell just how many sick bastards loomed over me.

I curled into a tighter ball on the floor.

I wanted to scream and fight, but the heat just kept punishing me. I reached for the incubus, hating myself even as my hand met his chilly ankle, and the temperature became a fraction more bearable.

"Don't do this," I urged.

Tears ran freely down my cheeks as I stared down the dark reality of what was about to happen.

The incubus stroked my cheek, ice in his eyes. "But I want to."

"What are we waiting for?" one of the horned demons leaning against the wall scoffed. "I'll go first."

The incubus hissed at the spiked male, his eyes flashing gold. "Back off. I found her. I'm first."

A great shattering sounded, and I jerked my arm up on instinct, protecting my face.

"You're all going to die," a familiar voice rasped manically. "So. Fucking. Painfully."

Chapter 28

The first scream pierced the thumping bass.

I whipped my arm down, taking in the madness. A dark being of smoke and rage tore through the room.

Killian clawed a demon's face and spun into the next male, sinking his fangs into the human's neck and tearing free.

A whirlwind of death, he brutalised demon after demon, black wings smoking with his violent need.

I whimpered, heat lashing at me all over again. I wanted to help fight, but it was all I could do to hold still on the floor amongst the blood spray and broken glass.

Killian's silvered gaze swept over me, and then he snarled at the demon rushing him, somehow upping his ferocity.

He wasn't going for clean kills.

Each demon he cut down was still alive, writhing in agony on the see-through floor. Like me.

He disembowelled the incubus who'd laid his hands on me, letting the screaming male hit the floor to suffer in a growing pool of his own blood and innards.

A demon rushed into the room, blood coating her hands like gloves. I vaguely recognised her as the woman behind the bar, black-and-pink hair framing her heart-shaped face. Neon-pink eyes glowed with rage.

"Shit. *Killian?* Well, I can see I was late to the party," she chuckled, but a darkness lurked in her narrowed eyes as she surveyed the dying males on the floor before staring the enforcer down. "You'd better be here to help her too."

Killian grunted, his eyes fixed on me with a sharp intensity, his nostrils flaring like a wild animal.

I whimpered again, "Kill." I swallowed thickly, tasting the blood and desire in the air. "S-Something's...wrong with me."

He stomped through the bodies, deliberately crunching bones under his solid boots and making his victims scream as he came for me.

"Nothing's wrong, sweetness. I've got you now." His voice came out as a low, rough rasp, silver-streaked eyes wild even as his words aimed to soothe. His inked chest heaved with every laboured breath, and the look in his eyes promised a dark hunger.

Without acknowledging the bloodied bartender, he scooped me into his arms. I moaned at the feel of his cool skin against me, even smeared with blood that I knew should still be warm.

"Fuck. I can feel your need. Your heat." His eyes blazed. "I've got you," he repeated, but I could barely hear his gravelly voice over the club's pounding music and my own hazed lust.

"Kill... I... I need you," I murmured.

Tears gathered in my eyes. I was frustrated and horny and desperate. And Killian was cooling and soothing. He was the glass of ice water on a hot summer's day, and I was fires-damned parched.

"Shit. I've never seen a heat this bad before. More idiots are coming," the bartender warned, spinning to face the direction of the stairway. Her unique pink eyes glowed as they pinned me. "Are you safe with him?"

That a stranger would care for my safety would have shocked me if I could think straight. I was a demon-mage hybrid. Even other outcasts would throw me away. But all I could notice was how beautiful she was with her innocent pixie face and long flowing hair dipped in a pretty dusky pink, and wonder what her petal-soft skin would feel like slicked with sweat against mine.

"Yes," I forced the word out, my claws digging into Killian's arm.

She nodded and pinned Killian with a hard stare. "Get her out of here. I'll deal with this."

Killian's voice was a guttural rasp. "Thanks, Aurora. I owe you one."

I didn't have time to wonder how they knew each other. Killian hugged me to his chest and leaped for the window. His wings wrapped me tight just before we hit the glass. It broke in a deafening shatter as we crashed through.

And then we were falling.

I sucked in a ragged gasp to scream, but his wings shot wide, and the air was trapped in my lungs as we were yanked upwards. He landed with a soft thud, setting me on my feet in what looked like another filthy alley just outside the nightclub. He pulled back enough to run his gaze over me fully, searching for injuries, but his hands never left my waist.

Lightning streaked through his stormy eyes. His wings were still pitch black, the feathers drenched in writhing shadows and painted with blood.

"Fires, Eve. Tell me you're okay." His voice was a pleading rasp, rough enough that I swore I felt it scrape my skin.

Was I?

That burning need had only slightly lessened with his body pressing in around me.

A group of strangers had tried to assault me.

Killian pulled me close, wrapping me in his arms and fitting my smaller body in the protection of his. I was shaking so hard against his solid frame, my fangs clattered together.

A hard length pressed against my middle, and I whined at the fierce need burning me up.

I was so far from okay, I couldn't see a way back to it.

But that blaze in my middle wouldn't let up, and it ate through my worries and fears until all I could do was *feel*. And hunger.

All for him.

"I need you," I whimpered, head tipped back to meet his gaze as I pressed myself harder into him, rubbing myself against the thick length trapped beneath his trousers.

He leaned down until mere inches separated his lips from mine. "You have me, sweetness. You've always had me."

Anticipation shivered through me, from the pointy ends of my horns right to my toes.

The bloody enforcer confused the hell out of me, but I didn't have the brainpower to overthink his words right now. Not when more heat lashed my insides.

I rubbed my thighs together, trying to ease that ache between them.

He groaned, running his nose along my neck. "Your scent is fucking irresistible. You're in heat, sweetness. Something must have triggered you when you came through the portal."

His deep inhales tickled the sensitive skin, and I moaned, trying to burrow closer even though he already had me trapped against his front.

His hand stroked along my spine, aiming to soothe. But nothing would except all of him.

"Killian," I hissed, my tone a demand.

A wolf whistle sliced through the moment. Killian jerked his head up, a threatening growl rumbling from his lips, peeled back to bare vicious fangs.

Terror slid down my spine before the heat burned through it.

A handful of roughened demons stalked through the alley towards us.

I knew I should be afraid, but the heat devoured any logic. I wanted Killian to tear them apart and then fuck me, covered in the evidence of his strength and dominance.

Primal lust hazed my thoughts.

I'd be side-eyeing myself if I could think straight.

Two identical male blood demons led the pack, with their telltale grey skin and red horns.

"That's a lush treat you have there," the one on the left said, forked tongue slobbering over his lower lip.

"Yes indeed. She smells positively *ripe*." His twin snickered.

I wanted to gag. But as a horny idiot in heat, I also wanted him to think of me as a fertile female in her prime. A desirable mate.

Killian's hand tightened on my hip, and his pitch-black wings flared on either side of me in an intimidating display.

"She's mine." He bristled with barely leashed violence but grinned manically wide. "Leave. Now."

The "or else" was an unspoken threat that had danger spiking through the night. Tension suffocated the alleyway, thickening the cold air.

My core fluttered at the possessive edge in Killian's voice, even as the sane part of me, buried way down, recognised that my pheromones were driving him almost as much as me right now.

"How's one weak mutt going to stop us taking what we want?" the eerie twin on the left mused. "I'll drain you dry, then your slut can drain my balls."

His other half snorted as if to punctuate their mocking.

Killian laughed, his unhinged cackle ricocheting off the brick walls. "Well, my pretty princess *does* deserve more birthday gifts."

Chapter 29

Killian grinned at me over his wing arch. "Run, sweetness. I'll catch up with your new presents in just a sec."

My mouth parted at his arrogance, but I couldn't help the moan that slipped free at how fires-damned attractive it was.

Moonlight bathed the demon, highlighting the sharp tips of his textured bone-white horns and the wild grin slashing through his handsome features. His black wings flared in challenge, bleeding smoke to blend into the night, claws flexed readily at his sides.

He was chaos incarnate.

A fallen angel of lore.

Despite his command, I was rooted to the spot.

Besides, there was no way it was still my twenty-second birthday. The day was endless.

The twin thugs bared red fangs, and one of them called out, "Over here, lads! We've found tonight's fun."

The pair charged as one. My heart seized as more blood demons appeared around the nightclub's corner, filling the alleyway with snarls and pounding footsteps as they all descended on the lone incubus.

"Fuck," I gasped, anxiety slithering in.

I wanted to throw myself at the horde and hump them all to death.

You know, to save Killian.

Heat punished me, pulsing in waves of fire from the inside out. I bit my lip on another whimper, fighting with every insane urge that cropped up.

And then there was no more time for thinking.

The demons were on Killian in a clash of fists on flesh and splattering blood.

Dark laughter rang through the night. Killian spun and slashed, claws finding arteries. He became a storm of violence and blood. His wing smacked into a demon's face, breaking his victim's nose, while he kicked out another attacker's kneecap with a nauseating crunch.

He took the group of demons apart. Piece by piece.

If I'd thought I'd seen Killian's violent side before, it had nothing on this night.

Within seconds, eight demons were nothing but broken bones and ruptured flesh. Fresh meat on filthy cobblestones.

One twin struggled on his back, trying to rise even though his arm had snapped the wrong angle and blood poured from a nasty gut wound.

The healer in me wanted to rush over, but the heat craved to watch my chosen mate defend me. Needed to see him prove his vicious prowess as worthy before he took his prize.

And I was desperate to be the spoils of his war.

He stalked over, looking down at the demon struggling at his feet. "You're going to bleed out. Slowly. Painfully. And while you die, I want you to remember that it wasn't because you insulted me. It was because you laid eyes on *her*."

He reached down, scooping his claws into the demon's eye sockets as the other male screamed and screamed. Killian cackled in response.

And. Popped. Both. Eyeballs. Out.

He yanked the connecting tissues free with a snap.

"You sick fuck!" The demon squealed, scrabbling at Killian's arms, blood pouring from the gaping holes beneath his brows. "This is why mutts are executed at birth!"

Killian crushed the demon's eyes in his palms. "Great, now you made me ruin her gift," he snarled, dropping the wet lumps back on the screeching demon's chest. He leaned down and wiped his palms on the man's shirt.

"Gods, Kill," I croaked.

At this point, I didn't know whether to clap or throw up.

He turned to me, silvered gaze clashing with mine.

"I told you to run, sweetness." His low voice was as feral as I'd ever heard it.

I swallowed thickly, but it was like my body wasn't my own, heat racing through my bloodstream and burning away logic.

I turned and fled, my boots slapping the cobbles as I charged out of the alley.

Manic laughter followed me.

And then he was right behind me. Hands clamped around my waist. He leaped, wings snapping wide and pumping hard. I choked on a scream as the ground fell away.

"You're not very good at fleeing, sweetness," his husky voice whispered in my ear. "Someone might think you wanted to be caught."

I shuddered, eyes closing as he ran his nose along my throat, scenting me with a low groan.

He turned me in his arms, and something cold hit my thighs, making me sit. I blinked wide eyes open.

Killian grinned down at me, wings pumping leisurely at his back, the night sky peeking behind him.

He balanced me precariously on a balcony railing.

"Killian," I gasped, gripping the chilled metal I perched on. I couldn't tell if it was ice or I was fire.

His boots touched down between the vertical slats of the rail, and large hands framed my hips on the metal bar.

His eyes focused on my lips, but his pupils dilated like he'd been smoking haze for hours. "Yes, sweetness?"

His wings beat the air in lazy strokes, black feathers seeping darkness that rose into the night. Even though his soothing touch tamed some of the blazing heat, fire simmered low in my body, demanding and insistent.

"Is this safe?" I squeaked, trying to encourage the logical, concerned side of me over the needy hussy who just wanted to spread her thighs and let Killian devour the ache between them.

The incubus pulled a stick of haze from his back pocket, placed it between his lips, and clicked his fingers with enough ferocity for his claws to spark. The tip caught, and a bright-red cherry burned the night as hot as the blood rushing through my veins.

"You're never safe from me, sweetness," he murmured, words becoming smoke that drifted from his darkening lips. "And yet I can't seem to stay away."

A feral snarl sounded from the ground far below, slicing through the moment before a voice boomed out, "Oi! I can smell that needy succubus you've got up there!"

My eyes shot wide, heart pounding. It only pumped the molten desire faster through my bloodstream. Even with the reckless need scrambling my thoughts, I didn't want anyone else to touch me.

I wanted Killian.

"Bring her down, or I'm coming up for a turn," the male sneered. "And you'll just have to scrape together what's left."

Killian took another deep drag and smirked. "Wait here, sweetness."

A dark cloud accompanied his words, the distinct floral scent washing over me and obscuring my vision.

He let go.

Killian stared up at me as he plummeted towards the concrete several stories below, haze stick blazing as he took another pull, not bothering to use his wings.

"Kill!" I screamed, gripping the railing tight as I balanced on the edge.

The psycho was in free fall and still smoking without a care in the realms.

I could just make out the vicious smirk on his lips, damn smoke between them. He finally twisted, flaring nightmare wings and landing on top of the demon stupid enough to anger the ruthless enforcer.

He was a blur of violence.

The sounds of flesh smacking flesh rang out. Killian smashed his knuckles into the pure-bred incubus's face repeatedly. His victim groaned, trying to rake his claws across Killian's arms, but the enforcer just laughed, catching the smaller male's hands.

The crack of breaking bones shattered the night.

Killian grabbed the male's bleached horns and, with a violent wrench, snapped each of the four off the male's skull and proceeded to stab them into the demon's stomach.

If I wasn't high on whatever was happening to me, his ferocity might have unnerved me. As it was, the brutal way he protected only made me want him more.

The psychotic demon grabbed something metallic from the other male's jacket. He held the hip flask over the groaning demon, liquid splashing over his victim.

Within minutes, he was flying back towards me, arrowing straight for the balcony he'd left me on. That damn stick of haze still darkened his lips despite its fiery tip.

Blood splattered his face, dripping down his chest until the predatory birds across his skin bathed in crimson rain.

Silver eyes gleamed with hunger.

It matched my own.

"Killian," I moaned. "Please—"

His hand shot out and gripped my throat, cutting me off mid-plea. His tail curled around the smoke stick in his mouth, pulling it free as he blew out a lungful of shadow.

His tail flicked the smoking drug over his wing. It tumbled, hitting the groaning demon below. Flames burst to life, under-lighting Killian in an ominous, fiery glow.

"Shh, sweetness. I know exactly what you need," he whispered, hazed lips barely moving.

And then they were slamming down on mine.

I moaned as he kissed me like a beast starved, all teeth and tongue and hunger.

Blood bloomed through the kiss as my fangs nicked his forked tip. The caramel flavour of him drugged me, mixing with the heady, smoky feel of his desire pouring into me until he was everything.

He wrenched back, and his hold on my throat while he hovered mid-air was the only thing stopping me from plummeting to the concrete below, already littered with the flaming body of his last victim.

"I'm going to take you like the ruthless bastard I am, sweetness, and you're going to scream for me like the good girl you are. Say yes." His accent thickened, roughened by the need hounding us both.

Heat blazed through me at his words.

"Yes." The word slipped free on a moan.

With a snarl, he tore open his fly, freeing his heavy cock. The feathered texture of his throbbing length glistened with pre-cum under the moonlight. I already knew exactly how deliciously his slick would tingle on contact.

But I craved to know how he would finally feel inside me.

The glorious bastard was hung like an incubus.

A giggle escaped me at the dumb thought, but the giddy high was replaced with the burn of lust and dark need.

Killian bared his fangs with a manic grin. "Laugh while you can, Princess. You're about to scream until your voice gives out."

I sucked in a breath as he clawed open my trousers, ripping right through the leather and my panties beneath. Sharp tips threatened my pussy enough to make my inner walls tremble. His tail lashed under my knee and yanked my legs wide.

He thrust in deep. All the way to the fucking hilt.

And I screamed.

Molten heat doused me in liquid pleasure. He throbbed inside me for a single blissful second, stretching me to my limit. I teetered on the edge. Feathered scales rubbed my inner walls as he vibrated inside me with each harsh wing-beat keeping him aloft.

He growled, like he was beyond anything as mundane as words. But his body was more than happy to speak for him.

The head of his tail slapped my clit, and I detonated.

High-pitched screams flooded the night as I writhed on his thick length, core squeezing the hard invasion, strangling the textured steel. Every nerve in me lit up. His grin was cruel as he watched me break for him while he held all the control, keeping perfectly still apart from his enormous shadowed wings stroking the night.

Time stuttered as I fought to breathe.

Bliss wound through me before the heat chased it, leaving me hungry and needy all over again as I panted on the metal railing, trying not to fall to my death as I clawed at his muscular shoulders.

And then the incubus went to war.

The demon pulled back and slammed back in. Deep. Hard. Vicious.

He unleashed all that pent-up fury, pounding into me over and over. His hand squeezed my throat, pinning me on the edge of the railing.

Every harsh thrust knocked a moan from my lips. Until every breath was a scream from the ecstasy. From the heat pulsing through my core. The slick friction and vicious stretch.

"Take. My. Fucking. Cock. Sweetness," he snarled, each word punctuated by a hard thrust that had my head lolling back onto his fingers.

The stars above witnessed our lust. My inner walls clamped harder around him. The rough friction of his feathered shaft was smoothed by the tingling slickness of the pleasure he seeped just for me.

"Kill," I moaned, claws scraping down to his forearms, blood slicking my palms. "Please."

He squeezed my neck tighter, stealing my air and forcing my head back to face him. To meet the silver lightning streaking through stormy eyes.

"I'm going to stretch out this pretty pussy, sweetness. Even though I shouldn't. I'm about to fuck you until you milk my knots so damn sweetly."

I mewled, the thought of taking his mating knots and power-laced cum driving me insane with desire.

"Such a greedy girl," he purred, eyes crazed with vicious need as he pounded me into submission. "Have you ever been knotted before?"

"W-What?" The question caught me off guard, and I frowned before another thrust wiped the expression. The next was hard enough to almost knock me off my perch.

"I'll take that as a no, then." He smirked, slowing his pace to a teasing glide through my slickness, making a lewd wet noise from the amount of cum I already dripped. "Good. I want to be the only one who makes you feel this fucking good when I break you, over and over. You're in a mating heat, sweetness. Your body craves my cum. I'm going to fill up this needy pussy of mine until it overflows. You'll draw so much power from me, and in return, I'll fucking breed you."

He laughed, a cruel sound, as a manic glint lit his silver eyes.

I had a single moment of alarm before heady warmth burned through that too. The thought of Killian trying to get me pregnant was hot enough to scorch my middle.

He gripped my thighs, claws pinching, and yanked me off the balcony.

Straight onto his thick length.

Something impossibly wide smacked my stretched lips, and my eyes shot wide.

He grinned and pushed me down harder onto his length. I had a frantic second to stare between us at the larger, scale-like feather patterns around his cock's base, swollen and pulsing as they bore down on me.

His *knots*.

They popped past my tight entrance.

My claws raked his chest as I thrashed against him with a scream, battling to accept the harsh stretch. Pleasure and pain fought for dominance for a heart-stuttering moment.

"Fuck!" He snarled, bloody chest heaving, eyes wild. His tail bumped my clit with a wet slap.

It shoved me right over the edge.

I screamed, body writhing as Killian shattered me.

"Yes, sweetness, that's it." He growled. "Break for me."

He upped his pace, pounding so hard my fluttering core ached in the best way. He bounced me on his cock as much as his swollen knots allowed. The incubus fucked me with a wicked fury I'd never felt before, wings working hard at his back to stop us both from plummeting to our deaths. His pointed tip punished my cervix, and I felt his ridges flare, rubbing harder inside me even as his thick knots trapped me on his base, sealing him inside me.

"I've never craved anything as much as you, sweetness. Does that scare you?" His voice had dropped to a guttural rasp. "Because it should."

I convulsed on his length, writhing and moaning and coming undone.

He snarled with his release, knots pulsing violently, tremors wracking his entire body hard enough to shake us both. He flooded me with a wet heat.

A brutal tingling swept my inner walls, forcing power and bliss through me. It mixed with the heat hunting through my blood and burst into flame.

I gasped as wave after wave of pleasure ignited through me.

Heat and bliss merged as I burned on an altar of Killian's making.

Roaring sound rushed in my ears. Killian growled again, his knots throbbing. More wet heat filled me to my limit.

Blackness edged my vision until reality narrowed to gleaming silver eyes.

And then darkness eclipsed it all.

Chapter 30

A soothing warmth shifted around me, and I snuggled deeper into its embrace. The lingering tease of a sinful dream clung to the edges of my mind.

I'd dreamt of Killian rescuing me dramatically and taking me hard, mid-air, trying to breed me with his unique knots holding me captive.

My subconscious clearly hadn't got the message that I was done obsessing over the untouchable incubus.

A thick ache between my thighs had me frowning, pulling from sleep's hold. The heady scent of sex and burned caramel registered, along with something too big wedged inside me, stretching me obscenely.

I blinked fully awake, swallowing back a groan as the light pierced my eyeballs like stabbing needles. But I'd caught the edge of a slate-purple arm wrapped around my chest.

It. Hadn't. Been. A. Dream.

How many times was I going to shout that inside my own head?

My heart pounded in time with my screaming thoughts.

I'd gone into my first heat.

And *Killian* had been the one to break it.

Could I already be pregnant with his child?

"I can feel how hard you're thinking." Killian's rough voice was full of mirth as he whispered in my ear, placing a delicate kiss to the column of my throat, so at odds with the aching stretch from his solid length still inside me.

I stiffened in his arms, unsure how to react now we'd crossed that line so fully I wasn't sure we were in the same realm as it.

Killian thrust lightly behind me, his hard length buried impossibly deep. His knot felt slightly less intense than I re-membered from last night but still swollen enough to hold us together even though he'd somehow changed our positions while I'd been unconscious.

Aftershocks of pleasure echoed through my abused core as I pulsed around his hardness.

"I've been trapped inside you for hours," he murmured against my skin. "And I still can't get enough of you. So fucking addictive. Sweetness... Break for me one more time."

His fangs sank into my neck as he thrust, pushing and pulling his knots stuck inside me. Bright sparks lit me up from the inside. His warm venom hit my bloodstream and kindled pleasure. It raced to my core, stuffed full, and ignited. I moaned, writhing in his arms on silken sheets as he followed me right over the edge into oblivion with a low groan.

Hot seed filled me to bursting, the pressure overwhelming before he pulled back hard enough to slip free. I gasped at the rush of wet heat between us, oddly tempted to turn around and lap up every power-soaked drop from his monstrous cock.

It was all I could do to sprawl limply in Killian's firm hold though. My chest heaved as I struggled to catch my breath and scramble for some sense of reality through the post-orgasm haze.

At some point, after I'd apparently passed out on his fat flying dick last night, he'd moved us to an opulent bedroom.

Gold-accented furniture gleamed around the expansive room, everything painted in rich cream shades, underlit with a warm glow from invisible strip lighting and a dramatic crystal chandelier that somehow mocked the early morning sunlight flooding through the sheer curtains, swaying in the breeze.

The incubus cuddled me closer in the softest covers I'd felt in this realm or the next, in a sprawling four-poster bed complete with romantic drapes at each corner in some rich queen's dream.

Shattered glass littered the plush carpet like spilled diamonds. The curtains danced aside with a fresh breeze, revealing the jagged edges of industrial-thickness glass within a sliding door.

That led onto a familiar balcony complete with a metal railing, now bent inwards.

A blush worked its way up my neck to warm my cheeks.

I mentally slapped myself, pretended I wasn't gushing wet with a knot-load of his cum, and rolled to face the incubus. "Hi."

"Good morning, sweetness." Glowing storm-blue eyes stared back at me, stunning with their silvered flecks. He had the eyes and wings of a mythical Earth-realm angel. But Killian practically dripped demonic sin.

Blood even smeared his bare chest, painting a gory layer over his tattoos. At least our rabid fuck fest had generated enough energy for him to heal every ounce of damage I'd done in the past few days.

His deep-purple skin contrasted the satin sheets, and for the first time I could remember, I let myself explore the exquisite detail of his ink. With his wings thrown back along the bed behind him, sunlight snuck between us to grace his defined chest.

An enormous widow-witch reached sharp talons towards where his heart would be. Feathered wings flared across his upper chest, one side wrapping around his neck.

Clasped in its foot was a single flower.

I'd always thought they were generic blooms, but each one had five distinct tapered petals surrounding an intricate ring of nectaries.

They were bloodbores. Each and every one of them.

It was the flower I'd tried to poison him with on his first ever birthday cake. The ones someone had carved into my front door and that had turned up in huge planters outside my house.

My favourite flower.

I held my breath, scanning the other birds I could see across his shoulder and neck. Clasped in their beaks or gripped in their talons was the same deadly flower.

It was all over him, hidden in plain sight. Inked in his skin permanently.

I didn't know what it meant.

He noticed my intense focus, and something in his flirty mask softened. "Did you think, all this time, that my loyalty was only to your brother?"

My breath hitched.

What was he saying?

Maybe it didn't mean anything. Maybe I was just delusional.

Barely a few inches separated our lips, and I fought the urge to close the distance.

Now that the blazing lust of my heat wasn't burning us both, would he welcome my touch?

Just yesterday, I'd woken up in bed with him like this, and he'd made it clear it was about feeding.

Not something real.

Was last night just about seeing me through my first heat? Had I forced him into this too? Was that what he meant by loyalty?

I chewed my lower lip, welcoming the pinch of my fang. "I'm...sorry...if I put you in an uncomfortable position last night."

I wanted to have this conversation, but this was possibly the worst way to have it. We were naked and pressed up against each other in a stranger's bed.

Sexual demons weren't usually fazed by nudity though. Our bodies were our weapons.

Given what he wielded between his thighs, clearly his more so than most.

Killian frowned, peering into my eyes like he could make sense of my words if only he looked hard enough. "Eve... What happened between us was one of the best experiences of my life."

My lips parted. "What? But... The heat pheromones..." I trailed off, hyperaware of the sticky wetness leaking between my thighs.

Of *him* between my thighs.

A furious blush warmed my cheeks.

His frown melted, leaving a roguish smirk armed and ready. "This wasn't the first time I've been around a succubus in heat, Princess."

The reminder of his incubus lifestyle churned my stomach. He was a few years older than me and had apparently lived a varied, full life while I'd cloistered myself away, working on my healing magic and pining after an off-limits enforcer.

I cocked a brow, forcing myself not to spiral at those words. "I'm sure it's not," I drawled. "How very...*experienced* of you."

He chuckled, smooth and rich. "Oh, sweetness, don't be jealous. I've never knotted or tried to breed anyone but you." His forked tongue darted out, a quick swipe along my jaw. "Yours is the only pretty pussy I'm desperate to overflow."

My brows shot up. He was serious? The psycho was actually trying to *breed* me.

"You're insane," I whispered, but damn if a part of me wasn't sucker punched at the thought of carrying his young. Of starting a family with him.

The idea of him holding a baby was making me all broody, and I needed to slap some sense back into myself. I was here on a mission to stop my evil magic hurting people. There was no way I could responsibly have a kid right now.

Maybe not ever.

And especially with a demon whose mixed signals made me want to claw his face off.

His chuckle darkened into a sharp laugh. "Of course." He inclined his head. "But that doesn't mean I don't crave you."

My eyes narrowed to slits. "And yet back at that house party...you told Zahara we weren't even friends."

His voice dropped to a low rasp, his eyes dipping to my pouting lips before slowly trailing back up. "Because, you and I? We could never just be friends."

I had no idea what to say to that. My thoughts spun in useless circles, reading into every little thing he'd said to me.

But really, I was being selfish. I'd left him behind to keep him safe.

I had no right to keep inflicting pain on him, no matter what he thought about last night.

"I...should go. I have to fix my magic," I said, unable to hold his gaze any longer. "Before I hurt anyone else."

"*We* should go, you mean." His focus locked on my lips like he was ready to devour, not get dressed. "Or are you planning to poison me again, little witch?"

I knew this was coming, yet all the reasons I'd left him behind were still perfectly valid, despite the guilt I felt at abandoning him.

"*Killian.*" I fixed him with my serious glare, only slightly ruined by the fact I was naked and leaking his cum. "You have to go back. It doesn't matter what Rex told you to do."

His voice pitched low. "Your uncle didn't send me."

"What? Then why...?" I trailed off, swallowing the rest of my question. It didn't matter. "The kingdom needs you."

His demonic smile hardened, sharp enough to slice. "What about what I need?"

My argument died on my lips, beaten down by more mixed messages and confusing signals.

The bastard was going to have me over-analysing every damn word he said. Every expression on his handsome, stupid face.

"I'm coming with you. Your safety is my priority," he said.

I barely suppressed the urge to roll my eyes. More at me than him.

"Of course it is," I muttered, shifting my head higher on the pillow.

"Oh no, a handsome incubus wants to keep me safe. My life is *ruined*." His voice took on a high-pitched whiny quality that was somehow meant to be me.

A surprised laugh burst free, even as I tried to scowl at him and failed miserably. "That sounds nothing like me."

He beamed right back. "It's too accurate. I almost got a semi just hearing your dulcet tones."

I gave him a flat look, and he sniggered, pulling me closer against his hard front and proving he had more than just a semi.

"Anyway, if you're going to keep ruining my life, then you need a glamour, and we need a plan. I went to that club last night to get information on the Sage Coven's location, but I uh...got sidetracked," I finished dryly.

Rage flashed across Killian's face, silver streaking through his ocean eyes like the flash of lightning. A muscle feathered along his jaw. He clenched it hard enough that I worried about his poor fangs.

"Maybe we should go back tonight and ask around," I said, slowly drawing out the words in a soothing cadence like I was talking to a feral animal.

Killian managed to unclamp his jaw to spit out a single word. "No."

I arched a brow.

"You're not going back there. Ever." He bared his fangs, chest expanding. "I'll murder anyone who looks at you the second we walk in."

I cleared my throat, shifting on the bed, still locked in his arms like it was the most natural thing in the world. My cheeks warmed.

"Well, you successfully eased me through my first heat. I think we should be fine to go back without my vagina issuing another call to arms."

Killian snarled, "Well, it's a good thing we won't have to test that." He drew a deep breath, glancing aside. "I already know where to go."

I raised both my brows. "You do? And when were you going to share that little titbit with me?"

An infuriating smirk curved his lips.

"I'm curious," Killian started. "When you decided to poison me in my sleep, was the next step of your devious plan to run around the human realm questioning strangers until you stumbled upon the right coven?"

I shot him a flat look.

After reluctantly leaving bed this morning, we'd taken turns to freshen up in the fanciest en suite I'd ever seen and stolen clothes from our unsuspecting hosts. Thank fires millionaires travelled a lot, because nobody came back to the penthouse Killian had broken into.

We'd kept our muddied leather boots, but I'd been lucky enough to find designer jeans and a cashmere jumper that fit my lean frame, readying me to face the British chill of late summer despite its low-cut neckline. Killian had dug the realm's softest grey sweatpants out of the dresser in the next room over, poking a hole through for his tail. They stretched indecently tight around his muscular thighs and an arse that made mine look pancake flat, but at least he was clothed. Of course, that left the distractingly sexy incubus topless like he didn't feel the cold, which compared to my weak mutt self, I supposed he didn't.

I'd managed to cast a human-looking glamour on us both without the vicious darkness in me rearing its head to tear Killian apart. We'd then spent the last few hours in the biggest hire-car we could find, on account of Killian's giant wings, driving south to the not-so-secret location for the Sage Coven.

There'd been flirting and teasing but also talking about home, laughing, and joking about the latest antics the other enforcers had been getting up to, and generally avoiding anything too serious like the fact he'd fucked my brains out the night before or that I was one wrong move away from accidentally killing him.

We'd stopped only briefly at a service station, using the facilities and stocking up on a million different snack options. I was a teensy bit obsessed with all the adorable shapes of buttery shortbread you could get here. They even had a cat-shaped pack, and I vowed to bring my death-kitty familiar back some as a thank you for saving my life.

It had been oddly reassuring to watch Killian get crumbs everywhere as he ate shortbread while driving, like a normal person rather than the viciously untouchable enforcer he was.

I huffed. "It was much more thought out than that."

Killian smoothly pulled the car into a parking spot, and we silently observed the other cars and humans milling about the gravel lot, one of many dotted through the New Forest.

Trees swelled on one side, elms and ash growing thickly. On the other two sides, wide plains stretched, leading to rolling hills of vibrant grass and tufted heather. The heathland was brushed in pinks and purples with tiny flowering buds.

In the distance, a herd of wild horses galloped across the landscape, led by a stunning dappled grey stallion.

"Beautiful," Killian murmured.

I glanced over, only to find his stormy eyes locked onto me.

Warmth suffused my cheeks, and I offered him a shy smile. "You are such a flirt. Even for an incubus."

A grin bloomed across his face, showing off pointy fangs.

"Come on, sweetness." His voice dropped to a husky octave, eyes flaring silver. "Before you tempt me into staying in the car."

I gaped at the wicked enforcer, fighting another heated blush. As much as I wanted to pounce on the sexy demon, I didn't want to accidentally murder him.

Since I'd feasted on Killian last night, that darkness skulking inside me seemed quieter, but I couldn't trust it.

I opened the car door and hopped out before that demon could tempt me to sin.

The moment I stepped out, the buzz of life thrummed through me like a string being plucked. I drew a deep lungful of fresh, cool air and focused on the ripples of power all around me.

Killian coming up beside me was a low vibration in my mind. Beyond him, small waves seemed to signal the humans exploring through the national park, and even further out, I could sense wild ponies grazing and birds flitting through the trees.

Everything pulsed so strongly, but that dark hunger inside me was ever-present, lurking just below the surface, like a monster from the deep.

I blinked my eyes back open, turning to Killian with a frown. "So... Where are we actually going?"

He ran a hand along the waved length of one horn, flashing me a too-bright smile. "Into the woods."

I frowned. "You do know where we're going, right?"

He waved his claws dismissively. "Of course. I've been there before. But...not for some time. It's where I go for glamour if I'll be in the human realm for a long mission."

I pursed my lips, a frisson of jealousy winding through my chest. He had a mage contact who just happened to be from the coven we were looking for?

How often did he come here?

"I usually fly from our portal straight here, but it has to be at night," he said, scanning the landscape.

I grimaced at the reminder of the scourge plaguing this world. The hunters.

My time in their tender care had broken me in so many ways that I wasn't sure I'd ever be fixed right.

Warmth enveloped my hand, pulling me back into the here and now.

"I won't let them hurt you." Silver lightning streaked Killian's eyes, lighting stormy ocean depths. "Not ever again."

It was almost as if he could read my thoughts. My throat closed off. His words were said with that quiet kind of conviction I believed more than if he'd shouted them from the rooftops.

I nodded, feeling a different sort of warmth spreading through me.

"I know," I whispered, fighting back tears. "You already saved me once."

"Come on, Princess, let's go find you some hippies," he said, his small smile heartbreakingly handsome.

I followed Killian towards the tree-line, leaving our hire-car and the wandering humans behind.

Gravel gave way to thick grasses as we walked. Long minutes passed, with the swish of heather brushing the tops of my boots the only sound. The damp tips painted the hem of my trousers with moisture that lingered in the air.

Nature pulsed with life around me, filling me with a strange form of peace I'd not felt in a while.

We hiked across the uneven ground, finally reaching the tree-line after what felt like an hour. It took another half hour, but we finally stepped out from the small patch of forest into another swath of rolling heathland.

I wasn't sure what I was expecting, but no magical coven popped up to greet us, dancing around a bonfire with their book of spells and judgy attitudes.

"Are you sure you know where you're going?" I asked, giving Killian a dubious side-eye.

"Of course." He cleared his throat. "Before we get there, there's something you should—"

"Wait," I hissed, holding up a hand for silence.

Something pulsed again in the magical currents around me. My heart rate picked up as my brain translated the disturbances into information.

"There're people coming. Humans. Males." I bit my inner cheek, unsure how I knew these things. "Violent."

Killian didn't question it. He just drew his glamoured sword from the sheath between his wings and turned to where I faced.

A human emerged between the thick birches of a distant copse of trees, coming from the direction of the car park we'd left behind.

We hadn't seen another person since.

"Hunter," I whispered, eyes locking onto the danger.

Almost a hundred metres separated us, but I could still make out the sneer on his scarred face.

"It's different ones," he hissed over his shoulder, waving someone closer. His voice was barely audible over the breeze and the distance between us, but my demon heritage was still enough to give my senses an edge.

Eight men emerged from the trees, dressed casually in hiking gear but with suspiciously bulky coats. My heart sank as they jogged towards us, eyes darting everywhere as if they expected more demons to pop out of thin air.

The way they looked at Killian and me told me they knew exactly what we were, and they were salivating at the chance to hurt us.

Memories flashed through my mind like a slicing blade.

Chains.

Bars.

Screams.

Fists.

Knives.

Bruises.

Blood.

Death.

I swallowed back the bile that tried to surge up my throat. The air had a light quality to it, almost like it was too faint to contain any oxygen.

"Easy, sweetness. Just breathe for me. They won't lay a finger on you," Killian murmured, shadows bleeding down his wings to darken his feathers. "They're dead men walking."

"How did they even find us?" I struggled for enough breath to voice my question.

If my glamour had failed, we'd have received far more odd looks back at the service station.

Killian shook his horns, eyes locked onto his prey. "I don't know, but they're here now. I'm going to need you to run for me, sweetness. I'll catch up once I've had my fun with this lot." He shot me a quick smirk. "Want another tongue? Or maybe I'll just gift you their eyes for daring to even look at you. Uncrushed this time."

I clenched my jaw against the nausea roiling my stomach, glaring at Killian. "How can you joke at a time like this?" I hissed through my fangs. "And I'm not leaving you. Obviously."

He huffed, but the hunters were only paces away now.

The group fanned out until they formed a semi-circle at an almost safe distance, hands hovering near their waists. No doubt where they hid guns.

The man in the centre looked like most hunters I'd met—grizzled and angry, steeped in scars and righteous fury. He looked ex-military, or maybe law enforcement, but the mean glint in his beady eyes told me he hadn't joined up to protect people.

He'd done it to hurt.

"This is our world, Hell scum. Come with us quietly, or we can drag you off in pieces. Our scientists will have to pick over whatever's left," he snarled, violent anticipation in his tone.

"Silly human." Killian chuckled. "None of you are leaving."

He didn't wait for a response.

Killian leaped onto the hunter who'd spoken, blade slashing the man's throat before he'd fully drawn his pistol. The hunter dropped to his knees, scrabbling at his neck as blood gushed down his front.

Gunshots boomed across the flat landscape as the others freed their pistols. It was the middle of the day. There was no way other humans hadn't heard it too.

I could hardly move as violence unfolded. Terrorised memories locked me in place.

Spelled bullets rained down on Killian. One slammed into his thigh, buckling his knee. He snarled, a whirlwind of pain as he sliced each hunter before they could even think to turn their weapons on me instead.

But it was still eight against one.

Killian was putting his life on the line for me.

Shot. Cut. Bleeding.

He was always the first to take the damage. His whole life was drenched in pain and sacrifice.

Rage consumed me.

My poisoned blades were palmed before I knew it. I launched one at a hunter firing wildly. His pistol buzzed with telltale traces of magic. My knife slammed into the human's chest with enough force to knock him flat on his back. The poison would kill him quicker than the hole in his heart.

And then *it* started.

That creeping, vile *thing*. It filled my veins with dark hunger. The need for blood and pain. I snarled, overcome with the desperate call of my wicked magic. My hands glowed red.

Power lashed my insides and burst free, shooting outwards in a wave of viciousness. It ripped into the hunters, tearing flesh and breaking bones.

The men screamed.

And so did Killian.

The horrifyingly familiar sight of his skin splitting open filled my vision. He grunted, stumbling for a brief second before he continued to hack away at the hunters, firing manically as they tried to process injuries from phantom claws.

"Killian," I whimpered, choking back a sob. "I'm so sorry!"

I fled.

My feet pounded the heather as I tried to put as much distance between myself and Killian as possible.

I knew I was going to get him killed.

But I'd selfishly wanted him to stay by my side anyway.

I should have pushed harder.

I stumbled, my ankle twinging painfully as it rolled in an unseen dip. But I didn't dare stop, limping towards the next patch of trees looming steadily closer.

The magic flooding me swelled, and my ankle crunched painfully as something in it was righted. I gulped down air as I sped up, blurring past the first trees and into the forest's embrace.

Chapter 32

"Over here!" a masculine voice boomed, and a lanky male barrelled through the woods, gesturing at me wildly.

I slid to a stop, panting hard after running flat out for almost half an hour since I'd abandoned Killian to save him.

A determined expression hardened a classically handsome human face. Magic washed over me in a harmless wave, leaving tingles in its wake.

A *mage*.

I braced for my magic to lash out at him.

Nothing happened.

It had stopped roiling inside me around ten minutes ago, but I hadn't dared turn back for Killian yet.

I'd gone so far I could no longer hear the echoing gunshots.

Or maybe they'd stopped for another reason.

"Miss!" the guy yelled again, arms pumping as he sprinted towards me. "Keep running!"

My heart leaped into my throat as his wide eyes locked onto something behind me.

I spun, grabbing a poison-laced knife in each hand as I readied to attack any hunter lucky enough to escape Killian's massacre.

A monster lunged towards me.

The biggest smile split my lips.

"Get back, vile demon!" the mage roared, and a ball of golden light whizzed past my shoulder, heading right for Killian.

The demon sneered, batting the sunlight aside. It fizzled, charring a patch of leaf litter beside him.

Pitch-black wings framed Killian's heaving chest. Blood doused him from too many open cuts, courtesy of my magic and a few ragged gunshot wounds.

Guilt and anxiety sank claws deep into me as I gaped at the damage.

He parted his jaws, exposing deadly sharp fangs, and roared right back at the mage closing in on us.

The mage leaped in front of me, using his body like a shield and raising a hand to ward off the snarling demon. His palm glowed like sunshine, matching his spun gold hair and molten eyes. The effect was like a supernova powering him from the inside out.

I side-stepped him with a glare. "Stop! What the fires do you think you're doing?"

"Go, I'll distract him," he hissed under his breath. His eyes darted to me before they narrowed on Killian. "You'll never lay a finger on her, demon!"

"What?" I blinked in shock.

Killian flexed his bloodied claws with a chuckle, a deep, husky sound that belonged in the bedroom. "Oh, I've done a lot more than that."

The mage lunged, throwing his glowing fist towards Killian. I stumbled back as the demon flared his enormous wings, shoving me away from them both.

Killian side-stepped the next sunlit attack with ease, a rumbling laugh falling from his lips. "That all you got, *pretty-boy*?"

Kind of ironic, coming from the gorgeous incubus.

The sunny mage sneered, throwing a ball of glowing light at Killian. I flexed my claws, preparing to intervene, but Killian held a hand up to stop me even as he dipped out of the path of the sizzling magic.

"No, no, sweetness. Let's see what your knight in shining armour has," he mocked, his smirk as lethal as his raised claws.

"Both of you," I hissed. "Stop it."

This was so dumb.

The mage frowned, backing up a step as he glanced at me once more. "You're...not in danger?"

I snorted, hiking a thumb at the battered incubus. "He's the one in danger."

If you couldn't laugh at yourself...

The mage's glow dimmed as he glanced back and forth between the incubus and me, an adorable pink flushing his pale cheeks with colour. "Oh, I'm so sorry. I didn't mean to assume...

But the way you were fleeing in fear with him running after you…"
He trailed off, gesturing at the demon once more.

"Sure. Because all demons are just trying to steal pretty maidens to devour, right?" Killian ran his forked tongue across his lower lip suggestively, but his eyes were predator-focused on the other male.

The mage had the good grace to look uncomfortable. "You were literally chasing her down, covered in blood. Excuse me for trying to rescue someone in grave danger."

I mean, he had a point. I'd literally been sprinting like I'd disturbed a phoenix's nest, no doubt with a haunted look on my face.

The last time a male had run me down and dragged me off, I'd have given anything for a noble stranger to jump in and save me.

I stepped around the bristling wall of feathers and fury. Holding my hand out to the mage, I offered him a tight smile. "I'm Eve. Thank you for trying to help me. That was really nice of you."

He took my hand with a sheepish smile that revealed a cute set of dimples. "Alvie." He turned my palm over and placed a small kiss to the back like some ye olde gentleman. "A pleasure to make your acquaintance, Eve."

Killian growled, so low the threat was barely audible.

My hand tingled where the mage's soft lips had touched my skin, and I pulled back, putting some space between us, ignoring the urge to wipe my hand on my stolen jeans.

Faint wisps of his desire reached me as he gave me a quick once-over, making me blush as his powerful energy trickled into my reserves with the faint taste of lavender and rosemary.

I couldn't help but stare at him right back.

Well over six feet, he was tall for a human and built with a lean, almost wiry strength half-hidden by his casual white tee and neat jeans. He had that handsome, boy-next-door look about him but with a dash of magical allure in his rich golden hair and eyes. His tanned skin was unmarred, perfectly smooth and untouched.

Next to his easy perfection, I felt more broken somehow. Like all his golden glory only highlighted my blood-soaked claws and writhing darkness.

Something about him just screamed wholesome goodness.

I didn't trust it.

He probably had a spider familiar or something.

I'd met few mages apart from Zoella and the bastard who'd slept with me, kidnapped me, and sold me out to demon-hating hunters to be tortured and killed.

So about a 50 percent chance for dickhead when it came to magekind.

Maybe Alvie was everything I'd been searching for though. Hope unfurled in my chest, brightening my smile despite my suspicion.

Killian's growl roughened, a clear sign blood was about to spill.

I glanced at the prickly incubus, shooting him a warning look.

He stopped growling but flared his shadowed wings in an intimidating show of size and strength.

I barely suppressed the eye-roll threatening to make my head spin. "This is Killian," I said, gesturing to the stubborn demon.

The mage looked almost as suspicious of Killian as before, but at least he cordially dipped his narrow chin.

"We're actually here looking for help from the local coven," I said, giving him my friendliest smile to cover my nerves. "I'm...half-mage, and I'm looking for help with my magic."

His eyes darted to the short horns peeking out of my hair. When I'd glamoured Killian, I'd also cast the spell on myself, hiding the small quirks of my demonic heritage. A strong mage like Alvie could see the truth beneath though.

It meant he'd seen a mixed breed mutt running for her life and still jumped in to save me. The realisation endeared him to me even more, easing some of the instinctive mistrust.

He nodded to my horns with a smirk. "I'd figured it was a little early for Halloween dress-up."

Killian snorted beside me, muttering something rude under his breath. I couldn't help but smirk at what he thought of the new mage.

Alvie continued as if the demon wasn't obviously irritated by him. "My coven isn't far from here, and it would be my honour to escort you to them. I would never turn away a witch in need."

"Thank you," I rushed out, the weight of my fears lightening for the first time since I'd torn Killian open at that damned house party.

He smiled, shining like the sun. "Of course, Eve. Can I ask what your magic affinity is?"

I nibbled my lower lip. Zoella had explained to me the branches of magic—mental, elemental, and nature. As a healer, I was a rare affinity within the nature branch.

"Healing," I said, voice tight.

His expressive eyes widened, like huge shining coins framed by the gilded flutter of his long lashes.

"Beautiful and talented," he murmured.

All I saw was a blur of purple and darkness as Killian lunged for the mage.

He had the poor male pinned to a tree trunk by his neck, claws pricking the mage's pale throat enough to spill beads of red.

"Killian!" I gaped. "Fires' sake, let him go!"

Killian snarled, fangs gnashing inches from the mage's face as he bristled with unhinged fury.

Like he suddenly realised his overreaction, his features transformed into an innocent smile.

"Oops." He patted the terrified mage's cheek sarcastically. "My mistake. I could have sworn your little sparkle fingers were glowing again."

He stepped back, releasing the mage.

Alvie scowled, swiping at the blood on his neck. "I would never hurt my own kind."

Killian bared his fangs in a fake smile. "She's *my* kind, actually."

I huffed loudly, drawing their attention before they could literally whip their dicks out and start pissing circles around me. "In case you haven't noticed, I'm both. Now, about that coven invite...?" I trailed off, throwing Alvie an encouraging look.

He frowned. "Of course, Eve, you're more than welcome. Your...*friend*, however..."

Killian chuckled, the sound harsh like a poisoned blade. "Oh, Sparkles, we're much more than friends."

"Are we?" I quirked a brow at him.

It wasn't long ago he'd emphatically told Zahara that we weren't friends, and my lips twitched as I poked the grouchy dragon. He might have explained what he'd meant by that statement, but apparently I wasn't quite ready to stop teasing him about it. Especially when I didn't know where we stood now.

Killian's smile turned wry. "You're not going to let that go, are you?"

My stupid heart did a little flip, and my even stupider brain decided now was the perfect time to read too much into his words.

Did he mean we were more than friends as in dating? Lovers? Or more like close friends? In a completely platonic way? Almost family?

Gah. I needed to slap myself. But I was trying to project innocent, sane witch vibes to our new mage acquaintance.

I pasted on a completely normal smile, mini fangs hidden. "He'll be good, I promise."

Desperate hope expanded in my chest. I could promise no such thing, but this was my chance to be rid of this curse. To fix myself.

To go home without the chance of accidental murders. Return as a valuable healer rather than a broken monster.

Killian grinned manically wide. "Oh, so very good," he purred, forked tongue swiping out to catch a stray drop of hunter blood from his lips.

Deep worry lines creased between Alvie's golden brows.

It was entirely justified.

<h1 style="text-align:center">Chapter 33</h1>

Alvie shot me a shy smile. "My coven isn't far. Really, you've managed to get so close on your own. Perhaps the sister goddesses were guiding your steps when you fled that demon." He waved a dismissive hand toward Killian, menacing just behind him.

I stifled a snort at Killian's intensity, falling in step with the mage as he led us off the path, walking deeper into the thick woods of the national park.

"I wasn't fleeing Killian." *I was fleeing myself.* "Hunters found us." My voice strangled as terror gripped me by the throat.

Alvie almost missed a stride, eyes widening in alarm. "*De-mon* hunters?"

With the immediate danger over, my brain tried to drag me back into the darkness of my memories.

I nodded mutely, airways too tight to breathe.

Warmth brushed my back. Killian's arrow tail stroked along my spine a second time, and my lungs finally remembered how to inflate as his touch anchored me in the present.

This comforting, touchy side of Killian was throwing me off. Maybe the recent blood loss was just making him loopy. He still had bullet holes in his arms and legs, after all.

"Don't worry, Sparkles," the incubus drawled. "I've already taken care of your pest problem."

Of course he'd have killed them all before chasing me down. Killian didn't run from a fight. Unlike the new, broken me.

"Thank you," I murmured, offering him a grateful smile.

His tail gave me one final soothing stroke before returning to sway lightly behind him with each prowling step.

A furrow dug between Alvie's narrow brows, an almost brooding silence falling over the group as we walked.

There were so many types of trees around us—silvered birches, broad ash, rough beeches, proud oaks—some of which resembled the types we had in the Bloodwood, only without blood-like sap and luminescent moss. Probably fewer poison wildflowers too.

Killian radiated intensity, stalking right behind Alvie in obvious threat. His feathered wings were semi-flared, ready to shoot out and slam the mage at any moment. At least they were back to their angelic white beneath the rust-coloured splatters.

I wouldn't be surprised if the mage could feel Killian's breath on the back of his neck though.

"Good." Alvie seemed to shake himself after a long moment, clearing his throat. "That's very good. Given my offensive affinity, I'm one of the chief protectors of the Sage Coven."

I frowned at his odd pause. But then again, who knew what kind of blood-soaked history he had with the hunters himself? He was probably frazzled at how close the hunters had come to his coven.

I wasn't exactly a model for healthy reactions myself.

I'd mistaken the psychotic voice in my head telling me to disembowel my enemies and feast on their organs as a fun form of trauma response. But really, my death-kitty familiar was just being a helpful cutie like that.

My heart ached to see her again. To at least know she was okay.

Killian rolled his stormy eyes at the mage but kept quiet.

"Can you tell me about your magic?" I asked, curiosity getting the better of me.

"Of course." He preened under the attention, a bright smile helping me push back dark thoughts of the hunters dragging me back to their lab of nightmares. "I'm a nature mage, like most of my coven. They're mostly healers, like yourself, but my affinity lies with the sun."

He tipped his face back, angled towards where the sun must be, hidden by the thick canopy and thicker clouds of the late afternoon.

"You can conjure sunlight as a weapon?" I asked.

What would it be like to hold that kind of power in your hands?

As if he heard my thoughts, he lifted a hand with a dramatic flourish. Light coalesced above his flat palm, and a warm glow bathed my face like I peered into a fireplace.

"Wow," I breathed. "No wonder you're so tanned in this icebox."

He chuckled, the sound as warm as his magic. "I know, I make a great sunbed. Don't worry, my services are free for a witch as pretty as you." He wagged his golden brows at me playfully, even as faint wisps of soapy desire seeped towards me.

A surprised snort had me sounding like a spike boar. I could just make out Killian's eyes narrowing in my periphery as he stalked behind us.

It was like the mage *wanted* to get his tongue ripped out.

"Enough about me, tell me about you, Eve." Alvie closed his fist around the sunbeam, extinguishing it. He steered us around a fallen oak, angling us through a denser patch of trees, and tucked a golden curl behind his ear.

They were rounded, just like mine.

"Well...my mother was a succubus, which I guess means my father was a mage, but he didn't stick around long enough for me to find out. I was born in Hell and live in the Hybrid Kingdom, but I love visiting the human realm when I can."

Or I had before I'd been sold to hunters on my last trip.

"How did you learn magic without your father to teach you?" he asked, his attention riveted to my face, hanging on my every word. The intensity would almost be flattering, if not for the uncomfortable topic.

"Mostly trial and error." I shrugged, lips twitching as a hundred memories bubbled up. "I threw whatever power I could at my poor brother until something happened. But now my friend and I have started our own grimoire. She's a nature mage, but from the Quartz Coven up in Riverside."

"That's one of the most inspiring stories I've ever heard. Not only is your magical intuition strong, but I can feel the energy radiating off you. You're incredibly powerful." The honesty in his golden eyes shone a light on something I'd buried long ago.

I'd never been called *powerful* before.

I wasn't a force to be reckoned with. Not like Killian, with his mastery of violence, or Alvie throwing literal sunbeams.

I was the outcast service provider people hoped never to see.

And now I wasn't even that.

"What's your coven like?" I blurted the first thing I could think of.

"Amazing." He flashed me a dazzling smile. "I'd do anything to protect my brothers and sisters in magic. Here in the Sage Coven, we have some of the most powerful healers in the world. We respect all life."

A sense of pride seemed to puff up his chest, and the picture he painted drew me in more than I'd have cared to admit.

"So...they're not going to try to murder me and Killian for being demons?" I asked, wondering again if following a random mage was a smart idea.

It hadn't exactly panned out well for me last time. Plus, Zoella's coven had been run by some evil dictator.

"What? No!" Alvie shook his head, aghast. "We're more open-minded than those other stuck-up covens." He gave me a subtle look from under his long lashes, leaking wisps of lavender desire for me to soak up. "Summoning isn't forbidden here. In fact, I know of a few coven members who've dated demons..."

"How very scandalous," I mock-gasped, clutching imaginary pearls at my jumper's collar.

Liquid gold eyes caught mine. "Yes, well, the boost of magic from demons can be...tempting."

Killian's growl was deep enough to rumble the earth beneath our feet.

My cheeks flamed, and it took everything in me to keep my gaze from raking the incubus. That carved door in my mind threatened to swing wide open and let my craving for him smack him right in his pretty face.

Even now, my core tingled from the...*power* he'd gifted me during my heat.

"Yup," I coughed, looking anywhere but at the two men looming closer. "I guess your coven's welcome policy is why my friend suggested I seek you out. Since my magic has started...acting up, I'm hoping someone in your coven has similar magic to teach me to contain it. Or well, just to heal me, I guess."

Killian scowled at the back of Alvie's angelic curls. "There's nothing to fix, sweetness. You're perfect just the way you are."

I shot him a look.

The enforcer was as confusing as he was frustrating.

I'd tried to squash my dumb obsession when I'd stabbed him in the Bloodwood, but since last night, he'd been saying cute shit and wasn't even fucked up on haze.

Alvie glanced over his shoulder at the demon, features pinching, before his attention returned to me. "Whatever is going on with your magic, I'm sure someone in my coven can help. I'll make sure of it. You're not alone anymore."

I felt more than saw Killian bristle. The demon was a second away from murdering our one chance at finding this coven.

"Thank you," I said, stepping closer to the mage in case I needed to protect him from Killian's irrational need for violence. The psycho was still covered in blood from his last fight. "We really appreciate you helping us like this."

"Yes, Sparkles," Killian drawled, a lethal bite underscoring his tone. "Thank you ever so much."

An awareness soared through my subconscious with a faint pulse of magic.

I held up a palm. "Wait a sec."

Killian was instantly on high alert, scanning the forest. "What is it?"

I cocked my head, trying to extend my newfound intangible sense outwards. A small smile tugged at my lips. "It's not danger."

Alvie squinted between the trees before resting his attention on me. "What can you sense? Did you hear something?"

A goshawk flew overhead, but that wasn't what I'd been waiting for.

Pounding thuds grew louder until a herd of wild horses raced by the forest boundary, metres from where we lingered out of sight through the tree-line.

I shrugged at Alvie, lips crooked into a sheepish smile. "I...can sometimes *feel* beings around me."

"An animal mage and a healer." He whistled low. "That's a strong, and rare, combination. Do you have your familiar yet?"

My thoughts leaped to the hellcat I'd left behind. "I think so."

Killian's gaze found mine, and genuine delight curved his full lips. "That pretty kitty."

The bastard was truly stunning when he smiled for real, his dusky purple features carved into heart-stopping perfection.

I fanged my lower lip, warmth suffusing my cheeks. "Guess having a psychotic hellcat breaking in all the time makes a bit more sense now, huh?"

Alvie paled to a chalky hue. "A *hellcat*?!"

Unease squirmed through me. I was already different enough without revealing all the little quirks that made me a hellish witch rather than a normal one.

"Yeah, she's kind of an arsehole, but cute enough to get away with it," I said.

Killian snorted, wings fluttering with the movement.

The mage continued to gawp at me before seeming to shake himself. "Wow. What other amazing powers are you hiding?"

My thoughts dipped to the vile darkness I harboured, and the bloodthirsty monster cracked open its eyes.

I swallowed thickly, frantically trying to shove it deeper into the abyss. "Nothing."

Chapter 34

"A moment, please." Alvie halted us in an unremarkable part of the woods, a good hour of tense walking later. Hordes of curious critters had peered at us through the branches as we'd passed by, helping lighten the general aura of hostility simmering between Killian and Alvie. The mage had frowned adorably with each new animal, though, pointing out which ones shouldn't even be awake at this time of day, the weak sun dipping low with the fading afternoon.

I stilled, finally sensing what had pulled us up short.

A faint pulse of energy radiated ahead, like a wall of power, invisible to the naked eye and almost undetectable if I wasn't already open to the currents of magic around me.

"It's the ward boundary, right? Just there." I pointed at a subtle line of dark stones, half-buried in the leaf litter.

Alvie beamed at me. "That's correct, Eve. Your natural abilities are amazing. I can only imagine what you'll be able to do with training."

Killian brooded in silence, his focus latched onto the mage.

I tugged at the hem of my jumper, unsure what to do with Alvie's compliment. "So, um, how do Killian and I get through it?"

"I'll let you in on a little coven secret." His smile turned smug as he leaned in close, the clean scent of lavender soap washing over me. "Since I'm our coven's protector and a high-ranking mage, I've been given access to the ward's keying spell."

"A secret or a chance to brag?" Killian mocked, baiting the mage.

Alvie ignored the demon, but his smile tightened.

The tension between them had only ratcheted higher and higher, and they'd just met about an hour ago.

"That's amazing," I blurted before the two idiots could come to blows. "I'd love to learn about warding."

Hybrids would always be hunted for our differences. We were slaughtered and enslaved. Rex always had to worry about our kingdom being invaded. If I could add another layer of protection, maybe I could make up for all the danger I'd put everyone in.

Alvie beckoned me closer with a crook of his finger, walking backwards to the invisible ward. "It would be my pleasure to give you a quick lesson."

I followed, curiosity getting the better of me. What things could I learn that I didn't even know existed?

Beyond my affinity magic, and whatever nature connection I'd yet to explore, could I do amazing things too? I'd spent my whole life suppressing my mage side, except to heal, trying to be the most demonic of demons. I'd still never fit in.

Could I have been looking at things all wrong? Was I more mage than demon?

Up close, static buzzed from the ward line. I stretched my hands out, combing my fingers as close as I dared. Sparks nipped me like tiny insects, the bites firmer the closer I got to the invisible wall above the carefully placed stones.

"You can feel the boundary, warning you away, correct?" Alvie asked, watching me intently as I fondled the magic barrier, a crease between his golden brows.

I nodded slowly, concentrating on the strange feeling. "Yes, it's giving me little shocks."

His frown deepened. "Hmmm, usually you'd be in a lot more discomfort, touching it directly." The expression melted into another of his bright smiles. "Another talent to uncover about the mysterious beauty."

I ducked my head, looking away. What did you even say to something like that?

He'd probably meant "abomination" but was trying to be polite.

"If you concentrate on the ward, you might get a sense of the area it covers. My territory is quite large," he said, a tinge of pride and something else lifting his tone.

I closed my eyes, focusing on the magic before me.

A wonky circle stretched out beyond the wall, blankness filling the vast space. The rest of the forest illuminated with sparks of life, great and small, but nothing shone inside the image of the ward boundary in my head. It reminded me of the dead zone around the portal.

"It spans for miles," I murmured, blinking my eyes back open.

Alvie nodded. "Yes, very good. Only a select few mages have their signature tied into the locking spell on it, but our whole coven and a few special guests have permission to come and go as they please. Though, the coven elder is alerted when someone crosses. He likes to keep a rather close eye on our movements."

The last part was said with a sour note. Apparently, Alvie wasn't a huge fan of his leader.

"Anyway, I'll let you and your demon...*friend* in as temporary guests. But we'll have to go straight to see the coven elder."

I flashed him a smile, ignoring the mix of emotions squirming through me at the thought of meeting more mages. "That's great. Really, Alvie, I can't thank you enough for helping us."

He returned the smile, reached for my hand where it hovered over the barrier, and squeezed. "Of course, Eve. Us mages look out for our own."

Killian muttered something under his breath—probably not very complimentary to our mage host. I pulled my hand from Alvie's, and Killian planted himself right beside me, radiating heat and threat.

The mage raised his hand, glowing with sunshine trapped beneath his skin, and whispered mysterious words I couldn't quite catch.

Magic rose as a crackling static sensation. It flared brightly for a moment, washing over me. Feathers brushed my back as Killian's wings rustled, flexing and tightening beside me.

As quick as it had come, the sensation fled, leaving me oddly energised.

"There, that should do it." Alvie stepped past the line of dark stones and beckoned us to follow. "Come on, I'm sure the coven elder is already on his way to intercept us with the new signatures registered, especially with one being non-mage." He glanced meaningfully at Killian.

With a deep inhale, I stepped past the innocuous line of stones, bracing for the sharp bite of magic. It smoothed over me instead, like a gentle stream. A warm, welcoming feeling enveloped me, nothing like I'd have expected from a spell designed to keep people out. It almost felt familiar, like a hug from a friend.

A rustling clued me in that we weren't alone.

The barrier's magic released me, and Killian stepped beside me, already laser-focused on the source of the noise.

"Wow, that was fast," I murmured, watching the stone-lined path winding between tall trees.

A small group of mages hurried down it towards us.

A lean, middle-aged male led the charge. Despite the towering enforcer beside me, the man's focus locked onto me, unwavering.

Something about him held my attention too.

A smattering of grey threaded through wine-red hair, his short and sensible haircut just long enough to curl at the ends.

Neat black slacks and a soft-looking button-down shirt gave him an almost casual style, but tension furrowed his hawkish features.

For some strange reason, he seemed familiar. Almost like I knew he was the source of that welcoming magic.

Killian bristled, claws splaying ready at his sides.

"Ah, Coven Elder, you're just in time for me to introduce you to our new guests." Alvie stepped aside and swept a hand towards us. "This is Eve and her acquaintance. Eve here is in need of our help with her healing magic."

The coven elder seemed unable to hear anything the younger mage said though. He didn't take his gaze off me for a second, merlot eyes blazing with some unknown intensity. "Lilabell?"

I froze, everything in me icing over at the name on his lips.

"No," I croaked. "But how did you know my mother?"

Chapter 35

The coven elder turned as white as bone.

An almost imperceptible shift rippled through the handful of mages clustered around their leader along the stone-marked trail.

Killian's wings twitched beside me. Tension poured off him. If anyone so much as sparked, he'd be on them in a blink.

"You...look just like her," the coven elder murmured.

I swallowed thickly. I'd heard that my whole childhood. My aunts had beaten me mercilessly for it, trying to punish me for stealing their beloved sister's face as well as her life.

"So I've heard." My voice came out as a dark rasp. I eyed him with the sinking sense of impending doom.

I just *knew* what was happening here.

"How..." He swallowed hard, voice trembling. "How old are you, dear?"

"Twenty-two."

"Yesterday, in fact," Killian hissed, tail rising aggressively over his shoulder, stinger peeking from the arrowed tip to glint in the dulling afternoon light.

A pained expression wrinkled the old mage's features. Everyone gaped back and forth between us.

Except Killian, who growled, shaking with rage beside me. He took a single step forward, and I grabbed his forearm, digging my claws in to hold him back. The contact helped me find strength.

I forced the next words out. "You're my father, aren't you?"

"I..." He seemed to visibly gather himself, drawing up straight. "I think so—"

Killian's vicious snarl cut him off. "I should cut you down where you stand. How could you abandon her? Your child?!" His tail lashed behind him, punctuating with words like the crack of a whip.

I'd wondered that my whole life, and I'd never been more grateful to have Killian at my side. He knew exactly what I'd gone through.

If I'd had a father to raise me after my mother died, maybe things would have been different. Maybe I'd have been protected and loved. Not abused and threatened. Not staring down the barrel of a life in the pleasure houses of a succubus kingdom.

"I had no idea." He stepped forward, hand outstretched. "Eve, *daughter*." He whispered the word almost reverently, a look of wonder replacing the shell-shocked expression. "Please believe me. Lilabell never mentioned she was pregnant. One day, she just disappeared and never answered my summons again."

"Save your excuses," Killian hissed.

A burly male beside the coven elder cleared his throat, catching the coven elder's attention and throwing a pointed look towards Killian.

The older mage seemed to shake himself, taking in the blood smears and bullet wounds across the incubus. "Goddesses, where are my manners? Are either of you in need of healing?"

His eyes glowed, shining like rubies, raking over me desperately as if searching for injuries. Their bright hue put Alvie's sunny glow to shame, making his power seem dim in comparison.

I shook my horns, unable to voice that I had such magic to heal myself still. "Killian does."

"I'm fine." The demon stared the coven elder down until his glow withered away.

Of course the stubborn enforcer would refuse. Apparently, he rejected all healers, not just me.

"If you're certain." The coven elder inclined his head. Some of the steel that must have earned him his position seeped in, and he met Killian's intense stare for a long moment before returning his attention to me. "Please, come with us. It's a bit hectic with tonight's initiation, but let's find somewhere to sit down and talk.

Unless demonic fashion has become a lot more macabre lately, you must be tired from whatever trials you've faced getting here."

He wasn't wrong. It felt like a lifetime had passed in a single day.

Kilian leaned down, whispering in my ear. "Even though this coven is mostly friendly towards demons, we can't trust them. Especially not him."

Curiosity nipped at my thoughts as I eyed the back of the coven elder's head, stalking behind him. How many times had Killian been here if he knew things about the coven's leader? Had they met before? Who cast his glamours when he came here?

He caught my hand in his, enclosing it in his warm strength. Storm-blue eyes, slashed through with slit pupils, bored into me as he brushed a loose curl back from my face, tucking it behind my ear. "If you want to leave, just say the word and we're gone. We don't need these people, sweetness. You never have. We'll figure something else out. Together."

His blood-smeared wings unfurled, readying to take off on my command.

My heart swelled. Killian meant every word. Even if it put him in danger, he'd take me away from here if I asked him to.

"I can't be the reason you get hurt again, Kill. Not you, or Rex, or Zoella, or anyone. I have to keep our home safe. I have to fix my magic and be a healer. Be useful," I murmured, rushing the words out through the tightness in my throat.

"Eve..." He trailed off, head bending towards mine in our own private bubble of intensity. "You're fucking perfect. No matter what your magic does or doesn't do for people. Your value isn't tied to what you let others take from you."

"Killian," I pleaded, licking my suddenly dry lips. "You don't understand. I'm doing this for you. For our family. Our home. I'm doing it out of necessity."

"You're doing it out of fear." Silver sharpened his gaze. "Fear that you're not good enough. That you're not worthy. But you are, Eve. No matter what magic you have or how big your horns are. No matter how many poisons you make for us. No matter how wild your curls are first thing in the morning, or how grumpy you are without coffee sweet enough to rot your fangs."

A muscle feathered along his jaw. The tattooed wing along his throat vibrated with the rapid beat of his pulse, but he held my gaze, unwavering. My own heart pattered with the same flighty cadence.

"You may not see your value, sweetness, but I've not been able to stop seeing it since you first tried to poison me with those damn flowers on that damn cake, and I'd eat every toxic crumb, just to be near you for a second longer."

My lips parted at his words. "Killian..."

Why was everything just so fires-damned complicated?

I wanted Killian. Every fibre of my broken being called out for him. My tattered soul screamed for it.

Yet how could I return home with him, knowing I was still a danger to everyone? How could I look Killian in the eye, knowing the next time he needed me, I could end up killing him instead of healing him?

I hadn't realised we had an audience until Alvie cleared his throat a few feet behind us. My father and his followers had stopped further ahead, all staring at us. We'd kept our conversation hushed enough to avoid human ears, but my cheeks still warmed.

"Kill...please," I murmured, squeezing his warm forearm. "I need to do this."

He nodded, eyes dropping to where my pale hand covered his rich purple skin, inked with silvery chains. "I'll follow you anywhere you want to go, sweetness."

I flashed him a tight smile and started after the group of mages, lingering a few steps along the trail.

Alvie had watched our exchange with a soft smile in place, but something churned in his sunshine eyes as he fell in step beside me. "It seems the sister goddesses have blessed our meeting as more than chance."

"Perhaps." I shrugged, and the three of us trailed after the coven elder and his cronies at a small distance.

My mind reeled as we continued in silence. The coven elder snuck glances at me over his narrow shoulders, brows raised like he was still shocked.

That made two of us.

Within minutes, the first buildings appeared through the trees, dotted along the path lined with mismatched paving stones. A luxurious village appeared in a large clearing, branching off the widening path that arrowed through the middle. Crescent rows of two-storey cabins sprang up from the forest, the neat squares blending in with the grey-hued trees surrounding the vast open area. In a way, it reminded me of a more uniform, lavish version of the Hybrid Kingdom.

Apart from the rogue hunters, their forest was pretty fangless though.

Mages of all ages and races milled around, giving our party curious gazes and friendly waves as we passed. Just normal people. Who could also do magic.

They seemed nowhere near as bloodthirsty or prejudiced as I'd have expected.

Children giggled, running around with colourful ribbons streaming behind them while harried parents tried to herd them. A cluster of young women sat outside a sprawling cabin we passed, tying bundles of sage leaves together and stacking them on a pile.

The deeper into coven territory we walked, the more buzz filled the air. Chatter, laughter, excited crowds, busy people. Flame-roasted meat, sage leaves, and wood smoke flavoured the cool air.

The coven elder passed the central row of buildings and stopped inside the last ring with his followers.

I avoided his gaze, taking my time assessing what looked like the heart of the coven.

An open-sided shelter spanned the middle, like an enormous gazebo with a rustic canvas top. In its centre, a pile of logs burned low within a raised brazier, its base ringed by ornate white stones and rows of cushioned wicker chairs, filling with people. I followed the path of the smoke, up through a tented gap in the roof and into the dusky sky above.

Two burly men hauled a platter of seasoned meats past our awkward group. They carried it towards an outdoor kitchen, sheltered within the innermost ring of buildings, and the pair loaded an enormous shiny smoker with slabs of herb-crusted joints.

They even had a pizza oven going.

Alvie and Killian eyed each other, another stare-off going down right beside me as we joined the leader.

The coven elder spoke quietly to the mages who'd accompanied him, and they each hurried off in different directions away from the main gazebo, leaving just the four of us in a bubble of hushed tension amid the hub of activity bustling around us.

I drew a full breath, scrounging up the courage to address the mage who'd apparently spaffed me out of his balls. "So... You're my father, huh? What's your name?"

I hated that a part of me was curious.

He winced, as if the awkwardness of the situation was hitting him too. "Orion Warren."

Warren.

Technically, if I'd been raised in the human realm, that would be my last name. Demons rarely bothered with such things though. I was lucky I'd been given one.

Eve Warren.

It was an odd thing to consider.

I'd dreamt of finding my father for years growing up. Until I'd fled and Rex had taken me in. That was when I'd learned that family was your choice, and clearly, my birth father had never chosen me.

"Cool." I shrugged. "So what can you tell me about fixing magic?"

Chapter 36

The coven elder paused, searching my flat gaze with shrewd eyes.

After a tense moment, he gestured at one of the empty picnic benches beyond the outdoor kitchen. "I think it's best we sit for this, daughter."

I watched Killian stalk in the direction my sperm donor indicated. Mages hurried out of his way, but nobody seemed that fazed by a gore-covered demon stalking through their midst. My eyes locked onto the faint tremor running the length of his tail. The bastard was in more pain that he'd let on.

And I was responsible.

Yet unable to fix it.

I blew out a harsh breath. "If I can change his mind, can you heal him?"

Orion glanced between Killian and me with a thoughtful expression, nodding. "I can patch him up, but I've not healed a winged demon in years. It might be best for him to see one of our more specialist healers."

Killian turned halfway to the bench, a stubborn clench to his hard jaw. His hearing was good enough that he'd have caught the whole murmured conversation, even with the background chatter from the coven members running around their forest resort.

"Please, Kill," I said. "I've seen you bleed enough in the past few days to last a lifetime."

He grunted, raising his voice so the coven elder beside me could hear too. "Fine."

"Alvie, take our guest to Jacaranda. She should be in the clinic still." Orion waved a hand towards one of the nearby buildings. "Hunters attacked a group on their way back from the coast this morning."

"Of course, Elder." Ice hardened the sunny mage's expression. "You'll be okay, Eve?" He asked, thawing a fraction as he looked at me.

Killian's fists clenched hard enough to drip blood to the packed earth. The demon radiated threat but stayed quiet, eyes dropping to the three remaining blades still strapped to my thighs. He knew me well enough to know I could handle myself against one healer, even a coven elder.

"Yes, thank you." I shot Alvie a forced smile.

The mage raked me with a lingering once-over before stomping off along one of the many tracks that branched from the central path, Killian on his heels like a predator stalking prey.

I watched his white feathers disappear into the nearest building before he reappeared in a ground-level window, staring out at me with his usual watchful eye. He even reached forward and shoved the glass pane open wide so he'd likely be able to hear me too.

I'd never admit it, but his stalkerish ways were more comforting than was sane.

Orion took a seat on the bench he'd gestured at before, and I grudgingly sat opposite him, barely resisting the urge to palm a poisoned knife under the table.

"Look, I know I'm not exactly Father of the Year, but I think you should be careful with that demon. I know he might be...*attractive*." He coughed, cheeks reddening. "But as a healer, you need to protect your heart more than most."

"What are you talking about?" I shook my horns. "Actually, it doesn't matter. I'm not here for relationship advice. I'm just here to fix my broken magic."

Thunder struck his expression. "You already gave it away?"

I frowned even harder. "Gave what away?"

If he said my virginity, I was going to throat punch him. Claws first.

He sighed, and his initial irritation drained to a distraught look. "I have failed you. In so very many ways."

The reminder stoked my fury, but I bit my tongue, waiting for an explanation.

"You are a healer, yes? Like almost every mage in our family line."

I nodded slowly, waiting for him to continue.

He took a moment, seeming to gather himself. "Healers can lose their magic...by giving it away. If you heal someone already falling into death's embrace, you'll give too much of your power. It might never replenish. *All* your magic will leave you. Is that...what happened to you, child?"

I shook my head, a niggle of fear worming its way in. What would life be like if I could *never* heal someone again? Just a few weeks without the ability was a nightmare.

The thing that made me valuable gone forever in a single act? Terrifying.

"No." I swallowed thickly. "My magic has turned...dark. Instead of healing, it hurts people."

The admission had guilt squirming through me. I wasn't particularly squeamish. Being raised in violence had a way of stripping that from you pretty quickly. To survive as a hybrid in Hell, you couldn't be afraid of getting your claws bloody.

It was that I should be helping people, and I wanted to, but I was only hurting them instead.

Something akin to relief slackened the elder's features. A few minor details seemed familiar, like the slope of his nose and the curl to his short hair.

It was strange, looking for myself in him.

"That which can be given can also be taken away." He chuckled with a relieved shake of his head. "It's perfectly fine, Eve. In fact, it's a sign of your power. It's the strongest expression of the healer affinity, to reverse the body's natural healing process." His merlot eyes gleamed with what I might have called pride. "When your magic lashes out with *darkness*, as you put it, it's your power unhealing old wounds. Some say it even siphons energy from the act. It's incredibly rare."

His words stunned me into silence.

Was my magic not just whole but somehow powerful?

Valuable?

I searched his beaming face for any hint of a lie. I'd never heard of such a thing, but then again, I'd been raised by demons, not mages. My chance to grow up as a happy, sheltered mage like Alvie was taken from me when the succubus who'd spawned me couldn't even be bothered to inform my father.

My fang found my lower lip as I tried to think it all through. "But why would it keep lashing out when I didn't want it to? And it's been stopping me from healing others," I said, struggling to believe that my magic wasn't as broken as my mind.

He shrugged. "My best guess? It's instinctive. A defence mechanism. Magic tends to manifest at times of high stress. Judging by the state of your...*friend*, you've been in quite the pickle recently."

Why did everyone think we were friends except the demon himself?

I shot Killian a glare through the windows of the clinic. A stern woman with bright-white hair held glowing hands over Killian's wing, concentrating on her work. The demon only had eyes for me though.

Orion cleared his throat. "Is that when you've felt your magic acting out? An animal backed into a corner will lash out to protect itself."

All the puzzle pieces were slotting together.

It made perfect sense when he put it that way.

When my darkness had first manifested, I'd been locked in a cell, battered and bruised and forced to watch one of my cellmates die on some sick scientist's operating table.

I'd hardly been able to heal anyone since then. My time in the hunter's clutches had damaged me to a point where I'd felt broken, and my magic had responded accordingly. As if the danger were still present.

The only times it had felt calm was when Killian had fed me, giving me protection and power and a sense of safety I'd never get enough of.

"I can see that you're thinking this through. It's a lot, all this too"—he gestured a soft-looking hand between us—"must be difficult to take in."

I bobbed my horns, thoughts still reeling.

A sympathetic frown rumpled his brow. "Eve, if I'd have known Lilabell was pregnant..." He shook his head, blowing out a breath like someone stepped on his chest. "I hope you believe me when I say I would have travelled through Hell and back to get you. I'd love the opportunity to get to know you now, though, if you'll let me."

I didn't quite know what to say to that. The old mage seemed sincere, but I'd never been one to trust easily. Life had taught me not to.

"You don't have to say anything right now." He held up his hands in surrender, showing neatly blunted human nails. A small sigh escaped his lips as he gazed up at the sky. "I know it's too much too soon, but the goddesses clearly had a plan because tonight is the coven's annual initiation ceremony for new mages."

I'd heard of a coven initiation before. Zoella had told me about hers, only half-completed, before she'd managed to remove her anchor mark, setting her free from the coven who'd been responsible for her pain.

Penetrating eyes met mine, so round and human. So similar to my own.

"There's a place for you here," he continued. "Your demon side won't be looked down upon. Especially not when you're clearly such a powerful mage. If you choose to join us, and I sincerely hope you do, I can teach you about your magic and how to channel both healing and harming sides. Just binding yourself to us tonight will anchor your power to us and help you start to control it."

My skin prickled like spiders crept along my arms.

A part of me knew coming here wouldn't be an easy fix to all my problems. Whatever was broken would take time to heal. But could I really move to the human realm and join a coven of strangers? How long until I gained control of the darkness?

If I stayed, how much would I learn about myself too? About my magic and the things I'd never known were even possible?

How many people would I hurt if I went back now?

"I... I'll think about it," I said, my voice slipping out in a hoarse whisper.

"That's all I could hope for." An encouraging smile curved my father's lips up. "We can provide you with a safe place to unlock your true potential, Eve. To be a part of our magical family, as you always should have been."

"Coven Elder Warren!" a high-pitched voice rang out. "It's time!"

Orion turned to a middle-aged woman dressed in a tailored shift dress, nudging a young man busy tapping his shiny watch towards the seats under the tented roof.

Orion stood from the bench and called back with a good-natured huff, "Be there shortly, Elder Reese."

Turning his smile on me, he continued, "I've asked for rooms to be prepared for you in our finest guest chalet for afterwards, but if you would follow me, everyone is gathering now to start the ceremony."

Great. So if I wanted to fix myself, I had to join my father's coven. And it had to be now.

I felt exactly like a feral animal backed into yet another corner.

The darkness in my chest stretched out, flexing its claws.

A weight crushed my lungs, heavy enough that I could barely suck in air. On the outside, I managed a tight smile for the coven elder.

"Jacaranda is probably about done with her patient, so I'm sure Alvie will bring your friend to join us shortly. He'll also show you both to your quarters afterwards so you can freshen up and rest, whether you decide to initiate or not. It seems our resident greenhouse has already taken quite the shine to you, though, pun intended."

"*Greenhouse?*" A rogue snort escaped me, the absurdity enough to loosen the tightness in my chest, even as I clenched my shaky hands in my lap to hide them.

"Did he not tell you about his powers?" His face scrunched up in a quizzical frown. "Alvie's power is sunlight. He's an asset for our vegetable patch."

"Errr, yeah." I rubbed the base of a horn.

Alvie had been nice to me, and his warm welcome and excitement at having me here felt genuine, but it seemed he might have been overselling his position as chief protector of the coven. I supposed everyone wanted to feel useful.

Maybe I'd fit in here after all.

I'd shied away from my mage heritage for so long, but was it time to embrace that part of me?

Nobody had sneered at me for being a mutt yet, or tried to snap my bones until they could feed on my agony.

A good start.

"Come, daughter." The coven elder held out his hand to help me stand, and with a steadying breath, I reached out and took it. "Join your true family."

Chapter 37

Clouds sped across the bruised sky, giving the coven a spooky feel as night crept in.

My father led me from the quiet picnic tables, towards the canvas stretching over part of the clearing. The chatter of excited voices spilled from beneath.

A flickering bonfire roared from the centre, outshining the moon and adding to the moist warmth trapped by the fancy tent.

The feel of so many people was an incessant tapping at my senses. Even my magic reacted to the shriek of so much life around me.

Darkness stirred in my chest, yawning wide enough to show its teeth.

My heart drummed a rapid beat. Panic slicked my palms before I rubbed them off on my stolen jeans, shoving down the hunger corrupting my blood.

Orion weaved us through the buzzing crowd, oblivious to the monster he led through his people, taking me right to the front. He gestured to the first row of plush chairs before a waist-high tree stump wreathed in frosted sage.

"Sit here with the other initiates, child." Heavy eyes pinned me. "I hope you'll let me and your destined family help you. It's the least I can do."

Saliva pooled between my fangs. The feeling of being trapped only poked the beast my magic had become.

"Thanks," I rasped, backing away and taking the furthest empty seat at the end of the row.

The coven elder watched me intently before a mage I recognised from the welcome party pulled him aside for a hushed discussion.

I could hardly bring myself to look at the handful of other mages, all around my age, already seated several chairs down, as close to the tree stump altar as they could get.

The nearest witch flashed me a pleasant smile, eyes sparkling as bright as the firelight catching the polished gemstone of her necklace.

I attempted to return the gesture. Judging by the rapid blinking of her false lashes before she spun back to the mage beside her, I needed to work on the whole friendly thing if I was going to stay here.

My breathing shallowed as the bonfire's heat washed over one side of my face, contrasting the chill smothering the other half.

Either I joined Sage Coven in the next few minutes, or...

Well, there was no other choice.

I couldn't go home like this.

Either I take a risk with the Sage Coven, go on the run from hunters in the human realm, or try not to get murdered by purist demons and hungry critters in Hell.

Two of the three options I'd already had a turn with, and I did not care for a repeat experience.

"Fires, am I actually doing this?" My breathing turned ragged, and I gripped the base of the cushioned wicker beneath me, snapping the woven fibres one by one.

The monster within writhed with the need to lash out, and I fought to keep a neutral expression plastered to my face.

"Everything's going to be okay, Eve."

I startled as hot breath fanned my ear with the whispered words.

Alvie leaned forward in the seat behind me and offered his usual sunny grin. "You're going to initiate, right? I'm so excited for you to join my coven."

His damp breath felt sticky against my neck, and I shifted away, my chair creaking in protest.

My answering smile felt brittle enough to crack my lips. "Where's Killian?"

He jerked a clawless thumb beyond the tent. "Jacaranda needed to dig the spelled bullets out manually before she could heal the wounds."

I looked for the building he'd been in, worry churning in my gut. He really had needed medical attention, and I'd just let him suffer for hours with bullets that could kill a normal demon. At least I'd been able to recreate the hunter's stolen magic poison, mainly by trial and error, so over the years, our people could develop a tolerance with carefully measured doses.

The demon I'd been searching for finally stepped out of the building, and I managed to uncurl my claws from the protesting wicker.

Even from this distance, Killian's glowing eyes found mine. He stalked through the moonlit clearing with all the intensity of a true predator. Utterly perfect, every inch of his muscular chest and arms had been knitted back together, wiped clear of the blood that had coated him.

Blood I'd forced onto his skin.

A surge of bile threatened to rush up my throat, and I swallowed thickly.

Killian towered over both the seated mages and the few stragglers still hurrying in around him as he reached the edge of the shelter, firelight warming his features.

"Oh my goddesses!" A squeaky feminine voice pierced the murmur. "*Killian*?!"

A stunning witch raced to my demon and leaped right for him. Killian's strong arms caught the woman on impact, and her legs locked around his waist.

He frowned, lips parting, and her mouth crashed against his.

It was worse than being stabbed.

I felt every cut.

Every slice into my soul. Hacking right down to the vulnerable core.

To the stupid hope I'd been harbouring since I'd been a dumb teen, baking him a poisoned cake.

His wide eyes shot to me as he kissed her. With lips that had been on my skin just this morning.

The incubus's hand wrapped around her throat and shoved back, dropping her, his tail lashing. "Get off me."

But it was too late.

"Let the ceremony begin!" my father boomed.

I hadn't realised I'd stood until the weight of too many eyes pressed on me. My claws stabbed my skin, blood slicking my palms, and I carefully folded myself back into the chair.

Darkness built and built in my chest. I tore my gaze off Killian's thunderous expression as he arrowed towards me, but the image of his lips pressed against another was burned into my mind.

It wasn't the first mentally scarring image of him I had, and apparently, it wouldn't be the last.

Not because he was an incubus.

But because he was *Killian*.

My father's voice continued, "Tonight is a joyous occasion! Not only is it the coven's initiation ceremony, but the goddesses have gifted me a powerful daughter, brimming with such potential."

"Oh, Eve, I'm so sorry," Alvie rushed out in a whisper. His hand reached over to squeeze my shoulder a fraction too hard. "I didn't realise he was the same *Killian* that Melody's been dating all these years."

Years.

My chest caved in. Crumbling into the dark abyss that waited to devour it.

Magic buzzed beneath my skin.

"Ow!" Alvie jerked his hand back and frowned at the blood dewing on his fingertips like he'd stuck his hand into a thorn-bush.

A furious presence reached us, but I stood before Killian could get close, taking a step away.

Right to my father's side.

"Eve, will you initiate into Sage Coven?" My father's voice rolled out over the crowd, echoing through my brain and bouncing around.

My gaze clashed with Killian's.

His chest heaved as he watched me, stormy eyes pleading. "Don't do this. It's not what you think. Please, sweetness."

My eyes burned with the threat of tears, but I bared my fangs with a hiss. "Thanks for making this easier."

Killian's expression shuttered. A cold, blank mask descended over his carved features.

I turned from him, staring up at my father instead.

His eyes gleamed in the firelight, chin lifting with his smile.

"I accept." My lips felt numb as the two words sealed my fate.

The crowd erupted in cheers behind me, but even their warm acceptance couldn't hold together the fractures splitting open my heart.

"Where would you like your mark, dear?" my father asked, hand raised and glowing a bright-ruby hue.

I swallowed thickly, heart pounding too fast, and pulled back the sleeve of my jumper. "My wrist."

He pressed two fingertips to my skin. A sizzling sounded, and a flash of pain fried my nerves, but he was already pulling away before I could react.

A magical tattoo lay in his wake: a small cluster of sage leaves shining with a faint silvery sheen.

"And now for tethering the anchor to your new family," my father said with an eager smile. "We usually let the anchor settle first, but I know you're strong enough to take it."

I braced for more pain, but he merely hovered his glowing hand over the mark. Something invisible tugged at my wrist, like a piece of thread knotted under my skin.

It didn't hurt, but the odd sensation made my stomach roil. The thread of magic dived through my arteries, weaving up my arm and into my chest. It collided with my magic store, and the tugging sensation tried to burst from my chest.

I fanged my lip to hold in a whimper, and the magic finally freed itself, taking a portion of my power with it. I got the sense of something large, just out of reach, and I knew instinctively it was the collective power of the coven.

Their energy mixed and roiled, soothing around each other, like a school of fish beneath the waves.

I rubbed my mark, trying to ease the odd push and pull. My skin was tender, but already I could feel it settling as my healing magic swept in.

My father beamed down at me. "I'm so glad to have you join me, daughter. You belong here, with your fellow mages."

I forced a smile back, still reeling.

The coven elder raised his voice, grabbing my hand and lifting it high so my new mark faced the seated crowd. "I give you our first initiate and new coven member, my long-lost daughter, Eve!"

The gathered mages applauded, whooping excitedly. Including the pretty witch who'd kissed my demon.

My gaze sliced to Killian.

But he was nowhere to be found.

Chapter 38

Rage lit a fire through my veins, burning hotter and hotter until I wanted to scream.

Magic spiked in my chest, but something curbed it before it could lash out, like it hit a wall of honey, sticky and soft as it slowly absorbed the sharp darkness.

It did nothing to stem my anger though.

I stormed away from my new coven as the next initiate was summoned to the tree stump altar where I'd just been magically bound.

"Killian!" I hissed, searching the darkness as I stalked between the picnic benches laden with wine bottles and iced buckets of beer. "Come back, you fucking coward!"

Wings fluttered overhead, and my eyes narrowed as the demon I hunted fell from the stars.

He landed on the stone-lined path, drenched in shadows that bled from his ebony wings. Silver eyes glinted through the darkness for a beat, and then he turned his wings on me and strode into the forest, back towards the way we'd come earlier.

I picked up my pace, hurrying after him and leaving the celebrating mages of my new coven behind.

"Hey! I'm talking to you!" I drew a knife from my thigh holster and chucked it after him. It sliced the night inches from his wing arch as he dipped it just in time. "Quit running."

He hissed, whirling on me as I snuffed out the distance between us. "That's rich coming from you, kid."

"Excuse me?" I scoffed.

He drew up to his full height and stood his ground. The second I was within reach, I shoved his chest, slamming him back into a tree hard enough to rain leaves.

"You heard me." He shook a leaf from his wavy hair, unfazed by the impact. "I was right all along. Your magic isn't *broken*, and yet you're still running from yourself."

"Fuck you, Kill. I had to join the coven to stabilise my cursed power before I hurt anyone else."

Doubt crept in at the edges as he snorted in cruel amusement.

"Did you?" He cocked his horns. "Or did your deadbeat dad just pressure a powerful new pawn into joining his coven? If this is just another aspect of your magic, then it's another part of you,

Eve. For years, I've watched you teach yourself complex healing magic. All alone. This is no different."

"It's completely different," I snapped. "And that's not why I followed you."

"What, then, Eve? What do you want from me? Because I can't seem to figure it out." His eyes blazed in the darkness.

"Are you being serious right now?" I snarled, rage and hurt bubbling up in a toxic mix. "You're the one seeing countless demonesses, and now witches too." Another blade found its way into my hand, somehow already pressed to his inked throat. "You bastard. I never would have touched you, heat or not, if I'd known."

He bared his fangs back, unafraid of the poisoned metal kissing his skin. "I haven't been with anyone since you were taken."

I stilled. "What?"

A sneer curled his upper lip. "You heard me."

"Why?"

Silver bled into his eyes fully, flashing brighter than sharpened steel in the moonlight. "You know why."

"Do I?" A harsh laugh left my lips, as cruel as Hell to a hybrid. "Because I know fuck all, it seems."

"Eve." A growl rumbled his chest. Wisps of shadow danced from his wings, rising and falling with each heaving breath.

"What. Are. You. Saying?" I bit out, fighting the urge to claw at him until he spilled sense.

"Dammit, Eve, it's *you*, okay?" His eyes burned into me, searing right down to my soul. "It's always been you."

Before I could do a single thing, he stormed the final gap between us, fisting my hair and slamming his lips against mine.

He devoured me with a kiss, crossing the line that had separated us for an eternity.

It was everything I'd dreamt of.

But could never have.

I ripped our lips apart, heaving for air.

"It's too late." My voice wavered as tears blurred my vision. "My place is here, and I'm not leaving until I'm fixed. However long that takes." My throat tightened, dropping my voice to a bitter whisper. "Go home, Killian."

"You're making a mistake. You can't trust these people, kid. That bastard who sired you already threw you away once. Come home with me."

Twin silver pools pleaded, screaming "choose me."

An image of my mother's lifeless body, sprawled in a pool of blood, flashed before my eyes. What if that was Rex? Or Zoella? Or *him*?

How could I live with myself if I let him down when he needed me most too? It wasn't just the danger of my bloody magic. It was the loss of my healing powers.

"You don't understand. I *have* to do this." I turned on my heel, dodging his claws as they grasped for my wrist. I couldn't look at him for another second or my resolve would crumble.

"Eve, wait!" he called after me.

My eyes burned as I picked up my pace, sprinting into the forest, leaving the shattered pieces of my heart at Killian's feet.

I struggled to breathe. My lungs squeezed tight and refused to obey my desperate need for them to expand with life again.

The ghost of Killian's lips still imprinted on mine.

I'd never felt more broken.

I hurried through the thickening woods, spindly trees looming over me as I fled the demon I wanted but couldn't have.

It would be selfish to trap him here in the human realm for years, stuck in a mage coven away from the life he'd built back in the Hybrid Kingdom. Or beg him to wait for me for fires only knew how long while I fixed myself.

As always, he was out of reach. Off-limits.

Something rippled through my subconscious. It took me a minute to connect the mental sensation to meaning.

A person waited up ahead.

A clean feeling I was coming to recognise, something magical, lurking in the forest and tripped my instincts.

"Eve! There you are," a bright male voice called out.

I turned in time to see a shock of golden hair, practically glowing under the dim moonlight filtering through the canopy. Alvie hurried towards me, crunching through the leaf litter.

I dashed the tears staining my cheeks and pasted on a smile as he neared. "Alvie, what are you doing here?"

Why wasn't he back at the ceremony with the rest of the mages?

He stopped within biting distance, flashing a friendly smile, but the expression didn't reach his yellow eyes. "I wanted to say congrats on joining my coven," he said before chewing his lower lip. "But... I also need your help."

I frowned. "Help with what?"

Something was off with the sunny mage. I just couldn't put my claw on what.

"It's the ward," he confessed, snapping a twig beneath his shifting weight. "The coven needs strength. Will you help me?"

"Sure." I drew the word out, trying to puzzle out what was triggering my instincts.

I may not plan to be here long-term, but I needed the coven's help during my stay. As a half-breed, I was a freak back home. If fixing the ward with Alvie encouraged people to overlook my differences, I couldn't afford not to.

"Excellent." Satisfaction radiated from the mage's golden eyes.

He snatched my hand, damp palm sliding wetly against mine. I barely resisted the urge to yank free as he tugged me along, almost breaking into a run.

The faint tingle of magic tickled my senses as we rushed through the dim forest, hinting at the invisible barrier protecting the coven's grounds.

My coven's grounds.

I stuffed down the burst of anxiety the thought brought on.

Alvie jerked me to a stop right before the wall of power, keeping my hand captive. At first glance, nothing seemed out of place. The line of half-buried stones sat untouched. Magic fizzed that same static from a few hours ago.

"Alvie...? What's wrong with the ward?" I peered around the hushed forest. "Was there a disturbance?"

Fear snaked through my middle. Had the hunters found us? Had I led them right to the doorstep of my new coven?

Danger stalked me everywhere I went.

"No." He cocked his head like he was considering something. "At least, not yet."

The hairs on my nape rose.

"What are we doing here?" I murmured carefully, stopping my friendly expression from slipping.

Alvie faced me, a serious mask dropping over his charming features. He squeezed, pressing my bones too close. "I need to borrow some of your power."

"What? Why?" I breathed, heart thudding.

The forest seemed to curl in around us, leaves whispering eerily in the breeze.

His eyes hardened at my reluctance, grip tightening further. "To strengthen our coven. I told you before, I'm our chief protector here."

Not according to my father.

But Alvie had tried to protect me in the woods. From a terrifying, blood-drenched demon. Whatever weird vibe I was getting was probably from my newfound coven binding and my stupid, broken heart.

"Okay... Anything to help the coven," I said, offering a tentative smile.

He finally released my aching hand, lifting his fingertips to my face. "Thank you, Eve. I knew you'd do the right thing."

I held back the urge to flinch as he stroked my cheek.

"Of course," I whispered.

Fantasies of ripping his hand off and shoving it down his throat played through my mind.

Too many men thought they had a right to touch something just because they wanted to. I'd lived it more than enough times.

"I won't let anything happen to you, Eve. We have a connection," he murmured, and everywhere his gaze roamed felt sticky.

Something wasn't right.

I peered through my blood-red lashes as he cupped my cheek.

"I know, I feel it too…" The lie spilled out on instinct, and I traced my lower lip with the tip of my tongue.

He followed the movement, and his eyes dropped to the scant cleavage peeking above my jumper's neckline. Hints of his soapy desire underscored his hooded expression. Energy rolled through me, wisps of his clean lavender flavour giving me a boost.

"But why would I need protection here?" I asked, nuzzling my cheek firmer into his hand, even as my stomach roiled.

He stroked through my curls like he was petting an animal. I fought the urge to hiss at the invasive touch.

"You won't." His grin twisted into an arrogant smirk. "Not when I'm coven elder."

I sucked in a breath.

His hands snapped around my wrists, tightening painfully. "Meos sumere. Meum est proprium," he chanted in a fevered rush.

Power bubbled up from my chest. It poured down my arms.

And into him.

Sunlight ignited the forest. Alvie became a supernova in its centre.

I yanked on his crushing hold, but something more than human strength locked us together. Energy drained from me so fast, I swayed like a drunk, crashing into Alvie's front.

My chest heaved as I thrashed against him, fighting to free myself.

He turned his head, unaffected by my pathetic struggles, and faced something beyond the ward line.

And that was when I felt it.

Life.

Rippling with the currents of multiple beings.

Intent on death.

Alvie lifted our joined hands, and sunshine blasted my retinas. Magic cracked through the air like thunder.

It hollowed me out like a soul-eater.

The ward shattered.

Chapter 39

A groan burst from my lips.

And I crumpled.

Dirt rushed up to greet me as Alvie let me fall.

My ears rang from the explosion of magic, and tears blurred my vision as Alvie's sunlight blazed painfully bright.

Fuelled by me.

I struggled onto my side, hollow and aching. Bone-deep pain cracked open my chest where my magic should have been.

Dark figures flitted into the light's edge.

Alvie loomed over my body with a victorious grin on his lips. "Well done, Eve!"

Faint blips of life rippled through my subconscious. Roughly fifty life forces pricked my magical senses before I lost count to the panic swelling inside me.

They weren't just any humans.

They were *hunters*.

"How could you?" I hissed at Alvie, trying to blink the world into glaring focus, but everything kept swimming. "They're your coven. Your *family*."

"I'm doing this *for* them." He sneered. "Your father is weakened by greed. All we do is summon demons and make deals for more magic and money. But what about what it costs the rest of us? Weak leaders weaken covens."

More shadows peeled from the trees towards us. I pushed myself shakily onto all fours, pain spiking my empty chest with every heaving inhale. My arms trembled under my own weight. I'd never felt so weak.

But I couldn't let everyone die.

This was my fault.

Men in black cargos and tight jumpers held pistols and knives as they approached on swift steps.

I stumbled to my feet, trying to veer away from the traitorous mage. My hand shook as I raised my claws.

I had to do something.

My father might not be the family I'd secretly dreamt of as a naive child, but I couldn't just let hunters take him and all those people. I'd barely survived my nightmare in their captivity.

And *Killian* was back there.

"C-Call them off," I slurred, gasping for each shallow breath. "Put the ward back, or you won't have a coven left to lead."

He rolled his sunlit eyes. "I'm not stupid, Eve. I've made a deal with the lead hunter. He's only going to take the coven elder. I'll keep everyone calm while they take your useless father."

"You fangless fool." I couldn't believe what I was hearing.

I didn't have time to argue with the traitor; the hunters were almost to the fallen ward line. The first few aimed spelled pistols at us as they closed in, scanning the area in a cautious sweep.

I couldn't take on over fifty armed hunters. Right now, I'd lose to five kittens.

The ward was my only hope.

I dug deep for the dregs of my magic. It was like trying to grasp a handful of syrup. Thick and sluggish, it responded slowly. I urged it on, mentally trying to reach for the void where magic should have sparked.

I threw my power at the ward line.

It bounced off the dead stones.

Alvie snatched my arm, tugging me back to his side. "Stop it," he sneered. "I was going to take you on a date after all this, but you're being an ungrateful bitch!"

"I'm devastated." I raked my claws deep across his arm.

He let me go with a hiss, eyes blazing. "I'll deal with your insubordination later. First, I need to greet my allies."

"They'll kill us all." I grabbed at him, missing his glowing arm by inches. "Fix the ward, Alvie!"

He peddled back, ignoring my urgent plea. I couldn't raise the ward myself.

But I hadn't been raised in magic. I'd been raised in violence.

I leaped at the golden mage, wrapping my legs around his waist and forcing him to stagger under my weight. I pressed my claws to his throat. "Do it, you idiot!"

The closest hunter lifted his pistol, magic sparking off its barrel. A grin slashed through his lined face. "Stupid fucking demons."

He fired off a round as I dropped from Alvie's back.

The mage jerked, stumbling. He fell to his knees with a whine, sunlight extinguished, clutching at the centre of his chest. Blood gushed down his pale shirt, the liquid almost black in the darkness.

The next bullet slammed into my shoulder, rocking me back. Another shattered my kneecap. Pain roared.

Burning. Scorching. Searing.

My jaw clenched on a scream.

I abandoned the traitorous mage in a pool of his own blood, clutching my shoulder and staggering behind the nearest tree. Every step was a hot poker to my blown knee. I half-hopped to the next trunk, trying to put distance between me and the hunters as I pushed my failing body toward the coven.

"Leave it," a male huffed. "It'll bleed out, anyway. We need to hit their satanic base before any of the other vermin scurry off."

Spelled bullets hurt so much worse than regular ones. Like acid being poured into the raw wounds.

Wisps of my powers jumped to the screeching joints, battling to reverse the damage. Hot metal worked out of my flesh, the blood-covered round flashing in the moonlight as it fell to the dirt. Warming magic soothed the pain, leaving behind a fierce ache and ragged holes in my clothing.

Dull thuds filled the forest as the hunters moved.

I wiped the sweat from my brow and tested putting weight on my healed knee.

I couldn't let the hunters reach their target.

The coven wasn't in any position to defend themselves. Most of them were healers, and probably drunk by now. They were unarmed and unprepared, even if Orion must have felt the ward break.

It would be a slaughter.

I peered around the trunk supporting most of my weight, tracking the hunters racing through the forest.

I drew a deep breath.

There was going to be a slaughter all right.

I stepped from my hiding place.

And reached deep into the abyss.

Dark hunger embraced me.

I craved their blood and pain. For every drop of mine they'd spilled. For every bone they'd broken. Every cut they'd carved into my flesh.

I screamed, throwing my hands out. Bloody magic raced forwards and slammed into the monsters.

They screamed back, dropping to the ground. Grunts of pain echoed. Bones crunched. The slick sound of blood splattered the forest floor.

Red swirled over my vision, tinting the gloom. Power flooded through my veins in bright lines of electricity as my magic devoured their essence, vibrating its way deep into my chest. Strength charged my limbs as my demonic side fed on the excess magic.

For the first time in my life, both sides of my heritage worked in perfect harmony, and it felt right. Natural. Like I hadn't been born a mistake.

Hunters raised their weapons, and gunfire burst through the night.

My heart squeezed as it rained bullets.

I dodged, zigzagging my way towards the frantic humans. Pain flared in bright sparks along my limbs as spelled lead grazed me. My magic swallowed the damage, but the pain threatened to buckle my knees.

A burly man staggered towards me, bleeding from multiple gashes on his arms. He bared his teeth, lifted his pistol, and squeezed the trigger.

It spat a magic round, whizzing past my ear. I snarled, eardrum ringing painfully, and swept low, gripping the barrel before he could get a second shot off and shoving it aside. It exploded in my hold, the percussive force mincing my hand, but the bullet found its home in another hunter, groaning on his knees beside us.

I swiped my claws through the hunter's throat, cutting short his yell with a wet gurgle as blood drenched my repairing fingers.

And then violence descended over me.

I spun and sliced, claws cutting flesh, fangs tearing jugulars. My magic latched onto most of the hunters, reopening countless old wounds, but not all, and they came for me in a blur of blades and bullets, their fury matching my own.

Pain ricocheted through my body with every slice and shot that found my flesh, until the world darkened at the edges, dancing with the red. My healing magic fought for my survival.

I stumbled as another spelled bullet smashed into my thigh, buckling my leg. I hissed, rolling through a pile of fallen leaves as I dodged the next round.

Gunshots boomed through the forest, pierced by their screams and my snarls.

A bright flare of life in my subconscious set my soul aflame, but dread chased on its heels.

Killian dropped through the canopy on shadowed wings, landing close enough for me to feel the gust of air as he used his body as a shield. His sword was already drawn, black blade angled towards the hunters.

"Get up, Eve. Run!" he snarled over his wing, but his focus never left the threats closing around us.

"Shoot to kill!" one hunter yelled. "We can still harvest corpses!"

I shuddered at the idea of their scientists getting hold of Killian, dead or alive, and lurched back to my feet, stumbling out from behind the demon my soul keened for.

With Killian here, I couldn't risk my darker magic cutting him down faster than the hunters, even if it wasn't completely spent.

So I tuned into the rhythm of violence, of the dance I'd learned long before any magic.

"Stubborn witch," Killian growled, blade slicing through the arm of a hunter, trying frantically to reload.

"Stupid demon," I hissed back. "As if I'd leave you."

Silvery eyes cut to me, filled with so much worry my heart ached. "Don't die."

Manic laughter spilled up my throat as I dodged another bullet. "I won't if you won't."

Killian and I cut through the hunters together. But with every bit of damage I took on, I could feel myself weakening—my healing power waning under the strain.

Something flittered at the edges of my consciousness, the tease of other living things on the horizon, but the signatures were all over the place, blending with the hunters and animals of the forest as my focus wavered.

"Traitorous bitch!" a voice croaked behind me.

I whirled, coming face to face with Alvie.

Ghoulish yellow light cast across deathly pale features. Blood covered his front from the bullet lodged in his chest. Angry red flesh was edged by charred fabric where he'd cauterised the wound that should have killed him.

But it was the glowing sunlight between his palms that shot me through with terror.

The deadly orb of power sailed straight for me.

Something slammed my side, knocking the air from my lungs and sending me sprawling to the ground.

Killian stood over me, wings flared.

Sunfire sizzled the air as it passed over me and smashed into Killian's chest, exploding in a blaze of vicious gold.

Chapter 40

The blinding light cleared, leaving my retinas burning from the overexposure.

The sight that hit me was horrifying.

Killian staggered a single step towards me and crashed to his knees. A ragged crater was all that remained of his chest, oozing black blood and clear fluid. I couldn't make out anything beating within. Just a gaping mess of flesh where his heart should have been.

"Killian!" I scrambled to catch him right as he collapsed.

My entire body shook as I eased his weight back onto his slackened wings.

The incubus blinked up at me, stormy ocean eyes glassy.

Glowing light built in my periphery. "One demon down," Alvie rasped, staggering to remain upright. "One worthless half-breed to go."

I struggled to tear my eyes off Killian, but a rage so hot it burned away the panic let me face the traitor.

With a snarl, I threw my vicious darkness at him. His flesh tore until every wound he'd ever had ripped through his mortal body. Bloody mouths shrieked across every visible inch of skin. His collarbone snapped, dropping his shoulder. Blood gushed from his crooked nose.

He spluttered as crimson rushed between his parted lips.

The glow brightened between his palms, his eyes stark with panic as he strained to pull enough magic to throw another ball of death.

But I wasn't just a mage.

With a snarl, I launched myself at him, crossing the distance between us at breakneck speed. My claws rent through his arm as he tried to block the death blow. I hissed, baring my fangs. With a rough yank on his glowing wrist, I tugged him sharply towards me. My short horn slammed into his eye with a wet pop.

He screeched, the sound like a dying phoenix.

My claws ripped through the delicate skin of his throat, tearing at everything vital.

And the noise died.

I let his body drop, ignoring the moist gurgling of blood bubbling from his throat wound as he rattled out his final breath.

I darted back to Killian, my heart hammering at the sight of him so still.

Impossibly, his battered chest twitched, so faint I almost missed it.

"Fires, Kill," I whined, blinking free the tears that filled my vision.

He peeled his eyes open, so painfully slow that my heart seized.

"Eve." His lips barely moved.

"It's going to be okay." My voice shook as hard as my hands, but I pressed them on either side of the cauterised wound hollowing his chest. "I can fix you. A-And w-we'll go back home. Together."

He was right. About all of it.

I summoned every scrap of energy I had left, and I poured it all into him.

He coughed, blood leaking from his pouty lips. "It's okay," he slurred. "As long as you live. You're all that's ever mattered."

"No!" I hissed, desperation shackling my tone. The energy drain was making me woozy, as was the sight of Killian's gleaming rib cage and burned flesh blurred between the flickering glow of my hands.

I pushed harder, forcing more and more of myself into my magic. Into Killian.

The normal warming smoothness of my healing magic sharpened, scraping at my insides with an awful, jagged sensation.

I whimpered, panic clawing at my middle. "Why would you do something so stupid?"

His inky lashes fluttered as he fought to keep his eyes open. "Because, sweetness... I love you."

The words knifed into me, cleaving my heart in two. His eyes didn't reopen.

I felt myself race towards a cliff. My metaphysical self teetered on a rocky ledge, hovering over a depthless ocean of black. I was at the point my father feared.

The point of no return.

Every shred of my being rebelled on instinct, fighting the overexertion.

But this was *Killian*.

How could my magic be worth more than him?

He was everything to me.

Whether I was valuable afterwards or not, it would be worth it, just to see his eyes silver with mischief one more time.

"I've always loved you," I whispered and leaned down, pressing my lips to his in a feather-light kiss.

I gave myself to him.

My essence slipped away. The very core of my being. The final light of magic drained into him and flickered out.

Bloodied skin knitted back together under my palms. It vibrated with a sluggish thump I was desperate to feel.

"Sweetness," Killian murmured against my lips.

Cool hands cupped my face, and I stared into a beautiful storm.

And then everything went black.

Chapter 41

The feel of being pulled into someone's arms dragged me from the abyss.

My rouge lashes fluttered until I was staring up into Killian's stunning features. He watched with a mixture of fear and relief that reflected my own heart.

"You're alive," I croaked.

"Because of you," he whispered, eyes raking over me as he slowly set me on my feet. His wings curled around my back, holding me steady against his front.

His *healed* front.

I marvelled at the smooth plum perfection of his skin, absent of ink. The lines of his tattoos turned to wisps around the edges of where a crater of flesh had once ravaged him.

A single claw tipped my chin up, forcing my gaze from the evidence of his near-death and up to his gleaming silver eyes instead. "Eve... What did you do?"

A hollow ache lurked deep in my chest. Right where the warmth of my magic, roiling and swirling like the core of a volcano, had used to live. The mark on my wrist, freshly anchoring me to the Sage Coven, was just as absent.

The destruction of my powers must have broken the mystical tie to a family that had never been mine to begin with. Somehow, I felt lighter without it.

But maybe that was the blood loss.

"What I had to." I met my demon's intensity, unblinking. "You're worth any price, Killian. You always have been."

A small line formed between his brows, something vulnerable in his eyes making my heart break all over again. His words were soft, drifting through the cocoon he'd created with his wings. "All these years... I thought you were rejecting me. I've been drowning you in energy for a long time, sweetness, and you never once mentioned it. You never even touched it. I couldn't blame you either. You've always been too good for a monster like me."

"Fires, Kill." A breathy laugh escaped me. "We're so stupid... I fell in love with you the moment I saw you." I swallowed, throat thickening at the memory. "Standing there battered and bruised, a million cuts across your malnourished frame and barely a handful of feathers left. Then you looked at me, and you lifted your damn chin. You dared me to think less of you. And I... I just knew you had the kind of strength I'd always craved. People have beaten me down my whole life, and I just thought to myself, if I was like him, it wouldn't matter what they did. I'd be unbreakable too."

Tears filled my vision, spilling over to wet my cheeks.

"You *are* unbreakable, Eve." He cupped my face in both palms and captured me with silvered eyes drenched in emotion. "You're stronger than I'll ever be. You saved me then, and every damn day since."

His words pierced my chest, and then he was closing the scant inches between us, lips fusing to mine.

It drugged me.

I couldn't think of anything but him. The feel of his tongue slipping past my defences. His body heat warming me. The scent of seared sweetness. The silk of his feathers shielding me from the world.

Even with the hollow where my magic used to live, my heart had never felt more full.

"That swine!" The coven elder's voice boomed through the woods.

Killian tore his mouth from mine, glaring in the direction the voice had come from. I followed his gaze as best I could with his wings and arms trapping me against him, refusing to let me so much as turn in his grip.

My father stormed down the path towards us, but his attention wasn't on me. It locked onto the mage I'd killed.

Sage Coven members already swarmed the area, standing over the bodies of downed hunters. They must have subdued the injured stragglers while I'd healed Killian and made out with him like nothing else existed.

My cheeks warmed as I realised anyone could have snuck up and tried to murder us both while I'd been absorbed in him. Knowing Killian, though, even half-dead, the enforcer wouldn't have been as easily caught off guard.

He was always protecting me.

The coven elder drew up beside us, glaring at Alvie's dead body like he could resurrect the mage and then kill him all over again.

"Apparently, my bloodthirsty side isn't all demonic," I mused, breathing in Killian's warming burned-caramel scent.

My father's expression pinched as he turned his attention to Killian and me, merlot eyes glowing bright in the dim forest now Alvie's light had been extinguished. Permanently.

"You know it was Alvie who let the hunters in?" I rasped, surprised he wasn't attacking us.

"I'm told he attacked you while you were trying to stop the hunters." His upper lip curled in disgust. "That boy has been after my position for years. Thankfully, my powerful daughter was here to protect her family." His lips stretched into a violent smile.

For a moment, I felt my own tip up in response. I'd never had a real parent, let alone one that would be proud of me.

The empty reality in my chest seemed to pulse, and I bit my lower lip, realising it wasn't just my magic I could no longer feel. I lifted my wrist, inspecting the smooth skin. The little cluster of sage leaves had disappeared, along with my powers.

"You stupid girl," my father snapped. Any hope I'd harboured at finding my birth father shattered with the look of disgust on his features as he gaped at my bare wrist. "What use are you to me magicless?!"

Killian moved before I could stop him, his hand clamping my father's throat. "Another word, and it will be your last."

Pain stuttered my breath as my father's words sank in like sharpened blades.

All I'd ever wanted was to matter. To be worth something. To belong.

Moonlight dappled one side of Killian's blood-spattered face through the trees. His handsome features honed to a deadly snarl as he strangled the gasping mage.

The coven watched on in silence, no one lifting a finger to protect their leader.

Until now, I'd been looking in all the wrong places. I didn't want to be here with a coven full of strangers.

I wanted to go home with Killian.

Back to my real family.

Killian glanced at me over his semi-flared wing. "What is he talking about, sweetness?"

"I... I won't need magic lessons anymore."

His black feathers ruffled against his back. "And why not?"

"Because I gave it all up. For you." I smiled up at him, cutting him off as he opened his mouth to protest. "And I'd do it again."

"Eve..." His harsh expression softened. "Why would you do that? I've been willing to die for you since the first time I saw you smile."

Tears sprang to my eyes again, and I hastily swiped them away. "I know, you dumb brute. But it's not your death I want, it's the rest of our lives. Together."

A broad grin split his lips.

"Come on, Kill. He's not worth it." I held my hand out to the incubus, and he dropped the coven elder, letting the old mage crumple to the dirt, spluttering for air. "Let's go home."

Killian threaded his blood-slicked fingers with mine. "Anything for you, sweetness."

He pulled me against his chest, the comforting beat of his new heart soothing the ragged edges of my strung-out nerves.

My demon hauled me into his arms, spread his wings, and launched us towards the stars.

Wings took flight in my heart and soared with us.

Epilogue

Two weeks later...

A hiss of laughter pierced the sunny morning.

I shifted on my knees in the short grass and shot a glare at the furball mocking me. "Really, Cookie? It's not that funny."

My enormous hellcat familiar sprawled on a plush fur blanket. I'd laid it in the sun behind my cabin just for her to be extra comfortable while I worked.

Ungrateful ball of fluff.

Her angular feline eyes, the same blood-red shade as mine, narrowed.

She gave an indignant meow and another hacking hiss. *It is, though, silly cub. Claws are for slashing the soft underbelly of your prey, not digging holes like some bored hellhound.* Her raspy words were spoken straight into my mind, clear enough to drip with mocking.

"It's called *gardening*," I huffed back, accidentally brushing mud on my cheek as I swiped back a stray curl, but my lips twitched at my familiar's sass. "My trowel broke, and there're only two more left to plant."

Hearing her voice in my mind—actually being able to *speak* to her—was going to be a double-edged sword from my absent magic, but I cherished it anyway. The hellcat had been a prickly kitty ever since Killian and I had made it back into Hell a week ago.

She'd waited for me at the portal the whole time. Days of watching and waiting, and if she was to be believed, many successful hunts of demons she considered stupid enough to become prey.

I hadn't asked too many questions about that part, but I had given her the cat-shaped shortbread I'd bought in the human realm just for her. A hungry hellcat was a dangerous one.

Reuniting with my familiar had been beautiful and heart-warming. Until she'd hissed at me for taking so long and tried to bite me again.

Even with my magic gone, the bond sang between us.

She hadn't stopped sassing me, but like a complete sap, I'd still used the last ingredients stashed in my pantry to bake her a whole batch of darkberry scones this morning. I'd saved a few for Killian too, but I had no idea where he'd snuck off to.

We'd only got back to the Hybrid Kingdom last night. After giving a quick summary of events for the monarchs and enforcers, followed by a long telling-off from Rex, we'd finally gone to bed.

Separately.

Until Killian had snuck into my bedroom in the middle of the night. I'd woken up this morning in his arms, feeling safer and happier than I could ever remember being.

I scooped another hole in the ground, getting even more dirt under my scarlet claws, and buried the next set of seeds in the mud.

Given how close my cabin was to the Bloodwood, the tall trees cast a dappled shade over the end of what I considered my garden. Nobody really bothered with fences here, but I was set on expanding my plant patch.

I may not be able to heal with magic anymore, but I knew how to make a mean salve or two.

Cookie lifted her head, angling her face over my shoulder.

I had a second to brace.

Something knocked into my side. White softness wrapped around me, and then I was rolling along the grass in a cloak of feathers. The sunny garden and blue sky blurred in a dizzying tumble.

Silver glinted in Killian's eyes as he cuddled me tighter than a basilisk, pinning me beneath him in a way that had my blood heating.

He flashed me a fanged grin like the psycho he was. "Need a hand, sweetness?"

I quirked a brow, barely resisting the urge to squirm beneath the delicious weight of his muscular warmth. "You've got mud all over your pretty pigeon wings now."

"Worth it," he murmured, eyes dipping to my parted lips. "Seems your gardening is going better than the last time I found you at the edge of the Bloodwood."

"You mean that time you stalked me in the dead of night like some creep?" I poked my tongue out at him, and a playful giggle bubbled up my throat.

His voice dropped to a husky rasp. "We both know I was stalking you long before that, and have been every day since."

I threw a mock glare his way. "You know, you're not meant to say crazy shit like that."

"And why not?" He pouted. "You're my future mate."

"How very presumptuous of you." I snorted. "You haven't even asked me."

He bared his fangs in the biggest grin. "Yet."

I sucked in a needy breath.

Demons claimed their mates at the height of passion. A wild, primal way to propose compared to the human style on one knee with a ring. Just the hint that it was something on his mind had heat pooling low in my body, sparking anticipation.

He pressed a chaste kiss to my lips, and my heart swelled.

We'd left my rotten father and his coven two weeks ago. Though the journey back had been easier than the way there, we'd still run into complications along the way: another hunter squad on Earth and some thieves staking out the Bloodwood that Cookie had thoroughly enjoyed mauling.

The danger hadn't stopped Killian and me from growing closer with each passing day.

And well into the night.

Killian's lips feathered over mine as he spoke. "Besides, I've already moved my stuff into your cabin."

My brows shot up to my horns. "What?!"

Mischief glinted in his stormy eyes. "You didn't think I had your pretty kitty out here distracting you all morning for nothing, did you?"

"Killian!" I gaped up at him. "You can't just do things like that."

He frowned, like he was actually considering my words, before the expression smoothed with an infuriatingly sultry purr, "And yet I did."

Before I could get a word out, his lips crashed against mine. He devoured any protests I might have had with his drugging kiss.

The persuasive incubus nipped my lower lip, fang stinging just enough to have me moaning into his mouth. "Killian…"

"Yes, sweetness?" His forked tongue lapped at the wound he'd created, stealing the tiny drop of blood. "Are you trying to play hard to get, little witch? I've already waited years, but if you really want to torture me longer, I'll kick your neighbour out and move in next door until you're ready."

I pursed my kiss-swollen lips. The demon was actually being serious.

"You're really diving in horns first here, aren't you?" I mused.

Storm clouds swirled in his expressive eyes. "When it comes to you, sweetness, how could I not?" He tapped the centre of his bare chest, where his tattoos had been wiped. "My heart is yours. It was even before you forged me a new one."

My own fluttered at his sweet words, but I pulled a face to cover how easily he made me melt. "An incubus with a honeyed tongue? Who'd have thought?"

"My sweet succubus." He leaned down, whispering in my ear, "Let me show you the other things I can do with my tongue. Or shall I get you another cake first?"

My cheeks flamed, and my greedy core fluttered at the thought.

"Eww, get off my baby sister!" a familiar voice boomed.

I choked on a strangled splutter, but Killian just chuckled, releasing me long enough to sit us both up in the grass.

Rex stood at the corner of my cabin with a fake scowl on his face. Fists planted on his hips, he arched his arrowhead tail over his shoulder in mock threat, stinger still tucked away. Sunshine caught his fiery ombre hair and set the bright shades alight.

Zoella swatted his arm with a playful huff. "What he meant to say was 'Aww, what an adorable couple you two make.'"

A dark beast stepped out beside them and woofed in greeting.

Before I could answer Alpha and the chaotic monarchs, a feral hiss rang out behind me.

This is my territory! The hellcat leaped right for the hellhound, and they clashed in a tangle of fluffy limbs and bared fangs.

Zoella's lilac brows shot up. "Wow, Alpha. And you said you'd made a new fur bestie," she teased.

I did not! Alpha woofed, batting his paw at Cookie's crimson tail tuft before the evil beast could stuff it fully in his mouth.

I blinked.

Apparently, I could translate Alpha's words now too. Before, it had been more of an intuitive understanding, like subconsciously reading body language.

The wicked witch snickered at her familiar. As usual, she looked every inch the badass witch queen. Her tattoos of spiky thorns and poisoned flowers were on display in a clingy sleeveless top and peeked through the tears in her ripped jeans.

Rex grabbed her hand and pulled her towards us with a smoky chuckle. "Don't worry, little mouse, if your mangy mutt perishes, I'll get you a new one."

Zoella rolled her eyes while Alpha growled in the king's direction.

I snorted, climbing to my feet and dusting the grass off my leathers. "It's a good thing they're only play-fighting, then, isn't it."

Killian stood, brushing off some grass I'd missed from my thigh. He wrapped his arms around my waist, resting his chin between my horns.

Rex's eyes narrowed as he closed in on us, tugging his queen along for the ride. The pair stopped before us, and I felt Killian tense at my back, but he didn't loosen his hold one bit.

The king cleared his throat, glaring over my head with a toss of his pointy horns. "You're sure you want this idiot?"

Zoella smacked his arm harder this time, grinning maniacally at me. "We're so happy for you both."

Rex rolled his bright-red eyes, the slitted pupil almost disappearing completely before he fixed his intent stare on Killian. "You're my best friend, Kill. But I will literally disembowel you if you hurt her."

I snorted. "Relax, *Uncle.* I'm grown up enough to make my own mistakes."

"Ouch," Killian drawled but hugged me tighter despite my teasing.

Rex chuckled. "Well, this is for sleeping with my little sister anyway."

His fist snapped out.

Killian released me as the punch caught him with a loud crack, knocking him back a step.

I gasped and bared my fangs up at my idiot brother. "Rex!"

Killian only laughed, working his jaw. Mischief twinkled in his stormy eyes. "Oh, we did a lot more than sleep," he purred.

Rex visibly bristled.

Zoella doubled over with laughter, waggling her lilac brows at me. "This is going to be so much fun. Double date tomorrow night?"

I sighed at them all and, without thinking, reached up to touch the faint bruising already darkening Killian's cheek.

Nothing happened.

My magic was gone. I'd not felt a spark since I'd given it all to save Killian, but I still didn't regret it. At times like this, I missed it though.

"Sorry," I whispered, awkwardly dropping my hand.

"Don't be," Killian said, voice fierce. "You've given me everything, and I can never repay your courage and kindness."

Soft fur brushed the back of my hand. Cookie rubbed her side against me, and something flickered in my chest as her blood-red eyes met mine.

I held perfectly still. My fingertips warmed, the faintest thrum of power running through me.

"Eve, look." Killian's voice filled with awe.

I stared down at my hand, marvelling at the red-tinged glow. Before I could freak out, I pressed my palm to Killian's cheek once more. Energy flowed through me and into the demon I loved, soothing and pure.

His eyes met mine, flaring wide. "Your magic…"

"It's coming back," I breathed.

Relief crashed into me. I'd thought it was gone forever.

Ugh, I'm the one bringing it back, actually. The hellcat sneezed, twitching her whiskers.

With a swish of her tail tuft into my face like a fluffy slap, she sauntered off, leaving me gaping behind her.

"Thank you," I murmured at her snootily retreating cat butt.

Cookie ignored me and sidled up to the imposing hellhound, sitting daintily beside him. Her tail flicked out, brushing the tuft over his nose. Alpha snapped his fangs at her, inches from biting off the end of her tail.

They didn't seem like friends exactly, more like frenemies, but it was adorable to watch.

"It wouldn't have mattered to me if it never returned, Eve. I love you no matter what," Killian whispered, brushing his thumb over my muddy cheek.

"Fine." Rex huffed, dramatically throwing his claws up. "If you're going to be all cute and shit, I'll stop punching you for being with my sister."

Killian bared his fangs at Rex in a wicked grin and swept me up, arms around my waist as he spun me around with a wild laugh, wings flared for balance.

"That's right, everyone knows you're mine now." He let me slide down his front, sending the most delicious shiver through my body, even with the eyes of my family on us.

"You mean, you're all mine," I teased, grinning so wide my cheeks ached.

"Sweetness." He pressed a delicate kiss to my lips. "I always was."

I'd just like to take a moment to thank you for reading this saucy tale!

As an indie author, it would mean so much to me if you could please <u>leave a review</u>. This helps other readers to find my wild stories and take a chance on me so I can keep on writing and living my author dream.

If you want more spicy paranormal and fantasy romance action, then sign up to my newsletter at <u>sakurablackbooks.com/ subscribe</u> for exclusive bonus content, character art and release updates.

Acknowledgments

This is just a quickie to say a huge thank you to my advance reader Emmy and my awesome beta readers—Mandy, Cheri, Kerry and Emma. Your comments helped me more than I can say, and I can't thank you enough for the time and effort you put in.

I also wanted to give my editor, Lyss, a big shout out for whipping this book into shape.

My ARC team has been simply amazing too. Thank you for your support in getting this book in front of more great readers like yourself!

Also By Sakura Black

Fae Mate Hunt Series *(complete)*: A spicy reverse harem monster romance novella series

0.5 – <u>The Nymph's Dark Pleasure</u>

1 – <u>Selected for the Shifters</u>

2 – <u>Hunted by the Minotaur</u>

3 – <u>Burning for the Fire Nymphs</u>

4 – <u>Fleeing the Feline King</u>

5 – <u>Their Concubine Queen</u>

1-5 – <u>Fae Mate Hunt: Complete Series Collection</u>

.

Monster Mate Hunt Series *(complete)*: A spicy reverse harem monster romance novella series

1 – <u>Rattled</u>

2 – <u>Get Foxed</u>

3 – <u>The Stones for It</u>

4 – <u>Reeled In</u>

5 – <u>Their Crown Jewels</u>

Playing with Demons Series: A spicy demon romance connected standalone series
1 – Take Me to Hell
2 – Capturing Sin
3 – Hellish Witch

For all the latest book release information, subscribe to Sakura's newsletter at sakurablackbooks.com and for a limited time, get a FREE bonus short story – The Nymph's Dark Pleasure – the prequel to Selected for the Shifters, all about Newbury's hot night with a dark stranger. Warning: it's a steamy one!

About the Author

Sakura Black is a writer of steamy fantasy and paranormal romance, often dreaming up wild stories about frightfully sweet monsters and the women they're lucky enough to fall horns over tail for.

For more saucy action head to Sakura's website: sakurablackbooks.com

You can also find Sakura's Author Page on Amazon or reach out on Instagram / Facebook / TikTok @sakurablackbooks - she loves hearing from readers (but is crap at social media so the best place to find her is her Newsletter)